My
COLD WAR

ALSO BY TOM PIAZZA

Blues And Trouble: Twelve Stories
True Adventures with the King of Bluegrass
Blues Up and Down: Jazz in Our Time
The Guide to Classic Recorded Jazz
Setting the Tempo: Fifty Years of Great Jazz Liner Notes

My COLD WAR

TOM PIAZZA

 ReganBooks

An Imprint of HarperCollins*Publishers*

HarperCollins books may be purchased for educational, business, or sales promotional use. For information please write: Special Markets Department, HarperCollins Publishers Inc., 10 East 53rd Street, New York, NY 10022.

FIRST EDITION

Designed by Judith Stagnitto Abbate/Abbate Design

Printed on acid-free paper

Library of Congress Cataloging-in-Publication Data

Piazza, Tom, 1955–
    My cold war : a novel / Tom Piazza.—1st ed.
       p. cm.
    ISBN 0-06-053340-4
       1. History teachers—Fiction. 2. College teachers—Fiction.
    3. Popular culture—Fiction. 4. Parent and adult child—Fiction.
    I. Title.

PS3566.I23M9 2003
813'.54—dc21   2003046649

03 04 05 06 07 BVG/RRD 10 9 8 7 6 5 4 3 2 1

FOR MARY

WITH GRATITUDE:

Cal Morgan, Amy Williams, Mary Howell, Lillian Piazza, Bob
Dylan, Dirk Powell, Kevin Rabalais, Ed Newman, Norman
Mailer, Stanley Crouch, Jeff Rosen, Bob Jones, Maureen
Sugden, Joe DeSalvo, Rosemary James, the Pirate's Alley
Faulkner Society, Josh Russell, Mary McCay, and the English
Departments of Loyola University and Millsaps College. A
special thanks to Yaddo and the Virginia Center for the
Creative Arts, where much of this novel was written.

And in memory of Joseph L. Piazza, 1923–2002.

I

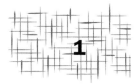

MY MOTHER HAD JUST MOVED to New York City from Eau
Claire in 1949, when she met Marie Kelso. Marie was four or five
years older and lived in the same women's residence on Thir-
teenth Street, operated by the Salvation Army. She always cut
through in the little black-and-white photos they used to take, so
sparingly, at parties. There she was, on the arm of the sofa, holding a cigarette and a highball like everybody else, laughing like
the others, but as if she were having an inside joke with the
viewer of the photo, a little voltage in the eye that spoke of knowing things the other girls didn't. She had been kind of wild—code
for premarital sex—despite being a Catholic, but maybe because
of that she became a sort of den mother to the younger women.
She was in her late thirties before she finally got married, to a
businessman named Bill. They never had any children.

My mother left the women's residence for her own apartment in 1951 and—you know how these things go—saw Marie
occasionally, but when she married my father and moved out to
Atlanticville, on Long Island, it got harder to maintain the old
friendships. A phone call now and then, and then no phone calls
for a long while.

Then, out of the blue, a call from Marie Kelso. It was 1962. She and Bill were living in New Jersey. "I wanted to see how the lovebirds were doing," she said. My mom talked to her for almost an hour, and by the end of the conversation, they had made plans for Marie to visit us in Atlanticville. As it turned out, Marie had something on her mind besides auld lang syne. She wanted my parents to join the John Birch Society.

———

MY MOTHER HAD come to New York to work in retail, for which she had prepared at Thellinger's department store in Eau Claire. New York—the great dream, as it still was. Not just a vehicle for making money but a destination, spiritual and material, in itself. She got a job at Saks and, over a year and a half, rose steadily from counter girl to assistant buyer. Her life was dotted with glamorous parties, encounters with movie stars; her clients included Rita Hayworth, and once she even brought clothes to Mae West's apartment. In pictures from that time, her honey-blond hair spills down over the shoulders of a beautiful striped silk blouse or a gray tailored suit, always a cigarette in her hand, laughing. . . .

She met my father one evening while she was pinch-hitting at one of the sweater counters during the pre-Christmas rush. Winking lights of Rockefeller Plaza, people rushing by on the sidewalks, the chill of December in the folds of their overcoats, smell of pretzels and chestnuts in the blue stove smoke. . . . He had stopped in to buy a sweater for his mother, and Mom had assisted him. He was still living with his parents on the far edge of Queens, working in the city; he came back the next week and hunted her up and they had a date, they began a courtship.

My father was very handsome—people said he resembled the actor Tyrone Power—but he had a slightly withered left arm. You had to look for a minute or two to notice it, and then only with his shirt off. He was also, it turned out, epileptic, although he didn't tell my mother about that until after they were engaged. It had kept him out of the war.

My mother had just come off a heartbreak. She was susceptible. Another year or so and she would have been a full buyer, and it would have been a corner to turn. She was at the corner already. In any case her life was rolling, but she was late getting married for those days—twenty-six!—and when the previous love withdrew, he left an emptiness that hadn't been there before. Suddenly New York and the life and the glamour were tinged with a hint of rue on the breeze, a rue that she knew could roll in heavier as the shadows grew. This is all speculation, basically, but that's where she was when my father entered the picture.

He wasn't making a lot of money, but he was doing something, electrical engineering, that had the potential for growth, something technical that had required lots of training, and he was smart, he could be funny, he had a good family—or, let us say, a large extended family with some material comfort. They got married.

———

ATLANTICVILLE. THEY BOUGHT the house for twelve thousand dollars, a decent chunk of money at the time.

Everybody else, it seems, had the same idea. Your own house, your own yard. All those boys and girls who had grown up in the tenements and alleys of Brooklyn and Queens or the Lower East Side and who had shipped out to fight the war, cigarette by cigarette, boot by boot. No particular education, except for those who came back for technical school on the GI Bill at CCNY or NYU. Atlanticville, and all the other towns like it, grew up for them overnight. Land that had been potato farms or marsh before the war was now bought up, filled in, and carved into little squares, like a tray of brownies. The developers named the streets with Indian words peculiar to tribes that had long since been driven off, or they named them for trees or for the developer's own children. My parents moved there because that was what they could afford; I don't think they necessarily planned on staying.

It was classic Levittown-style suburbia, the neighborhood laid out in a grid, the general effect of one block the same as another. One street, Alder Drive, made a kind of S shape, just to keep things interesting. The houses in the development were identical in their floor plan—split-level homes with single-car garages, on 60-by-100 plots, their facades distinguished only by the permutations of colors on their shingles and shutters. One house would be maroon with black shutters, the next one white with green shutters, the next one gray with blue shutters. . . . In my mind they sit quietly under the blue sky, on a cloudless, shadowless noon. . . .

This is my first memory:

Long, thin day. Sound of plane way up in springtime haze. Static afternoon, my head cocked, listening. Sunshine, the plane a silver-gray shadow, a sliver, against the sky. Laurel Avenue, around front, a long street, without history, waiting for its history in the noonday sun. Tiny trees, thin as a child's wrist, stabilized by guy wires along the curb strips.

Once in a while, a car goes by, but this is the middle of the day, 1960. People are at work.

In the partially submerged dens and finished basements, the laundry is being done, the ironing, the television going: *December Bride, I Love Lucy, Gale Storm, Love That Bob*. The beefy men's shows—*Dragnet, Gunsmoke*—came on later, in the evening, when the men came home. A toddler in midcrawl, hand stretching out to achieve a ball at the end of his reach by the radiator at the baseboard . . .

I went for a walk. I'm not sure where my mother was. How old could I have been? Four? The day seemed so static. Inaudible crackle of electricity in the wires above. I set out in the midnoon, headed off down Laurel Avenue. Every few steps, at first, I stopped and looked back at my house—an odd, playing-hooky feeling, a perspective I shouldn't have been having, not alone anyway. I kept walking, past the houses along Laurel, which I usually drove by with my mother, passing slowly now. Downstairs the laundry was being done, the ironing, the husbands off at work. Soap operas going. *As the World Turns. The Secret Storm.* Outside, the houses' sharp shadows swept slowly across the fledgling lawns as the afternoon slid by. And the sound of a plane way up in the spring-day haze. I was paying out the cable as I walked along, and then I forgot that I was paying out the cable and I just walked and looked. Lawns, fences. Way up above, the sky and haze, the plane sound gone now.

I passed Wonalancet Street where it teed into Laurel Avenue. Just before Manhasset I crossed to the other side of

Laurel Avenue itself. I was a long way from home; I could hardly see my house down the street. But I had a sense of where I was. I didn't want to go back yet—I hadn't really learned anything, hadn't pierced, somehow, the surface of this day. I rounded the corner onto Alder Drive, with its oddly sensuous curve in the street, leading first to the left and then around to the right, seeming to beckon, like a finger, or an arm, into the inscrutable afternoon. I followed the sidewalk. The houses were the same as they were on Laurel Avenue; in the yards a tricycle here or there. Striped plastic balls from the five and ten, permutations of the same colors and shutters, ironing, laundry . . .

At one point I turned to look back and realized I could no longer see the beginning of Alder Drive. The noon sky hung overhead, and I had the sensation of being suspended in curved space. Television music wafted faintly from inside one of the houses. I had gotten turned around, no longer sure from which direction I'd come. I was on a street that resembled my street in the aggregate but differed in particulars that were beneath the level of conscious notice. My reference points had been replaced with other reference points that seemed completely interchangeable with my ordinary ones, as if I were lost in the desert. But this was not disappearing off the radar screen into shifting dunes or dense undergrowth, with God's own inscrutability replicating itself; this was an exploration into something wholly man-made. I was moving laterally, not vertically, not going deep into a mystery but scribbling my way across its carefully constructed surface. The sky, one might say, was Their sky, not His sky. . . .

I started screaming and crying. Crying and screaming until someone came and took me home, I have no idea how. Six months later JFK was elected president.

IN THE EVENINGS I would go with my mother to pick up my father at the train station, where he would return from designing television circuitry somewhere amid the warehouses and rusting entrails of Jamaica, Queens. This was in the days before they raised the tracks on the Long Island Railroad, and the huffing engine would pull up right in front of you. It was romantic, I guess, the convergence at the railroad near sunset, the wives coming to welcome home the voyagers, how fared you today, the children rejoicing at the return unscathed. The arrival of the train, the reenacting of the troops' coming back into harbor, the satisfying daily replaying of the safe return home, the reaffirmation, how redolent it must have been to them then, in the lull between wars.

Years later my mother would tell me that those were some of the happiest moments of her life, the moments just before my father came home. Years later, when he cracked, my mother always told me to have sympathy for him, even as I saw her grow brittle and sad with the effort. I knew better. I kept my heart clenched like a fist.

CONTENTS OF THE bookshelf in the den downstairs: *The Sea Around Us. The Great Fog. Lost in the Horse Latitudes. Masters of Deceit. The Aspirin Age. The Naked Communist. None Dare Call It Treason. Flying Saucers—Serious Business. The Conquest of Space. Red Masquerade. McCarthy and His Enemies.*

The Many Loves of Dobie Gillis. Main themes: enemies, treason, deceit, promiscuity, invasion, loss of clarity and bearings, pain relief, and escape into outer space.

My father spent the 1950s doing something to television sets and other electronic items that ordinary people couldn't understand. He showed me—maybe I was six—how to tell the value of resistors by the brightly colored bands on the shank. Transistors had little flexible metal leads coming out of the bottom of the cap, like hairs out of a mole. I learned to use a soldering iron, and I invented nonsense circuits, dripping hot solder onto the reject circuit boards he gave me to play with. In the 1960s he switched to defense work, like everybody else. How many suburban kids got put through college courtesy of the Defense Department they would spend years railing against?

In 1961 I knew already that Russia was a place that would send planes or missiles to destroy my elementary school, and the walls would collapse the way they did in *Godzilla* as my schoolmates and I knelt in the halls and put our hands over our heads. But the stuff in my father's books was different. It was more personal. The cover of *The Naked Communist,* for example—bloodred, with a menacing, muscled silhouette looming behind the stark title. There were pamphlets lying around, really scary things, about how Communists would get up at their meetings and talk about slitting the throats of priests and children. "They like to sing about the blood? We'll give them blood . . . slit the throats of the little children on the altars. . . ." Now it wasn't planes, or missiles; it was people who looked just like ordinary people who would slit your throat in church. I was not scared of burglars when I was a kid, but I was very scared at night that Communists might break into the house and take me to a church for a blood sacrifice.

My mother didn't like my father's leaving that kind of material around where I could see it. She thought I read too much as it was and that I needed to spend more time outside. She kept after my father to teach me about sports, but his heart wasn't in it. He tried, I guess. We'd do it for a week or two, during which he'd show me what he knew ("Grab the football by the stitches and roll it out of your hand. . . .")—all good advice about ball handling, which he understood, and nothing about team dynamics, which he didn't. After a while there would be nowhere left to go. He would sit next to me on the cement steps leading up to our house's side door, drinking a glass of ice water, and say, "That was a good workout, wasn't it?"

Every Sunday we attended Mass in the gymnasium of the Catholic school across the street from our church. Father Hayden was one of three priests who said Mass at the gym, which had been conscripted to handle the overflow crowds from the regular church. On Sundays they pulled back the bleachers, which retracted against the light blue cinder block walls, and set up metal folding chairs on the gleaming, varnished wooden floors of the basketball court. High above, a lattice of beige-painted industrial-looking girders and beams crisscrossed the ceiling, supporting hanging lamps that cast a bright and shadowless light. The service was still carried on in Latin, and the odd, modal, singsong tones of the formal parts of the Mass stay with me to this day. At regular intervals somber men in dark suits strode down the aisles carrying long, bamboo-wrapped sticks to which were attached green-felt-lined wicker baskets for the collection. At each row they stopped and slowly pushed the basket down the row, and the parishioners contributed their money.

Each priest had a different style. Father Flynn was gray-haired and kindly; Father Dunn was gaunt and tall and had a five-o'clock shadow. But Father Hayden is the one I remember the best. With his spherical head with close-cropped hair and black glasses, he resembled the singer Allan Sherman. Most Catholic priests at that time were intensely politically conservative, but Father Hayden was openly and aggressively liberal. He delivered his homilies in a high-handed style laced with sarcasm and rhetorical questions: "Are you so busy at your incredibly important job that you can't help once a year at the church fair?" "If you are the kind of parishioner who spends more on his lawn in a week than you do in the collection plate in a year . . ." That kind of thing. He noticed everything that went on in the gym. If someone came in late during his initial announcements, he would interrupt himself to say, "Come in, don't stand around in the back with your hat in your hand. There are plenty of seats here in front." Or if someone was talking to the person in the next seat during his sermon, he might say, "I'm sorry—I was under the impression that I was delivering the sermon."

My father disliked Father Hayden under the best of circumstances, but when the priest applied that tone to questions of world events, my father would chafe visibly. "There are people in this world—I am sure this will come as a surprise to some of you—who don't spend Sunday afternoon after church Simonizing their cars, people who don't have enough to eat. . . ." These kinds of remarks irritated my father almost beyond endurance. For him, essentially, people who didn't have enough to eat probably just hadn't worked hard enough to get something to eat, and it wasn't his responsibility to pick up their slack. He would shift in his seat, muttering asides. My mother became extremely uncomfortable when he did this. It felt as if a fuse was burning. Sooner or later something was going to blow.

One Sunday, Father Hayden said something about praying for the people of Cuba, and even praying for Fidel Castro. This, finally, was too much for my father, who grumbled something out loud. Father Hayden heard it and said, from the pulpit, "What is it? If you have something to say, say it to me."

My father stood up at his seat, on the other side of my mother. "I said, why the hell do we have to pray for somebody who wants to come over here and kill us? Maybe we should wish him good luck, too."

There was a big murmur in the gymnasium, people adjusting, craning around to look.

Father Hayden said, "It's exactly the people who would do us the most harm that we need to pray for the most. And we should be taking care of our own house before we go around criticizing everybody else—"

"Don't lecture me," my father said, still standing. "I'm not a kid in your catechism class."

Next to me my mother had her head down, and I heard her whispering, "I don't believe it." To my father she said, sotto voce, "Frank, please . . ."

"Don't 'Frank, please' me," he shouted. Then, with everyone watching, he made his way out of the row and stood in the aisle waiting for us. There was a long moment of not knowing what to do, and then we got up and followed my father out of the gym.

After my father's shouting match with Father Hayden

(shortly after my first Communion), he stopped coming to church, leaving my mother and me to go it alone for several years, until my confirmation. Then we all stopped going. They still watched Bishop Fulton J. Sheen, a conservative political commentator and Catholic priest, on television, though. My father said, privately, that Father Hayden was a Commie. It was right around that time that Marie Kelso called.

MY PARENTS ENTERTAINED a fair amount back then. They had a low bar stocked with Canadian Club and other whiskeys, and shining chrome shakers and tongs for ice cubes and cut-glass tumblers. The photos show my father grinning, in a bow tie and short-sleeved white shirt, women in festive dresses. This was it, man; they owned the world, in a neighborhood built just for them.

But I never remember their preparing for anyone the way they prepared for Marie Kelso. My mother vacuumed and dusted the whole house, dusted the wall arrangements. I remember particularly a Chinese-looking fan in a fan-shaped frame. The house was decorated, like most of the houses I remember from that time, in a mix of styles in which the elements had been stirred up but not dissolved—echoes of American colonial in the wood-grained kitchen wall clock and the wooden tavern chairs around the Formica kitchen table, French grace notes by way of little paintings and a chair embroidered with a dark green fleur-de-lis pattern and a pair of frilly-shaded lamps on the heavy Germanic end tables, a hint of ancient Rome in a fluted column supporting a potted fern, inadvertent allusions to this and that, a scrap of chinoiserie here, British landscape painting in a French-colonial frame there, the whole postwar Levittown middle-class home-decorating Esperanto that everyone seemed, somehow, to have learned. I remember my father arranging a few magazines—*U.S. News & World Report, Scientific American, National Review*—in a kind of dovetailed effect on the coffee table, something I'd never seen him do. They made me wear a clip-on tie.

Whenever we went visiting or had guests over, my father got tight as a drumhead with nerves beforehand. The night Marie Kelso finally arrived, my mother helped him on with his white shirt, and he writhed, his neck muscles set in a rigid attitude of struggle; he looked up at her with his face contorted in frustration. "You see where I'm trying to put my hands? Pull the sleeve out." My father was constantly at war with his immediate environment, with tangled cords, with jackets that were too tight under the arms, or across the back, or in the seat, or all three. Objects became subjects, and he became their object. "You see what I'm trying to do?" he'd say. "Give me a hand. Don't just stand there. . . ."

Rarely did I see my mother express anger at him, but on this evening I remember her saying, "Put your own shirt on, then," and walking out of the bedroom. Mom was wearing a flamboyant blue silk blouse, perhaps in an echo of the old days. In my room I turned on my little record player and played the beginning of "Moody River" by Pat Boone, and she told me to turn it off. Marie Kelso's visit was making them both nervous. Finally the doorbell rang, a chime effect to which we had just graduated from the ringer we'd had. Mom went to open the door for her friend, with my father right behind her, and there stood Marie Kelso.

My mother raised both her hands as if to say, Here you are! and, like a reflection in a mirror, Marie Kelso did the same on the other side of the storm-door window. She was alone; Bill, it turned out, didn't participate in the Birch stuff. She opened the door herself and stepped inside; her hair was done exactly as she'd had it in the photos from a decade earlier, and she wore old-fashioned rimless glasses that gave her sharp, alert, suspicious eyes a severe cast. She wore a brown, nubby cloth coat and bright red lipstick, and when my mom went to kiss her, Marie turned her cheek and patted my mom on the back with a bare hand. She shook hands with my father and said, "Still handsome, Frank," looking at me as she said it.

"This is Johnny," my mom said. I stepped forward, smiling. Most guests greeted me enthusiastically; Marie Kelso gave me a forced half smile and a nod, and then she turned her attentions to the house. I remember her bending down to look at the names of the magazines my father had dovetailed, spreading them a bit with her fingertips and then turning away with no comment.

Dad took her coat, and Mom asked her how the trip out had been, and they exchanged a few words. My mom busied herself bringing out a tray of canapés, and my father asked Marie Kelso what she wanted to drink. She walked over to the bar, picked up a bottle of vodka and examined it, then asked for a highball.

"Well," she said, getting herself settled in the chair my father designated for her, crossing her legs and lighting a cigarette, as my parents perched on the couch and I sat in the "French chair" across from her, noticing the wary look she gave me. "The borscht has hit the fan."

My parents both smiled tentatively at this.

"I didn't know anybody could manage being Black Irish and

Red Irish at the same time, but Kennedy went and doo'd it," she said, taking a big slug off her highball and smacking her lips.

My parents were sitting in different body attitudes than they did with most guests. Mom sat on the edge of the couch, back straight, instead of sitting back and smiling at what her guest was saying. My father was leaning forward in his chair.

"Do you really think he's Red?" my father said, giving Marie an amiably skeptical look.

"He may have some trouble keeping it all straight," Marie said, "Khrushchev talking in one ear and the pope in the other. I'll admit that much."

"What about the Bay of Pigs?" my father said. "I thought he was trying to show some muscle. . . ."

Marie looked at him with a flat "Are you kidding?" look and said, "If you're trying to show some muscle, you don't send in a bunch of amateurs for hamburger duty."

I laughed out loud at this phrase, and Marie Kelso regarded me briefly with a raised eyebrow and a curious look. "Don't go softheaded on me, Frank," she continued. "You're an engineer. We have Yugoslav pilots training in Texas. Does this tell you something? Kennedy goes to sleep at night with Acheson singing him lullabies."

During this exchange I noticed my mother fidgeting, following the conversation to be polite, but I could tell from her eyes something wasn't exactly right. "Marie," my mom said breezily, "you never were one for small talk."

"There's no time for small talk," Marie said, giving my mother a knowing look. "You let the neighbors do the small talking. See what they say about their bassinettes and barbecues when the Russians are raping their wives."

My mom winced and surreptitiously tilted her head toward

me. Marie Kelso looked at me and said, "Maybe he shouldn't be here. If you don't want him to hear what's going on."

"Johnny, maybe you'd better—"

"I want to stay," I said. I wanted to know what was going on. If the Russians were coming over, I wanted to know about it.

My mom excused herself to do something in the kitchen, and I got up and ran after her. The dining-room table was set with the good plates and silverware. When we were in the kitchen, I said, "What is 'raping'?"

"Shush," my mother said, opening the oven. "I don't know if this was such a good idea."

"The roast?" I said.

She looked at me, puzzled, and then said, "Sweetie, why don't you go upstairs and play until dinner's ready."

"I don't want to," I said. I ran back into the living room.

"Look at Berlin," Marie Kelso was saying. "He sends Clay over and we rattle our swords and then when the time comes to fish or cut bait Kennedy handcuffs him. Why do you send him over there if you're going to put him in a straitjacket? Same thing Truman did to MacArthur. Different year, same story."

Of course I had no idea what any of this was about, but it was the first time I'd seen anybody but my father so sure of anything, and I watched her, fascinated.

"DINNER'S READY," MOM SAID.

"I want hamburger duty," I said.

"Good," she said distractedly, patting my chair. "You sit right here. Marie, you're in there, against the bureau."

My father liked to make toasts; it was a Sicilian thing. He raised his glass. "Here's to seeing old friends again," he said.

Marie Kelso raised her glass. "Here's to Kennedy. *Ich bin ein Commie.*"

We all drank. I drank grape soda and said, "Congratulations!"—a new word I'd learned.

"I heard a good one this week," Marie Kelso said. "What's black and white and Red all over?" There was a pause, during which I thought my parents were only being polite by not answering—everybody knew the answer to that: a zebra with the measles. When no one answered, she said, "Eisenhower in a tuxedo!" (A year later it would be "A bus full of Freedom Riders.")

They laughed at this. After a moment my father said, "I thought it was the *New York Times*." Marie Kelso smiled and tilted her chin upward, regarding my father. "That's not bad, Frank. Not bad at all . . . Did you see what Father Ginder wrote in *Our Sunday Visitor*?"

"Let's talk about something else for a while," Mom said. "I want to hear about Bill."

Now Marie looked at her old friend, my mother, across the table with the faintest of smiles. "Oh, Bill just keeps rolling along, like Old Man River," Marie said.

"You said he had a hernia operation?" Mom said.

"They trussed him up like a Thanksgiving turkey," Marie said. Then I saw a slight shift in her expression, and she said, "You remember Gladys Jorgensen, right?"

"Sure," Mom said. " 'Gladys to see ya—I'm Gladys!' "

Marie nodded exaggeratedly, twice. "Well, she came over—she's living in Chicago now. With a guy named Sobel, unfortunately, but . . . And she was in town, and we had her over, and she said, 'Bill, you are looking so *thin*,' and Bill said, 'I'm not thin; I'm just practicing a *containment* policy!' " Marie laughed heartily at this, and my mom laughed with her. Across the table my father was pouring himself another glass of wine. "Best line I ever heard him deliver. 'Bill,' I said, 'are you growing a sense of humor?' "

"Have you heard from any of the other girls?" Mom said.

"Oh, heck," Marie said, picking up the glass of wine my father had filled for her. "Jo Leahy called last week. They just bought a house in Riverdale, which is crazy, but that's what they're doing. Otherwise . . ."

They went on in that vein for a while. I noticed that my father wasn't paying attention to the gossip about old friends. He tended to get edgy when he felt unincluded, and he almost always felt unincluded. I had become a keen observer and anticipator of his moods. When he was unattended, bad humor seemed to collect, generating pressure that would be discharged with greater or lesser force depending on how much resistance it met. I recognized this now; he seemed to be waiting for a lull in the conversation.

Sure enough, as soon as there was a pause, he turned toward Marie with a kind of "We understand each other" familiarity that I already recognized as a sign that he was getting tanked.

"We have this priest," he said abruptly, like a car changing lanes without signaling. "This son of a bitch named Hayden . . ."

At this I saw my mother's face go blank; you didn't call a

priest a son of a bitch. Marie Kelso saw it, too, and I detected a flicker of quickening attention, perhaps even some amusement.

"For God's sake, Frank," Mom said.

He turned to her with his eyebrows up and an "Innocent little me?" expression on his face. " 'For God's sake, Frank,' " he said, in a caricature of a high, hysterical voice. " 'How awful. You said a bad word.' " He looked at my mother squarely, as if they were having a staring contest. Then my father ceremoniously turned back to Marie Kelso and said, "We have this priest. And he loves the masses. Oh, does his heart bleed for the downtrodden poor. He's always slapping us on the wrist for having more than the next guy."

Marie was looking at him; there was no way of reading what was behind her face.

"So one Sunday—when was this?" he said, turning over his shoulder toward my mother. "Huh?"

"I don't know," she said flatly, lighting a cigarette. "Sometime."

My father gave Marie Kelso a "See what I deal with?" look, a sarcastic half smile. "Let's say it was six months ago. He starts talking about the poor colored people. And how we have to make sure that everybody has enough to eat. And how we have to feel bad for the poor have-nots. And this, and that . . ."

Now Marie Kelso was smiling, watching him. My mother stood up and began clearing the plates.

"What am I, talking to myself?" my father said. My mother stopped clearing the dishes and stood still.

To fill the empty moment, I said, "Jesus said to feed the poor." This was something I'd learned in Communion class.

"Look, little boy," my father said, turning to me. "That's all fine for storybooks when you're a kid, but in the real world nobody cares about fairy tales."

"That's enough!" My mother was standing up; she had a plate in her hand, and I thought she was going to break it on the table. Her face was a kind of blotchy scarlet, and there was a high sound in her voice that scared me. "I don't want to hear any more!"

Marie Kelso stood up and got to my mother just as she started to cry.

"Franny," Marie said, "come on. You're right. No more." The two old friends stood there in a tableau of consolation, my mother's body bucking as she wept. I looked across the table at my father, and he looked back at me with a sheepish, conspiratorial smile, tilting his head toward them a little as if to say, "Look at the way they are," and I felt myself being invited, for the first time, into the world of men.

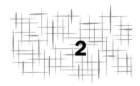

I HAVEN'T THOUGHT ABOUT THAT night in years. But lately I've been thinking about those days a lot. Those years.

I am on what Hollister College is officially, and generously, calling a sabbatical, ostensibly to write a book, which I can't write, from my position as Professor of History/Lecturer in Cold War Studies—a department I started at Hollister and of which I am the entire faculty. Other history professors (as well as Am Civ faculty, Lit people, whoever—it's interdisciplinary) do classes, but the heart of the major is the advanced-level seminar, conducted by me. In addition to a 100-level intro, every semester I cook up a seminar on some topic in Cold War Studies. "Face-ing the Cold War" is a popular one; it focuses on the cult of personality in the postwar superpowers, with lots of deconstructing of the actual pictorializing of the leaders—all the Mao stuff, naturally, thousands of people holding picture cards in a stadium, but also caricatures of Khrushchev and Nixon, why they put Kennedy's face on the half-dollar but never gave Truman a coin, stuff like that. "Lost Tribesmen" is another, about Jews who adopted alternate identities, like Bob Dylan, Norman Mailer, Ramblin' Jack Elliott, Werner Erhard. I do a music one, too, called "That Great Atomic

Power" after the Louvin Brothers song. We listen to Hank
Williams's "No, No, Joe," (a song about Stalin), Chuck Berry's
"Back in the USA," obviously "Masters of War" by Bob Dylan,
"Eve of Destruction" by Barry McGuire.

But the most popular seminar is "Hijacked," which I have to
offer every other semester. In that one we look at innocent people who become casualties of Historical Forces. We talk about
Leon Klinghoffer, whom the Palestine Liberation Front hijack-
ers killed in his wheelchair and threw over the side of the cruise
ship *Achille Lauro;* the Vietnamese girl photographed running
naked down the country road away from the napalm attack; pas-
sengers in the airplane hijackings of the 1960s; the testimony of
Hiroshima survivors. The kids love this course. They are fascinated by anyone's sudden plunge into a wholly discontinuous
experience. Very postmodern. Or maybe it's just postmodern to
think it's discontinuous.

I was one of the first academics to treat the Cold War as
pure phenomena, without getting into the motives of either
side, to examine its products—its flora, so to speak—without
getting caught up in history per se, in a story. I looked exclu-
sively at the surfaces of the Cold War, with the idea that the surfaces would tell you things about what was going on that you
would lose sight of as you went deeper and deeper into strategy,
politics, elections, treaties, all the messy anatomy of history. And
there's no question of evaluating right or wrong; we start with
the axiom that each side creates the other side.

Val, my wife, has a completely opposite view. She's a labor
organizer, one of the best known in the country, in fact. You've
seen her on *60 Minutes.* For her, everything is muscle against
muscle, meat, material. The traditional reasons are still in force:

economic self-interest, ruling classes trying to maintain power. The world is a wrestling match; the shift or twitch of one or another tendon or ligament makes all the difference in the nature of life for tens of thousands, if not millions, of people. The surface is only what the people in the cheap seats can see. We argue about it, or we used to.

Sometimes the less sophisticated kids will keep hammering and want to know who started it or who was right or wrong, and I tell them nobody started it and no one was right or wrong. The hipper students tend to begin with that assumption anyway, especially the ones who are into literary theory, film studies, French criticism. And yet . . . they all seem to be fascinated by the level of commitment on both sides during the era, especially during the 1960s. In spite of themselves. A lot of their parents were hippies, after all. They make fun of the more overt manifestations of it—the clothes, the hair—but still they're intrigued by the passion, or the belief.

The History Department (Cold War Studies is technically part of History; I've been trying to get Hollister to give it independent funding) used to feel very threatened by my approach, which is hardly orthodox history. One of the department dons, retired now, never approved my appointment and referred to what I did as "antihistory" during the whole time he remained on the faculty. But I am generally, if grudgingly, accepted now, largely because I bring a lot of notice to the college, am widely published, all that.

Five or six years ago, though, it was almost a comedy. I had an ongoing debate with a black professor named Coleman Silsbee—you read *The Black Mask of History,* I'm sure, or you read about it—an early "black conservative." Silsbee is a current star.

The Black Mask of History caused a big stir; Hollister paid a lot
of money to get him, and they pay a lot to keep him. He has
been working on the sequel for as long as he's been at Hollister.
He is a rarity among black writers, a big free-market flag-waver.
Whenever you talk about another country, it always boils down
to, Did they put a man on the moon? Did they win World War
II? His responses are basically a rejection of a frame of argument, not an answer. Val hates him. She thinks he's CIA.
Whether he is or not (dear old Hollister, nestled in the Connecticut hills, has been a seed farm for the Agency for fifty
years), he is certainly a propagandist, and he assumes I secretly
am, too. To Silsbee any expression of an idea is a form of propa-
ganda. In conversation his facial expression says, "You know, and
I know, that you're serving up some bullshit, and if I thought you
really took this seriously we wouldn't even be having this discussion." He'll say things like, "Yes, John, that's all nice about
Khrushchev's picture, but you know, and I know, that decisions
were made that affected real lives, and real people were killed,
and the question is, what kind of a system is less unjust?" And I
would say that these surface things had *become* life for huge
numbers of people, that most people's experience of systems, in
our culture at least, is of the surfaces that they present. And traditional history misses those surfaces. . . . And he'll look at me
with his "How long are you going to keep this up?" look and say,
"Well, that's the job of history, isn't it? To look beneath the surface?" That question has, in fact, become a raw nerve for me.

Anyway, until the unpleasantness with Rappaport, that was
the main avenue of criticism of the program. Otherwise, despite
the occasional grousing from the occasional grayhair, the snide
remarks ("History McNuggets" was one brilliant offering), the

whole Cold War Studies thing has become so popular that I am Entrenched. Yes, tenured, all that. I write books, I show up on TV. It's become an industry, almost.

And now this book, a chance to write my definitive statement on the Cold War. One of my former students, Gordon Kohl, a bright guy who graduated a few years ago, is an editor at one of the biggest publishing houses (a shock, of course, to realize that one is old enough to have students old enough, etc., etc. . . .). "Not a 'history,' " his letter read. "A phenomenology. The real John Delano take on it. Approach the Cold War strictly from the surface, as you do in class . . . the images, the mythoreligious underpinnings of it. . . ." He drew up a contract for more money than I make in three years, and there's a cross-marketing thing with PBS (a multipart special tentatively titled *John Delano's Cold War*—it's pronounced De-LAY-no, by the way); it can take any shape I want.

Fantastic, right? This is it. My opportunity to produce a definitive work, a synthesis of everything I've been talking about for the last fifteen years. But I can't write it. I'm at a dead standstill. I go to my office every day, on the top floor of Driller Hall, but instead of writing about the Kennedy-Nixon debates, or the media's treatment of LSD, I find myself daydreaming for hours, remembering family trips in vivid detail, my brother playing my father's violin, girls I made out with in junior high school. . . .

To be honest, I have been coming unglued. How can I explain this? I don't believe a word I write anymore. My whole approach to Cold War Studies, in fact, has started to feel like an exoskeleton into which I've crawled in order to hide from something. Suddenly everything I have done and thought, not only in my professional life but in my personal life, seems like nothing but a series of masks to me, and I find myself looking through the surfaces of those masks into a void. I seem to have been dealing with only half of . . . *something,* and not, apparently, the important half.

Did I mention that my father just died?

This was just after the Rappaport blowup happened. We don't need to go into how my father ended up in New Mexico; my mom had left him years before and in some ways never forgave herself for that extremely reasonable step, and that's a whole other story. My father's second wife, Estelle, was a meek, fatalistic woman who did her best. Years before, she had tried to be a glamorous wife to some Las Vegas type, who had finally left her because she wasn't brassy enough, and I think she must have decided, "Whatever else, not that." My father, at least, wasn't that type. They were both in their sixties when they met, and they decided to keep each other warm.

I hadn't spent more time with them than I needed to. In fact, I kept in the least possible touch I could without totally losing contact. One visit every two years at most. Our encounters flooded me with a sense of dread, of an undertow pulling me back into a person I had done my best to bury. The fact that I'd changed my name bothered my father no end, as did the fact that I had no children. He and Val did not get along, but then again he and everybody else didn't get along. . . . Don't get me started.

The Last Visit. I guess everybody has it. I hadn't seen him for two years, and I had some time at the beginning of summer. Val couldn't make it; she had a big labor conference she had to attend. Oh, how my father had aged—I don't know if it was the epilepsy medication taking its toll or what. His cheeks were sunken, and his glasses magnified his eyes, which loomed, confrontational and frightened, in front of me. Like all old men, he had discovered the Internet. For half my visit, he stayed in the darkened bedroom, in his pajamas, sitting at the computer, a folded towel underneath him on the chair, his face lit by the dim, spectral light of the monitor, like someone being interrogated by a ghost. Now, in addition to all my other reasons for being angry with him, I was angry with him for getting old and illustrating what would happen to me eventually, assuming I was lucky as we measure these things.

We circled each other warily, and the first evening went more or less all right. There were a couple of tight moments. At one point he asked me, "What do you hear from your brother?" This was a sore spot—he knew that Chris and I didn't speak. We hadn't spoken for eight years. He and Chris didn't speak either. We steered around it, though, and things were okay. But the second day, over dinner at the local Chinese restaurant (I had begun making notes to myself to think about the proliferation of Chinese restaurants as a Cold War phenomenon), he had a few glasses of wine, and he started acting ugly. As if he was scratching an itch, and I was the itch. On this evening Estelle was getting it from him as well. To keep from being sucked in, I began taking notes, right there at the table, on what he was saying. Here are a few examples, at random. My father on the molestation of children by Catholic priests: "Some of these kids went back for seconds, so what are they crying about?" On a recently deceased comedian: "He was nothing. He was a fat, stupid jerk. The only people who thought he was funny were other jerks." An exchange on the Orient Express, which had come up I don't remember how: Estelle: "How does the train get from London to Venice?" My father: "On tracks. How do you think it gets there?" On dieting (after Estelle refused dessert because of her diet and remarked how bad it was for your cholesterol): "Just because you can't eat it, don't make it lousy for me."

It went on and on. There was never any telling what, exactly, had triggered it or how long it would last. I had lived with it my whole life, and you'd think I would have gotten used to it, but I never did. We got back to their apartment, and it kept up, and at a certain point I said, "Dad, would you cut it out, please?" We were sitting in the living room, and Estelle was making coffee in the kitchen. He looked at me and said, "Cut what out?"

"The constant negativity."

"Look, sonny . . ."

This tone was impossible for me to take. So before it even got rolling, I held up my hand and said, "Listen, can I tell you why?" He stopped, and I thought, Now what? And I decided to tell him about the Rappaport thing.

Rappaport. A brilliant guy, no question about it. Younger than I was by about ten years, a kind of revisionist Zionist New Wave Holocaust theoretician. Very highly paid (I made inquiries). We had once exchanged a few unpleasant words over my "Lost Tribesmen" course, basically because he was by temperament extremely antagonistic toward assimilationist Jews in general, which was what the entire course was about. Anyway, we were on a panel together at a conference Hollister had sponsored, called "*Le Commencement du Siècle*—American Culture at the Beginning of the Millennium," and I had remarked that the turn of this century seemed to be notable for an increasing velocity and contrast in argument between sides on any given question. (I had suggested naming the panel "Things Fall Apart.") There were fewer and fewer gray areas; every argument was interpreted solely in terms of what power nexus stood to benefit from its implications. Hardly an unprecedented notion. I proposed calling it the Era of Bad Faith (professors love to name things—historical eras, art movements, moon craters . . .) and brought up abortion and Israel as two topics that couldn't be discussed rationally and that were rushing in to fill up the vacuum of absolute antagonism that had been left open by the dissolution of the Cold War. People, I said, needed a new Holy War to fight.

Well, Rappaport took my head off about Israel. He said that Israel had real enemies, who wanted to send in real missiles and destroy real cities, and that it wasn't a symbolic conflict, and I said, yes, well, and the antiabortion people believe they are saving real lives, and real things are always at stake in these conflicts, and what I was talking about was not the reality or the unreality of the conditions but the terms in which we frame how we think about those conditions, and Rappaport said this was a typical deconstructionist notion, and at a certain point people who live in History recognize that words only go so far to create reality, in fact they don't create reality, and if someone is holding a gun on you it doesn't make much difference how you frame the reality, your first question is what to do about the gun.

And I was about to say, yes, and how you answer *that* question has a lot to do with how you frame the situation in your own mind, but I couldn't get to that idea before he said, "And this entire premise is extremely irresponsible, that because there are two sides in an argument, neither side is right. Making the Cold War into a value-neutral situation is only an escape from analyzing the situation and asking which system has been more on the side of freedom, which system supports the existence of Israel, which system exterminates Jews wholesale, which system creates

Gulags. . . ." And on and on and on, and even the people there who agreed with Rappaport told me later they felt he had gone way over the top in his rhetoric, that it turned into a personal attack, and in a funny way it probably made my stock rise a little, since I didn't answer him angrily. But despite that, it left me with a depressed, nagging feeling. Did I really not believe in anything? Had I turned into some kind of wishy-washy, dime-store mystic? I'm susceptible to those kinds of doubts to begin with.

So I told my father all of this, and at a certain point I could see his impatience mounting.

"The guy's right," he said, breaking in. "I've always thought this whole course you taught was a lot of crap. What's the point of studying what Khrushchev's face looks like if you can't tell the difference between the United States and Russia in the first place? You're just . . . playing with yourself."

For the first and only time in my life, a switch flipped in me. I had evidently been under more strain than I realized. The arrogance, I thought. The years of obliviousness to the effect of his words and actions. Squadrons of resentment and anger, honed over decades into crack fighting trim by the drill sergeants of my subconscious, instantly mobilized for Red Alert; I was amazed in retrospect, the silos opening, missiles training in, total assured destruction. . . . Looking him right in the eye, I said, "Fuck you"— the expression of shock on his face was immediate and gratifying—"You want to know why nobody talks to you? You want to know why you spend all your time staring at that computer?"—the exhilaration, the free fall, like jumping out of an airplane, no going back now—"You're no good. You've never been any good. You're a mean, sorry excuse for a father. Your lousy attitude killed my mother, and it's not going to kill me."

Then I stood up, just as Estelle was walking into the room with the tray of coffee and cookies. "I feel sorry for you," I said. I grabbed my coat and bag and left the apartment, crossed the pool area of the gated community where they lived (I have a perfect, eidetic memory of the pool, covered with its blue tarp that sagged under little pools of rainwater, littered with yellowing leaves), went back to the hotel where the phone was ringing as I walked into the room—Estelle, calling in tears; I answered her curtly, hung up, and left the next morning. I never saw my father alive again.

Even before I left I began to feel the guilt, which I so richly deserved. Why did I have to lose it like that? What damage could he do me? Wasn't being old and decrepit punishment enough for him? Why had I let him get to me that way? And then I lost all chance of getting things straight with him.

The funeral. I was the only member of the immediate family there; no uncles, no aunts, no cousins. And my brother didn't come. The rest of the people at the wake were friends of Estelle's from New Mexico. Fifteen people, maximum. I looked at my father's face against the satin pillow, waxy, the skin ineptly tucked under his chin, making him look . . . portly. And burgundy-colored lipstick. Oh, please. I sat there, and I thought, There it all goes, up the chimney. One more life gone—the memories of World War II dance music, the Depression, Queens, Brooklyn, the early days of radio, whatever private sex experiences he'd had . . . all gone. All that pain— badly handled, for the most part, to be sure. Closed, swallowed up. Chris, my brother, didn't even send a card or flowers . . . nothing. His son. My brother.

There wasn't much of an estate to talk about. Estelle gave

me my father's old violin. I remember my father scratching away at it a few times when I was a kid. He hadn't played since high school. Inside him, I always felt, was some kind of crippled artist. At a certain point Chris had picked it up, and he played it all the time for about a year and a half. (I have no musical talent at all, unlike Chris.) I opened the case and took out the violin; it's always surprising how little a violin weighs. I looked at the grain in the wood, the eighty-year-old stain in its grooves. I almost went to pieces, really, but I wouldn't give my father that satisfaction, even posthumously.

I sat through two days of what I guess are the usual details. And then there I was, in middle age, with the last, and maybe the biggest, bridge into the past washed out forever. So of course I found myself looking back toward that past, across a rushing river, terrified. . . .

EVER SINCE THEN I haven't been able to get it together. I go to my office, but I find myself looking around, thinking, "What just happened?" "Where am I?" I try to write this book, but it seems so insubstantial to me, so dispensable. My mind keeps shuttling back instead to images of my own life, which I can't keep out, a forced march through the evidence of my own mortality. I am wearing out with this constant battle between what I'm supposed to be thinking about and what is obtruding itself on me.

Everything has gotten mixed up in my head. My personal life has always spelled extinction to me. It threatened to drown me in its apparent randomness. History, I thought, was what saved you from extinction. It conferred meaning from outside. It had been my escape. But obviously History was equally capable of completely extinguishing the individual—that, in fact, seemed in many ways to be its true job.

I don't know anymore what to put into the book and what to leave out. I lived through the Cold War. But what did it mean to say I lived through it? It meant that, say, JFK's assassination was part of My Life. But then, watching *The Jackie Gleason Show* the night my mother cut her finger to the bone, using the serrated bread knife to open a package of frozen broccoli ("What the hell did you use a bread knife for?" my father said) was part of the Cold War. Where and how did one's life join that Other Life of History? In writing about it, I seem constantly forced to make a choice about whether it belongs to me or to History. Everything cleaves into these pairs of mutually exclusive conceptual units, these contending absolutes. And if I don't *do something*, find some way of transcending these seemingly insoluble contradictions, I am afraid that my life, or my perception of it, will be shattered into meaningless pieces for keeps. I go to the office, and I try to focus, and I sit at my desk, fizzing like an Alka-Seltzer tablet in a puddle on the drainboard.

Gordon Kohl calls me periodically to check on the book, and my stomach crumples. I trump up some stuff, improvise a few riffs on different Cold War–era events. He always loves it, but I don't even know what I'm saying half the time. I'll go into some cadenza about the iconic relation between JFK and the Beatles, and he'll say, "This is great! Hurry! I hear cash registers ringing!" When I get off the phone, what I remember is my mother in a miniskirt, wearing an I LOVE PAUL button. It drove my father up the wall. Every day there is this weird overlay between my personal life and what I'm trying to write about, and I have begun to think, Well, maybe that is what I'm supposed to be writing about. But even my own life comes only as a series of surfaces, and that is the final dread. This, I think, may be the price I've paid for running away from it for so long, my own karma punishment. Now I want to break through that surface, and I don't know how. Where, I keep thinking—where have I been? How did I end up in such a limbo?

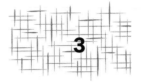

3

ATLANTICVILLE. ALL I EVER WANTED was to get away. Yet when I think about it now I can experience an odd longing. Almost anything, I have come to realize, can become an object of longing if you put a frame around it.

It must have been a lot like the prairie, with all that sky. In my memory an Aaron Copland ostinato wheels constantly in the background, imitating the drone of a plane overhead at midday. The sense of the men offstage at some muscular work and the women at home keeping order. Frontier characters still roamed the neighborhood then—ice-cream men, of course, but also milkmen, door-to-door salesmen, knife grinders steering their carts with the clanging bells, up and down the treeless streets, an echo of Brooklyn in that endless noon.

An image: Wonalancet Street, early afternoon; slowly a truck rolls past the identical houses, emitting a dense gray cloud of mist from its rear, a bored-looking county employee piloting it, checking the sideview occasionally. Behind him, like seagulls following a garbage barge, a group of boys riding their bicycles in tight, reckless circles, faces bright, excited—crazed with excitement—bobbing and ducking, jockeying for position to be next to ride inside the penumbra of thick mist, squeals pealing up from out of the great gray cloud. Inside the cloud they are both blind and invisible—fascinating and urgent concepts for young boys, first intimation of nonbeing for creatures who are pure being—except maybe for a leg and part of a bicycle wheel, apparitional near the ground, attached to a ghostly body enclosed in a mysterious fog. . . . The truck would make the slow, deliberate corner onto Laurel Avenue, spraying all the while, the kids following it like a carnival. I don't remember anybody's mother telling him it wasn't a good idea to ride a bicycle inside a cloud of insecticide.

I look back at it now and I can see it so clearly, the historical moment of Long Island postwar suburbia. It was all still balanced; the New had not yet outweighed the Old, the Old World still hanging on in Brooklyn and Queens and parts of Manhattan—people speaking Italian and Polish and Yiddish in steaming tenements, the tiled floors in the hallways under the single overhead bulb, the smells of cooking. . . . That Old World was still able to coexist with the denatured, accelerated New World of brand-new houses on cookie-cutter lots, the new classrooms in the just-built elementary schools, the fledgling shopping malls, the future as yet unfurnished, spreading like spores in a petri dish.

On Sundays we visited my grandparents in Garvey's Neck, where my father had spent his high-school years. Garvey's Neck was an old enclave on the North Shore, just outside the city line, a kind of annex of Queens with substantial houses from right after World War I and giant elm trees whose roots buckled the sidewalks. My grandparents' house, like all the houses on 135th Lane, was built in the Tudor style on a narrow plot on a street that ran on a steep incline down to Northern Boulevard, with its stores and restaurants. On a clear evening you could see the lights of New York in the distance. I was always aware of the combination of acceleration and increasing density as I got closer to the city—the traffic was thicker, the houses and stores closer together, the pressure of time and history increasing, the weight and pressure of the past.

The living room was filled with furry and nubbed over-stuffed velvet and brocade furniture from the 1920s, lamps with fringed shades, but we spent most of our time in the finished basement, a low-ceilinged room lined with varnished pine wainscoting and furnished with rattan chairs. My grandmother would lay out pieces of Swiss cheese on waxed paper on the table under the fluorescent-ring ceiling lamp. Upstairs was a sunny, old-fashioned tiled kitchen and the living room, and then, up a long flight of carpeted stairs, the bedroom level, where my deaf aunt had painted a swan on the pink tiles over the toilet. Through a door narrow enough to belong to a broom closet, a steep set of wooden stairs led up to a finished attic, which had been my father's room, where old books and photos were to be found everywhere in the four dormers. After dinner I would sneak away from the table to go up there and look out over the houses and trees and see the light in the clock tower at the top of Biener Pontiac winking against the sunset like the evening star.

On Sundays there were the big gatherings. Uncles, aunts, cousins. A houseful of kids underfoot, dressed nicely from church. The men in their late thirties, maybe. When we arrived, my grandmother would take my father's head in her hands like a cantaloupe and peck it with kisses, in front of his sisters and his cousins, and finally release it with an explosive *"Gia!"* "A prince!" she would say. The cousins would be watching, slit-eyed. They all had married good Sicilian girls from New York, but my father had found an exotic—a farm girl from Eau Claire. She was the object of numerous ostensibly well-intentioned double-entendre remarks, and she would, I now recognize, flirt back with them.

"Johnny boy," they'd say when I came in with my parents. Later my brother would be with us. Chris had blond hair when he was very young, although it darkened up some with time. My father came from a race of dark-skinned Sicilians, and my brother's unusual coloring was the topic of much ribbing. There was something otherworldly about him even then. They liked to pass him around from lap to lap, as if he were a big hydroponic tomato. A New World novelty. Look what grows here. But that was later.

After dinner Uncle Rudy would get started telling war stories. All my father's cousins—Uncle Rudy and Uncle Mike and Uncle Lenny and Uncle John—had been in World War II. Uncle Rudy and Uncle Johnny had sons, older than I was, who were bound for ROTC and eventual military service. My Uncle Johnny had captured a big Japanese flag in the Philippines, which hung in my cousin Paul's room. Uncle Rudy had fought in Europe, Uncle Johnny in the Pacific. They told stories about army life sitting around the table after dinner. They, children of people who had pulled up all stakes to move to this strange land maybe twenty years before the war, risked everything once again in order to be part of this new country. You had to admire it.

My father had a hard time with the stories. Memories of the

war gave everyone a shared history that, of course, he didn't share in the same way, having been medically exempt. It left its scar. The central event of his generation, and he was sidelined, unable to participate in what it meant, at the time, to be a man. While they were overseas, he was in college. None of his cousins went to college, even when they got back and it was available to them on the GI Bill. They resented him for having that chance, resented my grandparents for having more money and living in Garvey's Neck. But still, after all, they were family.

Uncle Rudy in his shirtsleeves, tie undone, everyone sitting around after dinner . . . He had the best audience in the world, he said, in my aunts and grandmother. Of all the cousins, he was the live wire, a short man in ill-fitting clothes, with reddish hair that hugged his head and a big wart by his nose. I don't think he had finished high school. He smoked constantly and eventually died of emphysema.

"You had the guys who were loading ordnance onto the big B-17s. . . . The planes would take off, and they would sit around and go back to whatever. We were billeted at Champfleury. You know 'billeted,' right, John?"

My Uncle John nodded, smiling.

"I don't 'know it,' " my father said.

"Well, Frank, you weren't there," Rudy said bluntly. One of my aunts giggled.

"So we were billeted next to a cheese factory, or like a cheese warehouse," he went on. "*Madonna mia,* you never saw so many cats all over the place." He did a mincing imitation of the way a cat would walk, carefully, head up, looking, then taking a few more steps. "We hated the cats 'cause they were always yelling in the night and waking us up, out behind the alley, making . . ." and he said something in Italian that made all my aunts squeal with laughter.

"These cats were always hungry. Because cats don't eat cheese; they're allergic to it."

"What are you talking about?" my father said, straining for a false heartiness in his voice, a one-of-the-guys sound. "Who told you cats don't eat cheese?"

"Who told me? My eyes told me, Frank," Uncle Rudy said.

"They make cat food with cheese in it," my father said.

"Frank, I wouldn't know; I don't eat cat food." This cracked up a couple of the aunts, as well as my Uncle Lenny, but my father rode in on top of the laughter.

"Well, listen," he said, wanting to clear up this important point, "we don't eat cat food either, but we buy food for our cats, with cheese, and they eat it."

"What can I tell you, Frank, you probably got a couple rats with long hair, *mangiare formaggio* . . ." and everybody laughed. I looked at my mother, and she was laughing, too, lighting a cigarette. My father sat there, unsmiling, frustrated that the truth wasn't being acknowledged.

"Anyway, a couple of guys had got these firecrackers—they'd been down in Marseilles and brought these back. And there was this one tomcat with the big tiger stripes and all this hair around his neck—he looked like the guys with the hats on the cigar box—"

"Dutch Masters," somebody said.

"Dutch Masters," Uncle Rudy repeated. "With the big thing around their neck. And this son of a bitch was like the Frank Sinatra of the whole cheese factory. He had every female cat screaming outside our windows all night long. Then in the morning you'd see him walking by, like"—and here he got up and walked half the length of the room with a smug expression on his face, flexing his shoulders as he walked, his butt switching. I laughed along with everybody else. My cousins were watching him, learning how to tell a story. "So one day we catch him, and this guy Mike O'Brien, a sergeant, he was from Passaic—he got killed in the Bulge he should rest in peace—he sticks a firecracker in this cat's rear end with the fuse sticking out and he lights it and we let the cat go quick. When the firecracker goes off that son of a bitch took off running, and we saw him later, walking like this," and he stood up and walked bowlegged, one halting step at a time, a perplexed expression on his face. Everybody laughed and laughed, and I glanced at my father and saw him looking at the floor, in a world of his own.

IT SOUNDS GREAT, right? The storytelling, the Oral Tradition. I hear them talk about it now, at the departmental meetings; the multicultural heads go on and on about the Elders this and the traditions that, and it makes me want to run screaming out of the room. The willed provincialism, the pride taken in the ignorance. . . . I ran as hard and as fast as I could in the other direction. All I wanted was to get away and be in some kind of pure America that was all motion and possibility.

My father ran, too, I guess. He moved with his exotic wife from all that Old World to the new, denatured suburbia. But he was never comfortable there either. Where he was comfortable was the ideal world of circuits and equations. Radios, televisions.

A place to stand that was absolute, not relative to the charisma of his cousins' experience.

"The great thing with math and physics," he told me more than once, "is that there's a right or wrong. You either have the right answer or you don't. It's hard, not soft."

But science isn't about reinforcing certainties. I once said to him that the great inventors were often surprised by what they found. He fluffed this off. And yet I know that he knew this. When he was a kid, in that big house in Garvey's Neck, he built radios from designs he found in *The Book of Knowledge*. The mystery of it, the voice, crackling but intelligible, like a message in a bottle from some faraway place. That yearning he must have felt.

ONE NIGHT MY father brought home a miniature reel-to-reel tape recorder. This was when very few people had them, and way before cassette tapes. I must have been at least seven or eight, because my brother was there, still in a high chair. We shared a bedroom; the tiny orange night-light at the foot of my bed cast muted, looming shadows on the midnight walls. Chris would stand in his crib holding on to the rail, and we would have conversations in babble talk; I'd tell him nonsense stories to make him go to sleep.

My father loved these things, gadgets. Everyone his age was gadget crazy. After the Depression and the war, the high that ensued. Look what you can buy! My uncles, even my grandfather. Christmas turned into a science fair. Electric blenders, stereos, electric hedge clippers, pneumatic cork removers, color TVs, dishwashers, lawn mowers, battery-powered toys for the kids . . .

I was already used to the movie camera, with its bright white lights mounted on a handheld rack, an antler trophy from a space animal. Nobody has seen these films since the night they were brought back from the photo place where they were developed, cousins and aunts and uncles all captured in jerky, accelerated motion. It was a momentary craze. I remember one night hearing some kind of commotion in my parents' room, laughter, subdued voices, my mother's voice saying, "No, Frank!" More laughter. My father walked out of the room holding the movie camera.

The tape recorder. It was small, like something you might see in an early James Bond movie, popping out from under a desk, the tiny reels spinning. The night he brought it home, we opened it up at the kitchen table after dinner. After removing the unit—it was about the size of a brick—from its packaging and inserting the batteries, he set it in the middle of the table, and the four of us sat there and looked at it. Into our small universe of homey-looking wallpaper and "colonial" chairs and trivets and pot holders had intruded an object from NASA. Chris was strapped into his high chair, kicking his legs in excitement. The machine sat in the middle of the table like an oracle. We would speak into it, and it would reveal something to us, about ourselves and our fate.

Or maybe that's not how it felt. Maybe it was just there and we hooked it up as quickly as we could, to have a little fun hearing our voices recorded for the first time.

My father got the microphone, a short, black plastic tube,

set up on a little stand, so that it was propped like a cannon, pointed upward, and we gathered on one side of the table; slowly, with concentration, he pushed the red "record" button and the "play" button simultaneously, and the reels started turning in tandem, at different speeds, like horses taking up the slack in the reins and getting along, the take-up reel spinning faster than the other, a relationship that would shift as the tape progressed. On the front a tiny red glass dot glowed like a ruby from within. The machine was recording.

"Hello," my father said with an insincere cordiality in his voice, as if he were an explorer greeting a group of natives who might or might not be hostile. "Here we are." He turned to us. "Say something," he said.

"Hi," I said.

My father looked at my mother. "Fran, say something."

My mother waved her hand in a vague gesture at the machine, as if she were waving at a movie camera.

"Come on . . ." my father said, "what's the machine going to do with that?" He adjusted the microphone so it was pointing more toward her. She shook her head a little and started giggling.

My father looked at me, as if for a helping hand, and he began talking. "Okay," he said, as if he were reading a radio dispatch from a foreign capital, "we're sitting here at the kitchen table, Daddy, Mommy, Johnny, and Chris. And Johnny's going to sing us a song. Take it away, Salt Lake City. . . ."

He was looking at me with an encouraging grin; it was a game. I started singing, "*A Fab wash is clean clear through and deodorizes, too; That's a Fab wash, a Fab wash, for you-u-u.*"

Applause from Mom and Dad. "Okay," my father said, as if

the party had really gotten rolling now. "Terrific. Fran, say something."

My mother shifted forward in her chair as if she were approaching a microphone, which she was, and said, "Well, I would just like to say that I am honored to be here tonight with such a great artist, such a great singer . . ."

"Thank you!" I shouted.

". . . and that . . . I . . ." searching for something appropriate to say, "I accept your nomination for president."

My father and I clapped and hollered.

"Okay," my father said. "You want to listen to it back?"

"Yeah," I said.

He pushed the "stop" button and the reels instantly stopped turning. Then, making sure he had the right button, he pushed "rewind" and they started revolving speedily in the opposite direction. My father looked up at us, smiling like a kid on Christmas morning. In a few moments the reel ran out and he stopped the machine, threaded the tape through the slot between the playback heads and back into the take-up reel and, taking a deep breath, pushed the "play" button. After a moment, out of the little speaker, my father's voice, or a tiny simulacrum of it, arose, like a thin, piping genie: "Hello . . ."

In amazement we listened to the sequence that we had just spoken, leaning forward toward the machine, squinting with the effort to hear, although we didn't need to. When my mother's part came on, she said, listening, "That doesn't sound like me."

"Yes it does," I said.

"Is that what I sound like? God . . ."

Then it was my father's voice saying, "You want to listen to it back?" and the sound stopping at the point where my father had turned off the machine. He looked at us now, and said, "Isn't that great?" My mother and I nodded enthusiastically. He reached toward the machine to press the "stop" button.

Before he could stop the recorder another voice came out of the speaker—a rough, croaking voice, saying something unrecognizable, surrounded by a fuzz of distortion, as if the person's mouth were too close to the microphone. *"Uncle Papa,"* the voice sounded like it was saying, *"Uncle Papa says 'ha, ha, ha . . .'"* Then again, repeating, *"Ha . . . Ha . . . Ha . . . ,"* speaking the syllables deliberately. In the background a kid's voice was saying, "Let me."

We looked at one another. Somebody else had recorded on the tape. Maybe in the store during a demonstration, maybe they had taken it home and returned it. . . . Who were these people? That heavy voice again, saying, *"Pa-pa . . . Pa-pa . . ."* thick-throated, mimicking a child's cadences. Then it, too, was cut off.

A moment of silence, then more sound—a rustling, confused sound of someone rubbing the microphone, positioning it, fiddling with it, then a clearer voice, perhaps a salesman, saying, "Whatever you want."

Pause, still recording, then another voice: "Over here?" The first voice said something indistinct. Silence for a moment, then the second voice saying, "Testing, one-two-three . . ."

Another voice, faint, a woman: "Go on, go on . . . do it. . . ." Then, up close to the microphone, in arch imitation of intimacy, a man's voice, tremulously singing, *"Ah, well-uh, since my bay-buh left me . . . I got a new place to go. . . . It's down at the . . ."* It trailed off, then another voice, also a man's voice, singing, distorted, too loud, *"Moon River . . . wider than the sky . . ."* Women's voices in the background, alternately derisive and feigning ecstatic delirium . . . the men in a convulsive parody of fame and adulation and misremembered lyrics.

Then silence. We listened to see what else would come; in the background our battery-powered wall clock ticked in stark relief, the second hand jerking forward with each click.

That seemed to be it. After a few more seconds, my father again reached toward the machine to shut it off. As his hand touched it, another voice shot out of the machine, high and shrill and vehement, screaming *"Fuck you! Fuck you! Shit! Fuck! Fuck shit . . . eat shit! . . ."*—a nasal adolescent's voice, and my father's hand jerked back as if he had touched a rattlesnake, and we stared at the machine as the little reels turned—*"Shit bastard fuck you! Fuck your shit! . . ."*

"Turn it off! For God's sake!" my mother was shouting.

My father reached out and after some fumbling got the "stop" button and stopped it. We sat there, collectively shaking. Chris was laughing and laughing in his high chair, looking at us in turn.

"That's horrible," my mother said. "Take it back."

My father looked at her as if she had advanced a crackpot theory of some sort. "What are you talking about, take it back? It's not the machine's fault. We can just tape over it."

"Take it back."

They debated this question for a while, as I remember. Neither of them looked at me.

"I feel sick," she said.

LATER THAT NIGHT I got up to go to the bathroom. I have no idea what time it was, but it was late. I saw a pale heightening of light across one of the living-room chairs downstairs, which meant that a light was on the kitchen. I walked down the stairs as quietly as I could. I rounded the corner and looked into the kitchen and saw my father sitting at the table in his pajamas, his hair neatly combed, the little tape-recorder reels revolving silently in front of him. He seemed way off in thought, or half asleep. His head jerked up when he noticed me.

"Jesus," he said, sitting back in the chair. "You startled me."

"What are you doing?" I asked him.

"I'm erasing the tape," he said, "so Mother doesn't get upset. If you just put it on 'record' and turn the volume down, you erase what's on there, and there'll be no more . . . untoward surprises." He had a way, sometimes, if he felt he needed to act in his official role as Father, of speaking in an unnaturally elevated diction, a kind of formality when he felt he had to discharge an official duty.

I pulled out a chair and sat down. He was younger then, by almost ten years, than I am now. In my mind I see him in his striped pajamas, his head slightly too large for his body.

"Come on," he said. "We can leave this running and go outside and have a smoke."

He pushed the chair back and stood up and opened the kitchen door, and we went out into the thin, black September night air and pulled the door almost shut behind us. It wasn't too cold, and we stood there looking up at the stars and the silhouettes of houses against the sky, over the Harkavys' house next door, which sat with its back to us.

"One night," he said, "I was out here having a smoke and I

looked in that window"—he meant the dining-room window in the rear of the Harkavys' house—"and I saw Mr. and Mrs. Harkavy walking around naked." He took a long puff of his cigarette.

I asked him if I could try the cigarette, and he looked down and smiled at me. Then he said, "Wait here for a second," and went inside. He reappeared in a moment with the cardboard box that had contained the tape recorder.

"Shut your eyes," he said. I did. A moment passed.

"Now open them." He handed me the closed box, turned me so that the light from the kitchen door shone on the box, and said, "Open it."

I opened the cover of the box. There, sitting inside, whitish in the light from the kitchen door, quivering in the box, sat a small cloud of cigarette smoke. I had seen smoke exhaled from his mouth and from my mother's, seen it piping up from the end of their cigarettes, but always moving, always going somewhere. I had never seen it just sitting someplace, like a cloud hugging the ground. It was a small miracle—as if he had made time stand still. I looked up at him and thought, What a great man my father is. What a great man.

THAT COULD NOT HAVE BEEN long before JFK was assassinated. Looking back on it now, there was that eerie moment of balance, the roller-coaster car approaching the high crest, about to plunge downward—the suburban idyll, the relative affluence, the barbecues, the fallout shelters, the Red Dread, the LSD experiments across the continent in California, the whole Camelot thing, the Peace Corps, physical fitness, *Mad* magazine, Hemingway's suicide, Marilyn Monroe's death—the impossible contradictions in the nation's situation wearing a bigger and bigger hole in the fabric of things as they appeared. . . .

I have, in fact, been trying to work on the JFK chapter, using my class notes. In my classes I stress the paradoxes of that time. I show them the stories in *Life* and *Look* about the need for community fallout shelters, complete with diagrams. One of them contains a letter supposedly written by JFK to the American public, encouraging them to build shelters. The grade-school kids doing air-raid drills, the Cuban missile crisis, and against that background the whole *Leave It to Beaver* obsession with normality . . .

I have a collection—one of the most notable collections

extant, actually—of Civil Defense pamphlets from that period, including shelter diagrams and information bulletins, which I have gathered over the years. The students' favorite is dependably the classic "Grandma's Pantry" flyer, from the summer of 1960. The cover is a drawing of what purports to be an old-fashioned pantry, bordered with a stylized rendering of gingham cloth. The text reads this way:

> GRANDMA'S PANTRY, *its shelves loaded with canned goods and staples, was ready for any emergency.*
>
> *And when Grandpa announced, "Pack up. We're moving west," Grandma put a portion of her pantry on the wagon, and was ready.*
>
> *Civil Defense figures Grandma had the right idea at home and on the westward trail. . . .*
>
> *Twentieth century "Grandmas" may be moving and moving fast—evacuating their homes—in a civil defense emergency.*

Then the pamphlet lists the things you need in the EVAC-UATION SURVIVAL KIT—a three-day supply of food and water, first-aid items, a flashlight, blankets, etc. There's a pen-and-ink illustration showing cans labeled "Fish," "Meat," "Stew," "Baby Food," "Fruit." At the end it says,

> IN THE FIRST DAYS *of a civil defense emergency everyone will have to be as self-sufficient as possible.*

The corner grocery store, the modern kitchen with its tap water, the light and power that come on with a flip of a switch—these and many other taken-for-granted services won't be there. IT PAYS TO GET READY WHILE YOUR THINKING IS STEADY.

Right afterward a drawing of a multipurpose kitchen tool, with a glowing halo around it, and the caption, "P.S. Don't forget the CAN OPENER!!"

The kids crack up at this, which is my intention, but it makes me feel a little guilty. It was not a joke; the copywriters who cranked out these pamphlets were not trying to be funny. People envisioned the need for the shelters and the stockpiles as a real possibility. Everything wiped out. People lived with this scenario day to day, at the exact same time that they watched projected images of themselves on TV on *The Dick Van Dyke Show* and *Ozzie and Harriet*—the apotheosis of the suburban dream. The governing hypotheses—total normalcy, abundance, and progress, along with the possibility at any moment of total global annihilation within minutes—had become so mutually antagonistic that something in people's sensibility turned absurdist. The angle, the no-man's-land, between The Official Version and anything that might resemble truth became the object of focus. This is where it started. At first it was a private joke that you giggled about in mutual recognition over a joint; then it gradually swelled into a suspicion of massive conspiracy and cover-up that opened the maws of every paranoia lurking in the collective unconscious and paved the way for the Era of Bad Faith. . . . We are so used to this now that it hardly seems worth saying. It has become its own cliché.

———

BUT JFK. MY students don't really get the whole JFK thing. The magic doesn't translate across the generations. It takes work to get them to see what it was. What I tell them is this: Kennedy was the fertility god of the Cold War, a satyr. When he was assassinated the issue went much deeper than ideology, as far as most people were concerned, whether they knew it or not. It was as if some integrative faculty went out of things. Spiritually.

They have a hard time getting a handle on this. Last semester one of my brightest students asked, "What do you mean? Like . . . integration? Like he was a spiritual leader?" (I have noticed this odd labeling faculty in so many of them. An anxiety to find a resting place for terms, to attach them, as quickly as possible, to already familiar concepts. The function of language has become primarily eliminatory, a lubricant to grease the tracks and get rid of complexities as quickly as possible, without having to engage them.)

"I mean," I went on, "that he served the function of a hero/god when he was alive, and when he was killed he became an actual god. Formally speaking, Kennedy was both the head, as president, and the genitalia of the country. He was a father figure, but also young enough to be virile and stimulating. A still-procreative father. This is a very healthy configuration for the state. When he was killed, all the sexual energy that had, through his agency, been invested in the state, was loose. Who was going to assume it? Lyndon Johnson?"

"That's so . . . *phallocentric*," one of the young women students, Maureen, said.

"The Beatles assumed it," I went on. "And suddenly there was a disintegrative split in the collective psyche, between the leaders, who were old, asexual, obsessed—like Johnson, prowling the White House Situation Room at midnight in his pajamas—and the young and creative forces in the society. . . ."

They don't get it. Have you ever seen *Mystery of the Wax Museum?* The scene where Glenda Farrell, trapped by the crazed Lionel Atwill, pounds at his head with her fist and cracks the wax mask he has fashioned to hide his horribly disfigured face? As those pieces of JFK's skull flew across the lunch-hour sky of Dealey Plaza, the surface of the time fragmented and revealed something beneath, but the interpretation of it is ambiguous to this day.

IN SOME WAYS the JFK chapter should be one of the easiest in this book to write. I've written, or maybe I should say produced, two books about him. *The Road to Dallas: JFK in Focus* was the big one, a series of photos of JFK from his first baby picture through the navy, the Senate, the whole thing, right up to the Zapruder frame of impact. The publisher actually insisted on ending with a photo of the Eternal Flame at Arlington National Cemetery, which I thought was a little hokey. The other was *Where Were You When Kennedy Was Shot?*, an oral history. I even had a hand in producing a ninety-minute special based on *Where Were You . . .* for one of the major networks (I can't mention the network; we're still in litigation over the use of the title).

Who shot him? I don't know, and I don't really care. I used to be way into it. Val is totally into the the-CIA-did-it theory. At this point it's like arguing over whether there's an afterlife or not. An answer is not achievable, so why bother? I guess I'm an agnostic. Val, on the other hand, is a believer. The CIA did it. Fine. Whatever.

Anyway, I have kept my campus office, at Driller Hall, one of several older classroom buildings that have been renovated on the lower floors to make computer labs. I'm up on four, where everything looks just the same as it did forty years ago. The old wooden doors, the twenty-five-watt bulbs overhead, the old-fashioned fire extinguishers, typed-up notices for summer rental villas in Tuscany. Outside, it is the beginning of a new semester, a new school year, and I am up here trying to reheat what I wrote in the other two Kennedy books. I have a good space, and the material is familiar, but I am getting nowhere. From my window I watch the students walking by four stories below, and anxiety floods my stomach. I have been avoiding people, and maybe, I thought, that was part of the problem. So a few days ago I decided to take lunch at the Hollister snack bar, something I haven't done for months. I thought I'd walk in and say hi to any of my colleagues who happened to be around, greet a few students, and remind myself of how it feels to be John Delano, star professor.

The snack bar has always been one of my favorite places on campus. It occupies a rotunda-like space on the ground floor of the student-union building, and its windows offer a sweeping view of a long, grassy lawn, Frisbee-playing freshmen, dogs with red bandannas around their necks. When I was teaching, I would often lead a happy troop of my students there after class for further discussion.

My visit on this day began nicely enough, greetings here and there. Nods across the room to Dean Gifford and to Ralph Powell, wearing his Irish felt hat and his goatee, both of which he began affecting after his divorce a year and a half ago. Sunlight, wood, small-paned windows, thirty different conversations bouncing off the varnished floors. Very agreeable. I took a tray from the hot, wet stack, fresh from the dishwasher, and moved it along the rails past the display cases full of pastries and fruits to the ordering area.

I had no sooner ordered my cheeseburger than I heard a familiar voice, loud, formal yet dosed with street diction, answering someone in baroque cadences; I heard the sound before I knew what he was saying, somehow overbearing and insinuating at the same moment. It was Coleman Silsbee. I braced myself; this was a bad card to turn up. As he rounded the corner of the cafeteria line, I heard my name.

"JOHN DELANO," his voice boomed, pronouncing it "DEL-ano" as he always did. De-LAY-no, I said, to myself. I've told Silsbee any number of times what the right pronunciation is. I have always wondered if he knows it isn't my birth name, and that's why he messes with the pronunciation.

"How's the Cold War?" he said, pulling his tray up next to mine. "Have we liberated Berlin?" He wore a long, dark green wool coat against the day's mild chill, with a huge wool scarf knotted at his throat, and a brown fedora.

To the woman behind the counter, he held up one imperious finger and said only, "Egg salad. No lettuce." The expressionless woman—middle-aged, wearing a hair net—scribbled the order on a little pad and said, without looking up, "White or wheat?"

"Do you have a roll, or a bun?"

"We can put it on a hamburger bun."

"Do that," he said. Noticing a slim, blond undergraduate who was no doubt working off part of her scholarship, pumping sodas in her uniform, smiling at him, he said, "How are you today, sweetheart?"

"Good, Coleman. How are you?" and she continued smiling at him over her shoulder as she went off to deliver the cup she had filled. Anyone else who dared to address an undergraduate as "sweetheart" would have been tarred and feathered, but Silsbee managed to bring it off.

"Extremely fine . . . ," he said under his breath, watching her walk away. Then, to me, he said, "So what are you working on?"

"I'm actually writing about the Kennedy assassination right now."

"Which one?"

"JFK." Of course, I thought. I still hadn't decided how to handle Bobby. A measure of how disorganized I had become. One more thing I needed to make room for. What was the book going to be? The Stations of the Cross of the sixties? Who needed another book like that? Beam me up, beam me up. . . .

Our orders arrived, and Silsbee said, "Come on, let's get a table."

This was the last thing I needed, really. Silsbee has a way of getting to your weak spot, finding out what's bugging you. I don't need anyone seeing into my weak spots right now. But Silsbee's personality is so compelling that it can be hard to figure out a rationale for not doing what he suggests. On top of that, in truth, I have always had the sense that if I spent time with him I would learn something. We went to one of the picnic-style tables, arranged like spokes along the long arc of the window bay that looked out onto the green.

"So when do you need to have the book done?" he asked, shaking a huge amount of pepper onto his sandwich.

Right away I felt a little sick. Breathe, I told myself. This was vintage Silsbee, a seemingly innocuous probe, a test. Was I nervous? Is there trouble with the book? Of course, maybe I was just being a little paranoid. "I basically have as much time as I want."

"A mixed blessing," he said, still shaking, not looking up. Nice, I thought; a wry allusion to his own difficulty in finishing the second volume of *The Black Mask of History*. I believe that the tally was somewhere around three different publishers, seven years and counting.

"Yeah," I said, encouraged. "Enough rope to hang yourself."

"So is it another picture book, or is it a history? How are you organizing it?"

Organizing it. Jesus, I thought, the guy is like a heat-seeking missile. "I guess it's roughly chronological," I said. "But I'm trying to focus on Big Images, or representative moments, and then kind of . . ." Kind of what? I fished for a word.

"Please don't say 'deconstruct.' I may have to move myself and my egg salad elsewhere."

"Honestly, Coleman," I said, "I don't really know what I'm doing."

As he heard this, he gave two short, convulsive laughs, looking down at the table, then another, his mouth full of sandwich. He reached his large hand over and grabbed a glass of water to chase it down, then sat looking at the table for a moment with his eyebrows raised.

"If all our colleagues were that honest," he said, "this *might* actually turn into an interesting place. So what are the big images? JFK assassination. What else?"

Images. "Well, it's not all images. . . . I'm planning a chapter on the Summer of Love—"

"Summer of poontango . . ."

"—one on Bob Dylan going electric at Newport, one on the presence of marijuana in the culture, images of Castro, fallout shelters, Levittown suburbia, the Moratorium, Kent State—"

I stopped; he was looking at me with one eyebrow raised.

"Yes?" I said.

"Please go on," he said. "But there does seem to be a major segment of American society and culture missing from the picture thus far."

Right—no black people.

"Huh," I said. "That's interesting. See, the thing is, I didn't grow up around black people. I never saw them, never talked to one until I was at college."

"Is this a history of the Cold War period," he said, looking me in the eye now, "or is it your autobiography?" Of course the angle between those two concepts was exactly what was bothering me. "I mean, if you're writing a *memoir*, that's one thing," he said, putting the remainder of the sandwich into his mouth.

"Does it have to be one or the other?" I said, noting the defensiveness in my own voice.

"It doesn't. But it's very difficult to do both. Books like that usually come from people who have actually been *involved* in history." Coleman tended to start italicizing words as he circled in for a kill, and I tensed up a little.

"Well," I said, "haven't we been involved in history?"

"What I mean is policy makers. Or those close to them."

"My questions still stands. Haven't we been involved in history? We have lived through history."

"Well," he said, smiling faintly and rubbing the backs of his fingers under his chin, "that's like saying a pubic hair has lived through sex. It's *there,* it is moved by the Big Event, but it isn't *involved* in the sense of affecting things." I thought I recognized the pubic-hair image from somewhere, maybe Norman Mailer. Coleman had a way of appropriating things others had said and using them as his own. We all did that, actually. But Coleman felt no shame about it.

"See, here's the deal," he said. "What is important in history is what moves things. Ligaments, muscle, bone. All the other stuff—what people wore, what women thought about when they cooked dinner for the king, how the servants furnished their rooms—that's all a function of the larger patterns. It might be interesting, but it's not fundamental. First you need to address the fundamentals. History is architecture, not interior decoration, which is what is wrong with your approach—"

"Hey, Coleman," I said, feeling my chest and neck getting hot. "Stop right there."

He looked at me as if I'd stiff-armed him.

"You're saying that the human dimension of ordinary people's lives is just 'interior decoration'? I mean, isn't that kind of . . . totalitarian?"

"How is that totalitarian?"

"Well, it's like saying individuals aren't important, just big historical events. I mean, what would you call that if you wouldn't call it totalitarian?"

"Hold on," he said, raising a hand now. "Relax. In what way, exactly, does focusing on pictures of JFK's face instead of, say, his civil-rights policy, lead us to the 'human dimension of ordinary people'?"

"Well," I began, "most of us aren't intimately affected by Big Events. . . ."

"Oh, really?" he said.

"The avenue," I went on, "into what individuals experience is the images by which they live. In the age of mass media, these images are charged like religious images. If you want to know what is really going on for most people, you need to look at the religious images they have fashioned for themselves. The ritual understructure, you could say." This, in case you haven't guessed, was a canned speech. Even as I said it I didn't know if I believed it.

"Like Santería," Coleman said. "Or voodoo. What is apparently happening is only a kind of visible shell for what's really going on underneath, which is the play of the supernatural forces."

"Right," I said. That was a good comparison. Silsbee had a treacherous way of summing up what you had said more pithily than you had said it and then, once it had been reduced to a manageable size, smashing it to pieces. My muscles tensed up even more.

"Well, Professor Delano," he said, pronouncing it correctly for once and wiping his mouth with the air of one who is about to bring one's lunchtime business to a close, "that, as we have said a number of times in these conversations, is . . . whatever it is. But whatever it is, is not history. It is, perhaps, an avenue into a study of mass hysteria or social pathology, but it is not history. Since the beginning of time, people have been projecting their fears onto totem animals, et cetera, et cetera, but the project of the West has been, one hopes, to shed light into those dark crevasses, to learn to think and evaluate information with the faculty of reason, which I will agree is in some jeopardy in our time, and perhaps even in the hallowed halls of Hollister College. In fact, *especially* in these same hallowed halls, and others like them." The inflated tone was a sign that he was winding up for the pitch. . . .

A student, an underclassman with red hair and freckles, had approached the table; without looking at him, Coleman held up one finger and said, "Just one minute." The kid took a step back.

"And this notion," he went on, "about the images is, quite frankly, some bullshit. Most people don't live in terms of religious images; they live in terms of their annual raise, doctors' visits, home repairs, as much sex as they can get, vacation. . . . In fact, one could argue that the notion that people's reality consists of these *images* might possibly be *construed* as a tad more totalitarian in its implications than my humble contention that history affects people's lives. I would recommend that you reread the novel *1984,* by George Orwell."

Maybe if I hadn't been having such a hard time, I could have come back at him with an imaginative argument, but what I felt at the moment was tired. Tired and dumb, as if I'd let myself be overmatched and then pinned to the mat. And, of course, in truth I wasn't at all sure anymore that what I was saying made decent sense. I felt as if I were stuck going around in a worn-out groove; I was missing some essential point, I had made some kind of similar mistake before. And then I had a memory, just an image really, of a long-distant afternoon, sidelined, something happening elsewhere. Where was that? I wondered. . . .

. . . A LARGE, DARK room; a bright doorway. I knew where this was. Outside, the afternoon flowed heavy, hot, and golden through the Dallas streets; the late sunlight clanged off the sides of buildings and filled the air, viscous and radioactive, like some kind of atomic beer syrup; through the open door, it leaked into the cavernous bar where we were sitting and spilled across the maroon-painted cement floor.

We had made it out to what was left of Deep Ellum, a historic black neighborhood that my friend Lee had wanted to see. Lee and I had been best friends in college. We'd been out of school for a couple of years—this was sometime around 1979, 1980—and he was about to go to business school, and it was a Last Trip, a kind of commemorative thing. It was before I made the final turn into the academic life, before I'd decided to finish my doctorate, and actually it was on the trip that I had the idea for the first of my Kennedy books.

They hadn't yet done any of the renewal stuff, and Dallas was a blasted heath if ever there was one. History itself seemed to be decaying, decomposing, like a tooth rotting from underneath. . . . It was that whole late-1970s inner-city interregnum between white flight and gentrification, as with Beale Street in Memphis or Eighteenth and Vine in Kansas City. The storefronts had been preserved, some of them at least, but the streets were empty, the lots behind and between the buildings full of garbage and sad-looking dogs. Most major urban areas had this place in them by this point, this rotting area that would eventually be swabbed out, sutured up, and recast as a museum of itself—a Historic District, if they were lucky enough to have a past that people would travel and pay to look into, once it had been fully replaced by a conceptualization of itself, put under Plexiglas.

The process had not yet begun in Dallas. We spent the earlier part of the day downtown, at my insistence, mainly in Dealey Plaza. There was something almost too much in being there. You got a kind of emotional sunburn just standing in the plaza. It had been only seventeen years since the assassination then; there wasn't enough filtering yet. The images were so charged they had irradiated the very landscape—the brick bulk of the Book Depository, the grassy knoll with the pergola behind it, unchanged, the sinuous design of the streets themselves in the plaza, funneling the traffic down the drain toward the triple underpass—the ground you stood on was radioactive with image. We had gone up to where Abraham Zapruder stood and shot his film, went around behind the fence at the top of the grassy knoll and looked at the railroad tracks, looked down from the overpass, but Lee seemed a little distracted, and after about an hour, he was ready to go out to Deep Ellum.

Looking back, I can see the glue of the friendship cracking and drying. He had given up wearing his faded dashiki; his Afro was now a very managed close-cut job, and he was wearing Brooks Brothers shirts and feeling a bit defensive about it. At college we'd been famous friends; few indeed were the interracial friendships outside of a sports team. We formed the film society together. Lee was one of the best-read people I've ever known, and he had a fine sense of irony that he maintained, like a flame under a chafing dish, about the condescension that he met constantly from the children of the WASP elite. Because I'd come from lower-middle-class Atlanticville and A-ville High School myself, neither of us was considered particularly worthy on the face of things, and we had formed our own mutual-admiration society. We were the ones who brought Kurosawa films to the campus, and speakers like Allen Ginsberg (that was me, actually; Lee wanted Gwendolyn Brooks). We read the same books—Ralph Ellison, James Baldwin, F. O. Matthiessen's *American Renaissance,* Constance Rourke's *American Humor,* Suzanne Langer's *Philosophy in a New Key.*

By senior year most of our classmates were on track to go to business school, law school, medical school, or into banking. At that time we both looked on a decision to attend business school as the mark of some terminal deficiency of imagination. For Lee, in addition, there was the loud ambient static of a certain stratum of people claiming that you weren't black enough if you did anything mainstream at all. Although, or perhaps because, he was from a solidly middle-class background, he was susceptible to this accusation.

Still, a couple of years of being out of school, family expectations, and seasoning in the real world, will have their effect. Lee eventually decided that he wasn't going to be the next Ralph Ellison, and he applied to b-school and got into Wharton with a full scholarship. He was understandably proud of this, but he was also touchy about it.

Anyway, we decided to go to Dallas, on a last hurrah before Lee went to Wharton. He had had relatives in the Dallas area, although they weren't there anymore. He was curious to see where they'd lived, and I was a big JFK-assassination bug; I had all the books that had been published at that point and had digested them thoroughly—*Six Seconds in Dallas, Rush to Judgment;* I think Anthony Summers's *Conspiracy* had just come out. It was interesting to move around the plaza and try to picture the angles, see the places I'd only read about—the little railroad house where Lee Bowers had sat, the pergola. . . . Dealey Plaza had been frozen in time. I would have spent all day there.

All told, we must have spent close to two hours at the plaza, although Lee spent the last forty minutes or so sitting on the grassy knoll reading *The Quiet American*. Then we took our rent-a-car and drove straight out Commerce Street to Deep Ellum, maybe twenty blocks away. I didn't see much of interest there, particularly—low one- and two-story buildings with faded and chipped brick, old 1920s commercial architecture gone to seed, crumbling sidewalks, boarded-up facades, no trees, a handful of winos, and a number of vacant-eyed younger black men with outlandish Afros. We found a place to stop in and have a beer, this cavelike space, and as there was very little to take my mind off the supercharged images of Dealey Plaza I started thinking out loud about the sight lines, the angle from the fence and whether the kind of damage JFK sustained could have been caused by a shot from the knoll, the possibility of the witnesses' on the underpass actually seeing a puff of gunsmoke under the trees by the fence. . . . Lee was quiet, seemed not to be listening. But most of all I remember expressing a kind of bewilderment at the contrast between the enormity of what had happened and the almost banal day-to-dayness of the architecture and the activity going on in Dealey Plaza.

"It's as if time stood still," I said. "Like a long scream. Those pictures Zapruder took, the moment before the bullet hit him in the head, and then the moment after, it just keeps replaying in your mind. The grass was green, everything was the same. But one moment reality looked one way, and the next moment it looked another."

When I said this, Lee looked at me in a way I'd never seen him look at me. I actually noted this at the moment. "Looked one way to whom?" he said.

"Well," I said, "reality was shattered, the reality of the presidency, the society, and the possibilities that Kennedy represented. . . ."

"I mean," he said, evenly, "for whom was that moment such a reality-shattering blow?"

"What do you mean?" I said. Now I realized something was going on, but I didn't know what it was. Something in Lee's sound wasn't quite right.

"Fifty years ago," he said, "this street had black-owned businesses on it, and black people walked around here who looked like normal people, trying to make a go of things. They looked like people who thought they had a shot at being Americans. They went to restaurants, they went to church, they had newspaper routes, they owned barbershops. They bought carpets for their living rooms, got out the good china for important company; they woke up in the morning and decided which tie to put on, listened to the radio, worried about their families. . . ."

At his best Lee was very smart, funny, and down-home. At his worst a high-handed rhetorical streak came out, as if he were preaching to a congregation instead of conversing with a friend. That was the sound he had now, and I felt a muscle cramp of defensiveness starting inside me. I felt wary of some element that was entering the conversation.

"I'm not sure what you're saying, Lee." I said. "That things are worse for black people now?"

"Well, in fact, since you ask, they *are* worse for black people in some ways. Better in other ways. But the idea that the death of a good-looking white man is the be-all and end-all of what this city is about is kind of irritating."

I was stunned, or disoriented, by the eruption of this sound in the conversation. I felt as if he'd slapped me in the face. " 'A good-looking white man'?" I said.

"I'm not interested in this mystical thing you have about the assassination," he went on, ignoring me. "That was seventeen years ago. Assassinations happen all the time. People get fucked over constantly. Constantly. I mean, my great-uncle was lynched, right down the road, in Fort Worth. Shit . . . Texas is a barbecue culture. They just dug a pit, shot him in both legs, and pushed him in and poured gasoline on him, set him on fire. They had to shoot him another couple of times to keep him from crawling out of the pit. This kind of shit happens all the time; it's an aspect of daily life for black people. It's not some abstraction. It's not two-dimensional."

Where had this come from? I felt as if he were pointing his finger at me. I was floored by the force behind his words.

"Black people," he went on, "have had more sustained threat to their community than anyone, and not just because their icons are under attack. When King was shot, and Malcolm X, people were shocked and disgusted, but nobody thought in terms of having their innocence shattered. It wasn't a matter of 'Oh, where is Camelot?' "

"I see." I said. My face was hot. This was the place where we should have stopped it, or I should have just backed out of the conversation. But I didn't. He was, I thought, saying I was just another fatuous white man. Because my great-uncle hadn't been lynched. All my grandparents had done was leave everything they knew behind, got on a boat to come to a new country where they knew nobody, and made something of themselves. That counted for nothing. I was in much deeper than I recognized, and as I went on, something that had been lurking, disguised, emerged. . . . "The great and noble black community," I heard myself saying, "which is so much wiser and less callow than that of the whites, who cherish their misty illusions.

The buffoonish, dismissible whites, who have been handling all the most intimate details of world-caliber crises, big, big things. But we are callow because the death by assassination of the leader of the free world seems to have more resonance than the fact that a couple of barbershops closed down. . . ."

Even as I spoke I seemed to hear myself from outside, shocked now at the force behind my own words. Where had that intensity come from? It was as if it had been programmed into me to say these things, feel these things, that I didn't even know I'd felt. Had I been a closet racist for years? But then, I thought, what about Lee? He'd started it. . . .

Lee sat on his stool, looking at me, his lips in a half smile. "No," he said. "*I* see." An appraising look. No—not appraising. The appraisal had been made. He was looking out over a vista from a vantage point toward which he had been climbing. The look said, "What did I expect? Did I really think this white man would be any different from the rest of them?" And he was right. That was the horrible thing.

LEE AND I never spoke again after that trip. And I never told anyone about that conversation. I was astonished at how quickly, even between old friends, bad faith and mutual suspicion blew up, because . . . of what? I felt some of that same sense of acceleration now, talking to Silsbee. The black irritation with the white obliviousness to black reality, and the white irritation with the black insistence on black centrality. The Original Sin of our culture, apparently insoluble. Had I learned nothing in twenty years?

"Well, Coleman," I said now, "maybe you're right. . . ." All for a cessation of hostilities.

"I am right," he said.

"But then," I began, once again lamely picking up the sword that was too heavy for me, "what do you make of the insatiable hunger for *People* magazine, and celebrity idol worship, people's obsession with these figures—"

"People have too much money and too much time on their hands. It's that simple." It was always just that simple.

BACK IN MY office, I sank into a serious depression. The book was there, in folders, the JFK research folder open, and I thought, What is all this? What am I doing? A mishmash of history, myth, my own personal experience . . . a big mess. Was Coleman right? Is it all an elaborate denial strategy? I was missing something, and I didn't know what it was.

I remember that I started shaking, as if I were cold. I didn't know what to do. An image, I thought. Find an image. If I quieted my mind, maybe I could summon some image that would contain it all, make it all add up. I sat quietly. And little by little an image, a mood, floated up, like a photo developing.

I was home sick from school. I was watching television downstairs in the recreation room, when the news flash came on. The weird combination of enormity with the banality of sitting in the den, which was unchanged; everything was the same, yet something big had happened, which would affect all of us yet not affect us. . . .

I ran upstairs to the kitchen, where my mother was washing

the floor. I remember very clearly saying, "Mom, somebody shot President Kennedy." And after I said it, I laughed. Was it the incongruity of such grave news coming out of my own eight-year-old mouth? I remember thinking, even then, I am laughing at something that isn't funny; this is an interesting phenomenon.

My mother regarded me blankly for a moment. Then she said, "Oh, my God," dropped the mop, and ran past me downstairs, as if I had disappeared from the room. I stood in the kitchen, trying to process that moment. I had apparently vanished in the glare of History, like the moon in the morning sky.

I had never seen my father cry, but I did that weekend as we watched the funeral, his hand over his mouth muffling his sobs, as the caissons rolled along the crisp, sunny autumn streets of Washington and the band played "Hail to the Chief." Tears coming out of his eyes.

And then I see his waxy face on that satin pillow, and me walking out of the apartment, and Estelle, later, on the phone, crying and saying, "No, John—you don't know how much he loves you; he just can't express it. . . ." And me hanging up.

5

IN JULY 1965 WE WERE on vacation in Cape Cod. "We" means my family, sitting at lunch, looking out toward the beach from the windows of a restaurant called the Red Jacket. Suddenly there was a trembling in the air around the table, a heightened alertness, an odd electric fizz or warpage, and I heard my mother hiss the words "Stop it."

The waitress had just brought our food, a late lunch. My father had ordered flounder; I remember this because that's what he always ordered. And suddenly he was blubbering, crying, into his hands, at the table. People were looking.

"Stop it," my mother hissed at him.

I looked back and forth at the two of them. "What's wrong?" I said.

"Jesus Christ," my mother said, throwing down her napkin. She wasn't relating to me at all, and that scared me. "Get hold of yourself," she said to my father.

He sat there, crying and making a kind of hooting noise, a keening sound. His face in his hands. After a minute the waitress came over. People were looking at us now, openly. "Is anything wrong?" she asked. We got Dad out of there and into the car, and an hour later my father was being injected with a sedative at a small hospital in Hyannis.

———

BREAKDOWNS, AS I understand the word, result from insupportable tension. Two competing demands are placed on a given system, neither of which will give up or allow the existence of the other. What is needed is some degree of transcendence.

My father had a series of them for two years. Most involved his taking to his bed for anywhere between a couple of days and maybe a month. I can still hear the disembodied voice coming from the darkened bedroom: "Turn the music down." He was finally hospitalized in the summer of 1967. Up to that time, you could almost make believe things were normal.

I see my father in a bow tie, working on his equations on the couch, all by himself after dinner. My mom wore short skirts, her honey-blond hair long and luxurious. Walking around with Chris on her hip, singing "Close your eyes, and I'll kiss you. . . ." wearing blue jeans with an Indian beaded belt. My father hated the Beatles, but my Mom thought they were great. I have some vague memory of discussion among The Relatives. My mother, for her part, had not come all the way to the Big City from Eau Claire, after all, just to sit around like an old Italian lady in a black dress.

———

WHAT IS HISTORY? As opposed to "a history"? Obviously it's not any one given version. But it's not just the cumulative accretion of detail either. If you could write down, hypothetically, everything that happened, would that be History? Isn't History, almost by definition, a version? Doesn't it imply a point of view?

"What is significant" does not necessarily imply relations of cause and effect. It can imply something that transcends the domain of cause and effect. This is part of why they say what I do isn't History. The idea that there is a cause for everything is finally one thing both sides of the Cold War could agree on. Anyway, the whole thing has become "no central point of view." So there is no History anymore. Only "histories." But aren't "histories" affected by "History"?

───────

GORDON KOHL CALLED again this morning to see how the book is going. I told him I'm working on the chapter about when Bob Dylan went electric at the Newport Folk Festival in July 1965. Which I'm not. But I will be. Gordon was a decent student, and I was his hero, maybe six years ago. One of my acolytes, I guess you'd say. He was from Oregon. He would come to the parties I used to give and sit there looking through the records and books. He talked like me, dressed like me. It's one of the gratifying things about being a professor. Later the roles are subtly reversed—they get to New York City and begin to realize how insulated from reality their professors are. If they can do something for us, a hint of obsequiousness creeps into our manner, a hint of condescension into theirs. It's natural, I guess. Gordon is a Dylan fan—it's fascinating to me how Dylan has maintained his charge for people Gordon's age.

"Great," Gordon said. "You've got an audience. Tell me where we're at. Paint it for me. I need a shot of pure crystal meth here." It sounded in fact as if Gordon had already had his shot of crystal meth for the morning. "This book is going to blow everybody's pipes out," he said. "They need it. I need it. Give me a taste, big guy. Lay it on me."

"Okay," I said. Focus, I thought. "The basic thesis of the chapter is that Dylan's appearance that weekend was the central event, the pivotal point, of the 1960s. It was the 'Iconic Moment' "—this was a little term I had coined—"that illuminated the end of the Old Left's hopes, the rise of the New Left, and, finally, the transcendence of both in the consciousness-expansion movement."

"I love this," he said. "Go on."

"Well, you know," I said, "in retrospect it is amazing how quickly everybody forgot about the JFK assassination. Or not forgot about but moved on. The Beatles were a big part of it. That fresh-faced reaffirmation of life in 1964. Reborn with the New Year. It was almost as if JFK's assassination had temporarily discharged some insupportable tension in the country. Like lightning. A circuit breaker, or a short circuit. The circuits were getting overheated. Then it all started building up again. In some ways 1965 was the last year of innocence. Kennedy's death was far enough behind so that you didn't live with it every moment. But society wasn't a big psychedelic theater yet either. Almost everything was still under the surface. Like a soup with a skin on top. But if you looked closely, something weird had entered the mix. You know the Beatles' record *I Feel Fine*?"

"Sure," he said.

"It's optimistic and exhilarating, but there's that weird feedback at the start, like a warning that something was about to blow. . . . The flip side was 'She's a Woman,' which was basically a blues, but stark and odd, with Paul singing in that slightly strangled voice, hysteria bubbling just underneath it. . . . The record itself was straddling some line—"

"Jesus," Gordon said. "Go on."

I was having a good time. I always had a good time when I could just riff like this for Gordon. That weekend at Newport was sort of a pet obsession of mine anyway. It wasn't just the way that Dylan looked and played that night, in his black leather blazer, betokened a shift in attitude. It was that that was when attitude itself moved to the center of people's attention. The fact that one was doing something loomed larger than the actual substance of what one was doing. Actions became rhetorical. And rhetoric started to become a kind of action.

"You have to understand the Newport Folk Festival," I said. "It was more or less the property of the big-time, old-time Leftists, guys like Pete Seeger, for whom folk music was the expression of the People, through which a better, more equitable world was going to be forged. It had been going for a few years at that point; George Wein started it as an offshoot of the Newport Jazz Festival. The Folk Festival presented blues singers, old-time fiddlers from the Appalachians, gospel groups, topical songwriters. The household god was Woody Guthrie, who was of course Dylan's first big hero, the prototype of the wandering proletarian balladeer. By the time the festival got rolling, Guthrie was out of commission with the disease that would kill him. But Dylan was writing and singing stuff like 'Masters of War,' 'With God on Our Side,' 'Only a Pawn in Their Game'—the greatest 'protest' songs ever written. It must have seemed too good to be true. Somebody that talented and charismatic in the service of the Movement.

The great Movement, overseen by the older generation of disciplined Leftists who knew what was best.

"In 1963 they had closed out the festival with everybody holding hands, Dylan in the middle, singing 'Blowin' in the Wind.' Now it's 1965. Suddenly Dylan wants to do his Sunday-night set with the Paul Butterfield Blues Band backing him up. The year before, the kid was still dressed like Woody Guthrie in his work shirt and blue jeans, and now he's wearing Ray-Ban shades and a big polka-dot fencing shirt and tight black jeans and Cuban-heeled boots. What happened to him? Albert Grossman and Alan Lomax actually had a fistfight over this, supposedly. Right at the festival."

"Who is this, now?" Gordon said.

I was surprised that Gordon didn't know, so I gave him the short version. Albert Grossman was Dylan's manager at the time, very successful and powerful; he also managed a lot of the best-known folk acts, like Peter, Paul & Mary. He began as a club owner, with a place called the Gate of Horn, in Chicago. He was heavy, dour-looking, a bearlike, forbidding presence. He really understood how to market and sell what was thought of as non-commercial music. As the sixties went by he got sucked into the counterculture more and more; he grew peyote buds in his office.

Lomax, on the other hand, was one of the pillars of the Old Left cultural front. His father was John A. Lomax, who discovered Leadbelly. They were both folklorists for the Library of Congress, used to travel around with heavy recording equipment during the Depression and record chain gangs singing. Alan never stopped interviewing the Simple Folk, pumping them for proletarian truth. Evidently Lomax had an unfortunate personality; he was supercilious. Even the people who liked him didn't like him. He had an agenda behind the agenda with everything. He liked things or didn't like them for ulterior motives. The same might have been said about Grossman, but the motives were different. For Grossman they stood to make money. For Lomax it was the eventual establishment of the workers' paradise.

"See," I told Gordon, "the Old Left social technicians thought they knew where society, or History, was going. Then along comes Dylan, their poster boy, with this injection of electricity into the carefully handmade philosophy of the Folk Festival, this eruption from the subconscious, this rolling of the dice. Woody Guthrie had a sign on his guitar that read, 'This machine kills fascists.' But Bob's electric guitar . . . nobody knew what that machine could or would do. That was sort of the point: Let's have an adventure without knowing the outcome, or even wanting to know it. It was both an aesthetic and an ethic.

"So on Sunday night, when Dylan came onstage wearing a black leather jacket, with Butterfield, doing 'Maggie's Farm,' and playing loud—really loud—the Old Guard saw it all laid out in front of them, the lid that was being pried up. Total id running around screaming in black leather . . . what happened to jeans and work shirts and solidarity? Lomax actually tried to pull the plug on Dylan's performance. Or maybe it was Pete Seeger. . . ." Actually, I wasn't sure. Which one was it?

"Right," Gordon said now, sounding distracted. "Right. Listen—I've got lunch in five minutes. Give me the visual, give me the image. John Delano, do it for me. Bring it all back home. What's the image that crystalizes the whole thing? Can you do it? Remember—this is *John Delano's Cold War.* We don't want to get too far into all the boring history stuff. Give me the image. . . ."

The boring history stuff. I taught him well, didn't I? He wanted the Iconic Moment. The image. That was easy enough—you just juxtaposed a photo of work-shirted Dylan from the 1964 festival with a 1965 shot of Dylan in his black leather blazer with his electric guitar, and there you had it, on one level. But what was really going on was Grossman and Lomax. The meaning of that image of Dylan going electric was really, as always, behind the image itself. But who would sit still for it?

. . . the haze, the day overcast, the faint smell of decaying fish on the air, early afternoon. It was actually the day before. But who even remembers that accurately? Grossman eating a corned-beef sandwich at one of the picnic tables in the Artists section, the tent's scalloped edges luffing listlessly in the mild breeze coming down off Narragansett Bay. Grossman, a man about fifty, wearing tinted granny glasses, looking like a cross between Beethoven and Ben Franklin. Mississippi Fred Mc-Dowell is two tables away, dressed not in the sharecropper over-alls certain members of the board wanted him to wear but in his best black suit and a thin tie, talking to another musician's wife about something down home, laughing a little. Kids walking by outside the fence area, looking in. Lomax, large and inelegant in his goatee, his shirt buttons straining against the pull of his belly, comes over and stands before Grossman as he is eating. Grossman does not like interruption. As placidly as a Chinatown gang lord in a Fu Manchu movie, Grossman says, "What can I do for you, Alan?" Looks up at him balefully, the old camouflage.

It is some small matter, but things simmer underneath. Grossman has brought in a different spirit, and it is met with a mixture of contempt and fear. Lomax, Seeger, Theodore Bikel— these men knew what Discipline was, the submerging of the self and the ego and its bottomless appetites in the name of something larger and more important. Grossman is the great Panderer. You can't make this stuff commercial in that sense. You begin to let in factors other than the long-practiced judgment of the ideological elite, too. . . . How can people know what's good for them? It makes them feel good? Selfishness in full regalia, the bourgeoisie showing their eternal True Colors, of course. . . . Grossman tries to get people excited for the wrong reasons. To buy, to spend. It is an end in itself with him. With the Old Guard, it's okay if people spend, but only on the Right Things. . . .

They settle it, whatever it is; Grossman goes back to his corned beef. Bob is at the hotel. Ordinarily, by this point, Grossman would be there with him, but he has other things to which he must attend on this particular afternoon. The rough spot is the presence of the Butterfield Blues Band, an electric band led by a young white harmonica player, on the blues stage. Lomax has been making snide comments since the Butterfield Band began being discussed. He was outvoted by Peter Yarrow and other members of the board, but Lomax wouldn't give up gracefully. Defeated, he would hold up the flag, still.

Grossman had long since abandoned any pretense of liking these people or even needing them. What he was selling was something that would sell; the point of his presence there was to sell it, and it did sell, in a way that the board's final bosses could not possibly ignore. And Lomax knew that, too, and hated it, and jockeyed for every inch of moral and political high ground to ease the pain of his imminent shunting aside from relevance. Grossman sitting alone at the table, a rare moment of rest from the line of petitioners that has formed outside the circle of his attentions, waiting to be let in. . . .

Of course, there was Bob, too. Their little battleground. The battle for the soul of Bob Dylan. And such earnestness—Irwin Silber, Izzy Young, their solicitude for Bob's political soul. As if he, not they, were the one being lost to History. . . . He was in the clutches of Grossman, the Great Bear. . . . His songs had grown steadily less disciplined. From "Blowin' in the Wind" to "Chimes of Freedom"—well, at least that one was still about Freedom, even if nobody could tell what the hell he was talking about. But "Subterranean Homesick Blues" . . .

The afternoon blues workshop set is due to start in forty-five minutes, and Grossman chews slowly, past, present, and future flattening out and making a path for his digestive efforts. Later that night there's a party on the Lorillard yacht, where a European promoter named Nacht would be, with whom Grossman wants to talk. These kinds of festivals were in their infancy at this point, but Grossman had a vision of a series of festivals like this, all over Europe. Nacht himself was dispensable—who wasn't?—but the idea was worth taking advantage of. In any case Grossman would lay the groundwork for next year's European tour. They were going to try France, not just England. And maybe Australia. That promoter who had said, "There's something wrong with him, isn't there?" Fucking troglodytes, Grossman thought. No wonder the English got rid of them.

What did the Old Guard want? They wanted to keep it under their own control. Their own little folk terrarium. Theo Bikel singing "Tzena, Tzena," looking like your Uncle Morry. Or Cousin Emmy popping out "Georgia Camp Meeting" on her cheeks. That's all right—he'd booked them all at the Gate of Horn—but Lomax's attitude toward Butterfield . . .

Lomax. Everything was an element of The Agenda. The Folk, baby. Keep 'em pure for their own good. He can have the Harvard education, of course, but God forbid The Folk should want one. "Clarence, why do I like your country music so much better than I like the music I hear up here in New York City . . . ?" That mixture of obsequiousness and condescension . . .

That was in that movie he'd seen, some little one-hour pilot film, black and white, shot in Lomax's apartment. It began with Jack Elliott and some eager, progressive boys and girls going up the stairs and Lomax ushering them into his apartment and then addressing the camera: "Well," he said, cigarette in hand, fat belly undisguised, hipster goatee, homemade haircut, "you're in Greenwich Village now, where people come to get away from America. It's not jazz around here anymore, it's folk music. Jazz is high-hat, and aging. Young people have gone mad over ballads and blues, guitar playing and banjo picking. We're recording here tonight; we're having a party, so [gesture of welcome] come on in. . . ."

Grossman picks something out of his teeth, allowing himself some drift, just a few moments. That was right before Bob came to town. Or maybe right after. Lomax was always a little suspicious of Bob. It was a funny movie. Lomax had Memphis Slim playing on some wheezing home organ, Willie Dixon thumping away next to him with that preoccupied and beleaguered look. Lomax zeroing in on Roscoe Holcomb, the banjo player, right up from Kentucky, the only one in the room with a tie and jacket on except for Memphis and Willie. He kept his hat on, too, a beige fedora; you could feel the man's discomfort as Lomax put his face too close and asked things like, "How many tunes do you know, d'you suppose?" The youngsters gathered around, listening to Lomax debrief the Wise Elder, the Folk Man, and Rossy shrugged, smiled, half embarrassed, half amused, without meeting Lomax's eyes, said, "Well . . . I wouldn't know." Lomax tried again: "Why d'you suppose it is that people sing high lonesome down there in the country you come from?" And Rossy shrugged again, half laughed, kind of embarrassed, eyes glinting: "Beats me."

Grossman's dislike for the Old Guard had grown. It wasn't really a political disagreement per se but a question of style, maybe even of philosophy. Such self-satisfaction, such smugness. Such trumped-up reverence mixed with a well-disguised contempt. He thought back to one night at the Gate of Horn, in the back room with Josh White, the Negro folk singer. Josh had had his experience with these guys, figured Grossman to be one of them, and was pulling his oppressed-minority, I'm-a-plowboy-who's-been-exploited-all-my-life routine—Josh White, who knew his way around the wine lists of Paris—and Grossman finally said, "Look, man, you're not dealing with one of these fucking morons right now, do you understand? We can step outside and you can pull out your knife and I'll take my .45 and we can discuss the fucking workers' revolution, and you'll never see Montparnasse again." White had just laughed, and then they got down to business.

Besides, all that fucking solicitude for the poor and downtrodden was bullshit. They didn't know how to see anybody as anything but a tool. He could still hear the old man's voice—John A. Lomax, Alan's father—on the Blind Willie McTell Library of Congress record, coaxing Blind Willie to rake some muck. "Don't you know any complainin' songs, Willie?" he said in his Southern planter's voice. "Something like 'Ain't It Hard to Be a Nigger, Nigger?' " And Blind Willie squirming around, saying poor white folks had it hard, too. And then, of course, there was the March of Time short from whenever the fuck it was. Back in the thirties somewhere. Bob loved this shit, had people collect it for him. They had Leadbelly dressed up in a convict suit, stripes and all, playing guitar and singing "Goodnight Irene." Then begging the senior Lomax, who was standing there, among the bestriped convicts, all black, to take one of the recordings Lomax had just made to the governor of Louisiana, O. K. Allen. Saying that if the governor heard the song, he'd turn him loose. And Lomax saying he'd do what he could, take it to the governor in Baton Rouge tomorrow, and Leadbelly saying, "Thank you boss! Thank you suh! Thank you, thank you boss!"—strumming his guitar in a caricature of pure Negro jubilation. Then the next scene was Lomax at a desk, typing, in what was supposedly his office and Leadbelly showing up with a bandanna around his neck like an extra out of Show Boat, saying "Boss, here I is." And Lomax looking up, saying "Leadbelly! What are you doing here?"

"No use trying to run away, boss; I come here to be your man. I got to work for you the rest of my life. You carried a record of my song to Governor O. K. Allen, and he pardoned me."

"Well, I certainly am glad. But, Leadbelly . . . you can't work for me. You're a mean boy; you killed two men. . . ."

"Don't talk that way, sir boss. . . . Please sir, take me with you, boss. I'll tie your shoestrings. You'll never have to tie your shoes as long as I work for you."

"All right, Leadbelly. I'll try you out."

And then they had Leadbelly clapping his hands and all but jumping up and down, shouting, "Thank you suh, boss! Thank you suh! I'll drive you all over the United States and I'll sing all my songs for you. And you'll be my big boss and I'll be your man."

So much for the workers' paradise, Grossman thinks. A few years later they had him singing "Bourgeois Blues." And now they're calling Bob an anarchist. That reminds him: He needs to *call Pennebaker to see what he thinks his timetable is. They're probably going to bring him along next year on the European tour. Shoot in color this time. . . . That's it; he wipes his hands on a paper napkin and gets up. He'll go over to Area Two and make sure things are set up for Butterfield.*

———

Alan Lomax, back at the blues stage, chewed absently at the patch of beard along his lower lip. The haze, the overcast, the young gathered, sitting on the grass, watching and learning. It had been a good day—not too hot. Pete Seeger was over at the Broadside stage; they'd had the Freedom Singers. Lomax was irritated, having been rebuffed in his attentions by a young woman working for the festival. Miriam Edel. They called her Mimi. All of twenty-three. Short skirt, hair back in a kerchief, carrying a clipboard and routing artists here and there. Son House, with his ribbon tie and funeral-parlor shirt, had been trying to get in her pants, and she had been rebuffing him with a good-natured brio. Lomax had been trying intermittently to pick her up, too. She had rebuffed him the same way, good-naturedly, etc., but it had hurt his feelings, made him feel old. What did she know anyway? Lomax didn't brood over it, exactly; he dismissed her as an idiot. But it put him in a foul mood.

And Grossman, sitting there with the strings of corned beef in his teeth, looking up at him as if he, Lomax, were the intruder. Grossman was a money changer, nothing more. He knew how to get water out of rocks. But the disrespect. Alan had been making recordings with his father at Parchman Farm while Grossman was probably still trying to sell hot radios. All Grossman knew was how to pump up people's egos and sell them. And twist and destroy them. Van Ronk had told him that Grossman had tried to package him as Olaf the Viking Blues Singer. He could see the change in Dylan, too, the little snot. Not that he hadn't seen that one coming from way back. A little opportunist, out only for himself. Just Grossman's type.

Then this. Four white kids blasting everybody's ears out with amplifiers. Two black guys, on drums and bass—what else?— and some frizzy-haired Jew boy on guitar davening up and down while he plays a string of overamped clichés. . . . What were they thinking about on the board? Was this supposed to be the project of the festival? Ego in tight pants and cowboy boots? No discipline, no pointing toward the bigger goal. The festival and what it stood for were supposed to be bigger than any individual performer. Wasn't there enough electronic junk, and posturing, on network television? Did the Folk Festival have to have it, too? The money guys had moved in to colonize this world, and this was one world that was not going to fall prey to commercial imperialism. Grossman would sell dog shit if he thought he could convince people it was gold. His God was the dollar, nothing more; everything else was in the service of the dollar. These guys looked like rejects from West Side Story. *Plus, it was earsplitting. It was a disgrace to put these kids on the same stage Son House had played on. It was an insult.*

He was in fact saying this to one of the board members, who was trying to do something else, as Grossman walked up. No preamble; looking at Lomax gravely, sepulchral gravity coming from the heavy-browed eyes, over the Ben Franklin glasses. Grossman said, "What seems to be the problem, Alan?"

Lomax confronts him, belly to belly, no quarter given, no mood to back down; the people who were there heard him say something about Leadbelly, and Grossman, evenly, but suggesting great force under control, looking out from under the heavy brows, says, "Leadbelly, wonderful as he was, was playing for a different time and place," and the next thing anyone knew, they were tussling, grabbing, trying to get leverage on the other's rotundity . . . and a fall, and they were on the ground. . . . It didn't last but a minute before they were separated, Grossman emitting a string of profanities: "You fat pig hypocrite bastard . . ." and Lomax, his shirt buttons pulled open up to the sternum, redfaced, angry. . . .

"THE IMAGE," I said, "would have to be Dylan practically lunging at the microphone, pouncing on the words, 'I-I-I-I-AIN'T gonna work on Maggie's Farm no more . . .' in his leather jacket. Sunday night, July twenty-five. That was the real Declaration of Independence of the sixties. Not on *your* farm and not on *their* farm. Three days later, LBJ doubled the size of the U.S. troop commitment in Vietnam—the real start of the war, you could say."

"Wow," Gordon said. "Can we get pictures of Dylan in that leather jacket for the cover?"

"That's something to think about," I said. I had forestalled disaster yet again. How much longer could I keep this up?

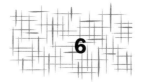

6

MY FATHER PULLED OUT OF IT, whatever it was, but it came back. First the absent look, then the trembling hands. Hypercritical; everything externalized. Over the next two years, finally, the hospitalizations.

What caused it? I don't know. I didn't then, and I still don't. All I knew was that my world had suddenly become infirm. Like a pink Spalding ball ruptured along its seam. It still looked like a ball. But squeeze it a little and it showed you where the crack was, showed you the dark, empty interior. I began shutting down, like someone closing the shutters on his house before a storm.

I WAS JUST hitting puberty. Everything had turned weirdly physical—music, colors, food. I haunted the library and discovered the paintings of Giorgio de Chirico, from just before World War I, with their mood of afternoon longing, train smokestacks and towers and deserted piazzas with their arcades in deep shadow. Everything hinted at some meaning just beneath the surface or just around the corner. I also discovered *Playboy*. At that time the magazine was inviting—not glossy, but printed on lusciously smooth stock, stapled and curving and erotic in itself. Inside, everybody looked as if they were having a great time. Men in velvet jackets, people naked together in hot tubs. The Playmates looked like real human beings. You could see the pores on their skin.

The fundamental thing for me became to get away from where I was, wherever that was at any given moment. Anything to keep me aloft, above the field of ashes in which I'd found myself. I would sit in my room and listen to records and read about the Beatles, Bob Dylan, Muhammad Ali, Martin Luther King, Robert Kennedy, Malcolm X. What was going on in my life made no difference, I decided. It was off the radar screen. What was important were these transcendent images. It never occurred to me that these figures led moment-to-moment lives, made decisions about laundry, clothes, bills, mortgages. . . . How could I know? Who was going to tell me?

Up until I hit adolescence, my brother, Chris, had sometimes been a good escape for me. We would sit on the living-room couch and play a game I invented where we would look upside down at each other's face, so that the bottom of the other's chin became the top of a bald, eyeless, egg-shaped cranium. When we started laughing at this image, the laughing mouth, viewed upside down, became a grotesque death rictus, which of course made us laugh even harder. We would do that and laugh and laugh for what seems in memory like hours. I was maybe ten, and he was maybe four.

Chris was the most beautiful kid. He was kind of otherworldly. "Elfin" isn't exactly the right word. People wanted to be around him. He had my mother's honey-blond hair and full lips and long eyelashes, even as a baby. Strangers would come up to him in the supermarket or on vacation and just want to touch him or say hello to him.

And he was talented. When I was in junior high school, he pulled out my guitar, in which I had lost interest, and taught himself how to play. Then it was our father's violin. I don't remember him ever taking lessons on either one. My father would sit and listen to him play "Danny Boy" on the violin, and he'd cry. Chris was a genius in art class, too. He could draw things well, almost by instinct, without the usual awkwardness and lack of proportion. . . . Chris had some beautiful flame in him that needed to be protected. I recognized that even then.

Chris idolized me. I would say crazy things to him to crack him up. We'd be driving with Mom and Dad, and I'd whisper something to him, like, "Let's go get a gas burger with some fried aspirin," and he'd laugh uncontrollably, and my father would get mad. One time I said I felt like eating a juiceburger with plastic sauce, and he laughed so hard he peed in the backseat.

But by the time he was really old enough to engage, I was doing everything I could to get away, in every sense. He was always around, a constant witness to my presence in that reality. Chris's need for me was bottomless. He had no other outlets. He couldn't bike into town yet or read a book. I was his escape. I started doing cruel things to discourage his attentions. I had a fluorescent orange KEEP OUT sign on my bedroom door, and over it I made another sign in orange Magic Marker, trying to match the letters, saying CHRIS. He tried to follow me everywhere, a nagging reminder of the conditions of my own life, and all I cared about was nullifying those conditions.

In the middle of my junior year at college my parents separated and Chris moved with my mother into a depressing apartment right on Merrick Road in downtown Rockville Centre, over a travel agency in a block of two-story brick stores. He metamorphosed into a nervous, skinny, hypersensitive adolescent. All the things that had come easily and naturally to him— the music, the art—seemed to have evaporated, stranding him with my mother. On my visits home, I noticed that he had taken on some of my father's worst traits in conversation, as if to compensate for his absence. He smoked cigarettes and was both pathetically needy and brittle and defensive. I couldn't handle it. But that was later, years later.

———

MY FATHER WAS hospitalized in the summer of 1967, the Summer of Love. My mother and I went to visit him at Sand Hill State Hospital, way out on Long Island. My mom was a trim thirty-eight years old, wearing a sort of flowered hippie dress. Suntanned legs, honey-colored hair. I don't know where Chris was; sometimes he would stay with one of the neighbor kids who would baby-sit him.

Why my mom thought it was a good idea to bring me out there, I don't know. Probably someone told her that at age twelve I was old enough to handle it. I was already turning into a cocky kid with a shell. I said it was fine with me. Inside I was scared out of my mind.

It was a beautiful, sunny day. At Sand Hill we had to go through a couple of checkpoints in the parking lot. No trees around anywhere. Mostly I remember the ochre brick facade of the building, with its rows of barred windows flush with the aging walls, like a face with no eyebrows.

Inside, an orderly came to accompany us to see my father. He was a thin, hollow-cheeked, youngish man with graying hair and a mustache. "Okay," he said, looking at some papers in a manila folder, "Fran and Johnny. You," he said, looking at me archly, "must be Johnny." I nodded. Walking ahead of us, he escorted us to the biggest elevator I'd ever entered. It had bare metal sides. Two women in hospital smocks stood inside, both wearing ribbons in their hair, holding hands, accompanied by a bored-looking orderly. One was short, with strawberry-blond hair and girlish features and an unlined face, looking placidly into space; the other was a large black woman who stared fixedly at the top of the elevator with an expression of fright and fascination that remained constant for the whole, slow ride. At the second floor the door opened, and I heard music playing from a transistor radio; just outside the elevator, a smiling man with Asian features was bouncing up and down in place wearing a big blue felt hat and no pants; from nearby a woman's stern voice repeated, "Elmo . . . *Elmo* . . ."

We got to the fourth floor finally, and the two women got out before us and walked down the hall, to the right. We stepped out into the hall, which was lined with light green ceramic tile, and our orderly motioned for us to follow him. We passed a room where a few people were sitting watching television, and then we came to a chipped, orange-painted metal door, which the orderly opened. He said, "Frank . . . we have some visitors." Then we were walking into the small room, which had bars on the windows and light green glazed cinder-block walls, a sickly bare beige linoleum floor, not even a little rug, and my father was sitting on the side of a cot looking at us. He was wearing a white undershirt and pajama bottoms. His hair was uncombed, and he was unshaven, and his eyes were red-rimmed, as if he had been crying.

I felt my mother squeeze my hand; I hadn't even realized until that moment that we had been holding hands. Dad looked from one of us to the other, as if he were having trouble placing us, as if we were waking him in the middle of a nap. On a small table in front of him were several sheets of paper covered with unintelligible scrawls, a pencil, and a small red pencil sharpener.

He looked at us as if he wanted to say something, opened his mouth, started, but before being able to form words made instead a croaking sound, dissolved into tears, looking right at us; my father, crying, stoop-shouldered, abject on the bed, crying helplessly, looking right at us.

"Oh, come on now, Frank," the orderly said, walking in, taking charge. "Be a big boy." He walked right up to my father, pulled a tissue out of a box; my father looked up at him imploringly; the orderly wiped my father's face, saying, "You don't want Johnny and Fran to see you crying, do you? Come on. . . ." My father looked up at the orderly as the orderly wiped his eyes and his nose.

When that was done, the orderly said, "I'll be right outside. If you need any help just call out, or come out."

IN THE CAR as we left the grounds, my mother was quiet, gazing straight out the front window, saying nothing. She seemed angry; I couldn't tell if she was mad at me for something or not. We headed down the parkway, back the way we had come, I assumed; it was a part of the island we had never visited. I opened my window, felt the breeze on my arms. Everything in the world was in some kind of free fall. Mom turned on the radio, and there was that song—"*If you're going to San . . . Fran . . . cisco . . . , Be sure to wear some flowers in your hair. . . .*" All that summer it made you feel as if you were missing a party that was going on somewhere else. Mom lit a cigarette, scratched her leg, sang along absently.

We turned off at an exit, and I glanced over at her. She seemed to be thinking about something. She had taken off her sandals and was driving barefoot. Something was up.

"Where are we going?" I asked her.

"I thought we'd take a ride and stop in on a friend." She looked over at me, right into my eyes. "Can you handle that?"

"Sure," I said. I could handle anything.

We drove down a scrubby section of four-lane highway, sandy along the edges. It was a funny, crappy-looking area. I asked her where we were, and she said Kings Park.

Eventually we came to a completely unremarkable street that ran at a right angle from the road we were on and alongside an empty field where people had dumped some garbage, and then we were in a kind of subdivision, full of cheap, smallish houses with brown lawns, trashy.

"Who are we going to see?" I asked her.

"A friend of mine."

A friend of hers. I assumed this was someone from the Old Days. There was something about the way she said it, though. A friend of Mine. I began circling my wagons inside myself.

We pulled up in front of a house, a little bigger than the others but also with a brown lawn. I saw Mom looking at the house, moving her head a bit, as we approached, as if to check whether anyone was home. The garage door was open, and the back of a car was visible.

"Okay," she said to herself, turning off the ignition and opening her door.

I didn't know why, but my heart was pounding. I had never gone on an errand like this with my mother or father before. There was something weird and clandestine about it. It was not scheduled, not on the list of understood destinations.

"Coming?" she said, standing there. I got out of the car and slammed the door. "This is a good friend of mine," she said. "I just thought it might be fun to visit for a little while." As she was telling me this, I could see that she was uncomfortable herself with what was going on. She didn't usually need to explain herself to me.

I followed wordlessly, up a gray cement path through the weeds to the front door. She rang the bell.

After about a minute, during which she craned her head to try and peek in the window, the door opened and a man appeared, wearing a white undershirt and blue jeans, with a surprised expression on his face. He had black hair combed wet, straight back from low on his forehead, and a face that started wide at the temples and narrowed to a pointed but weak jaw, like a fox's. His eyes squinted just a little and he had a mustache. Below his blue jeans he was barefoot.

"Surprise," my mom said. He looked at me like a home-steader in a western, spotting trouble coming over the ridge. He invited us in.

We stood on the bare wood floor of a sparsely furn-ished living room. A green couch faced a TV, which was going. Over the couch, a painting of three clowns on a pink back-ground.

"John," my mother said to me, "this is Danny."

"Hey there, John," he said, bending a bit at the waist, toward me, holding out his hand for me to shake. He definitely didn't need to bend toward me. I ignored him. There were three steps up into what appeared to be the kitchen.

"How about a Coke?" he said. "You want a Coke?" I didn't answer. I knew something was wrong now, because ordinarily my mother would have told me to watch my manners.

"So," he said. I could tell he was groping for words. I didn't even want to look at my mother, so I looked around the place. The windows were too high on the walls, too. The kitchen table had only two metal chairs, cheap chairs.

"Laurie is still out with her friends," the guy said. "It's too bad."

"Do I get a Coke?" my mother said.

The guy laughed. " 'Do I get a Coke . . .' Get a load of this," he said. She followed him up the three steps into the kitchen, where they talked awhile in low voices. No books, no magazines, no newspapers lying around. Wrong; one book, jammed be-tween couch cushions. I went to see what it was. It had a picture of a pyramid with an eye in the top. *Secrets of the Masters,* by E. P. Koretzky. I put it back.

I didn't know what to do with myself. I wasn't going to go up into the kitchen. I sat on the couch. It was a beat fake velvet thing. I sat on the edge of it. And what I thought was, I am lost, lost, lost.

———

WE WENT THERE maybe three times. It didn't last long, whatever it was. I poked around while they disappeared. In his basement I found records on labels I'd never heard of, with pictures of models in lurid Technicolor on the covers, some even bare-breasted. They were so tawdry that they didn't even get me hot. They had songs with titles like "I'm a Virgin, but I'm on the Verge," or "Tit for Tat." One record was called *The Iceman Cometh . . . and Other Party Favorites,* on Laff Records. On the cover a woman in a kitchen, wearing a see-through negligee, with lipstick, red hair, a cigarette holder, and a guy in a delivery uniform—her looking at him, him looking at camera. We had nothing even faintly resembling this at our house.

The guy, Danny—I never called him by his name—had two daughters, one of whom still lived at home. Her name was Laurie. She was maybe fifteen, and I was thirteen. On our last visit there, Laurie and I made out on an old couch in the basement, and she gave me my first blow job.

Mom stopped seeing Danny right around then. It was winter, turning the corner into 1968. My father came home from the hospital right before Christmas. Everything had begun to seem arbitrary to me. I would look at an ashtray I'd seen on the same end table my whole life and ask, Is this the ashtray in the house where I live a normal life with my parents, or is this the ashtray in the house where my father no longer lives because he's in the nuthouse, or is this the ashtray in the house where my father has returned as a shadow of himself . . . ? Everything around me began to float free of its moorings; somebody had untied the ropes. Of course, I myself was one of those things whose definition seemed very conditional at best.

The next year all the shit hit the fan—the King and Bobby Kennedy assassinations, the Chicago convention. The whole country seemed to be falling apart. My father held forth at the dinner table, snarling about law and order. He should, I thought, have had the decency to be at least a little sheepish after his breakdowns. We watched the Democratic convention on TV that summer. At one point the camera cut to Allen Ginsberg, who looked right at the camera and gestured, as if to say, "See? What did you expect?" My father laughed at that, for which I give him credit. Yeah, I thought. We can all relate, can't we?

7

MARIJUANA.

Suddenly it was there. In the culture, at the parties. A sacrament for the secularized. It made everything both more objective and more subjective. It objectified subjectivity. . . . You walked down the street, and the trees had a spirit under the streetlamp. The fence had a personality. The visible facts spoke in a coded way of something more profound, more serious, that lay underneath, teasing you to discover it. . . .

In the affectless, or seemingly affectless, world of A-ville, it lent warmth to objects. It lent the objects, you could say, a subjective life and gave your own subjectivity an oddly objective quality. You didn't just use the things around you; you cohabited with them. Marijuana brought you in touch with the tangible. But it also fed paranoia. There was a sense that more was going on than just what met the eye. Something not wholly accounted for by the visible facts. Under the surfaces of events, like cockroaches swarming in the lathwork behind a freshly painted wall, were millions of reasons things happened as they did that were wholly unapparent to the naked eye. It opened the world of the spirit, but also the world of total conspiracy.

A NIGHTTIME PARTY, in Massaquogue, the next town over. Mid-July; I was about to leave A-ville for good, for college. A little more than a year after the shootings at Kent State. Evening crickets going, the sense of something just around the corner that you couldn't anticipate. The party was for people who were working on the congressional campaign of Allard Lowenstein, the antiwar candidate who had spearheaded the "Dump Johnson" movement. My friend Corey Tarnopol had been the coordinator for A-ville High School. Then he had abruptly dropped out of the campaign, although he still knew the others who were involved. The Vietnam War had sucked everyone into activism of some sort. It engendered an activist stance, whether you were for the war or against it. However you felt, it seemed to matter.

They held the party at the house of some older activists and campaign contributors, the Lampkins. Massaquogue was a different thing from A-ville—richer, more Jewish, more cosmopolitan—and it lent the evening extra mystique. Light spilling out into the backyard, claiming a few square feet of lawn before dissipating in the deep shadows under the pin-oak and sugar-maple trees. From speakers in the windows came that high voice, McCartney's, *"Get back . . . Get back . . . Get back to where you once belonged . . ."* with that humid, hazy, muted guitar riff, the night and summer stretching out before you, the smell of dope smoke wafting on the still air. The party wound its way around to the front lawn and then into the street—

campaign donors, district organizers, high-school group leaders, and street canvassers. People sat on the back steps, getting high, talking. The whole night had an erotic charge; possibility was the air we breathed.

I was standing in a group listening to Ken Randall talk. He was the district organizer for our area, in his late twenties, with longish sandy-brown hair and a mustache, wearing a flowered shirt; he stood with his arm around his beautiful, barefoot wife. Ken exuded the Greening of America sense of optimism and polymorphous awareness that was still possible at that time.

"What we're looking at here," he was saying, "is a nodal point in history. History has nodes, times when lots of different elements feed into the equation"—he gestured authoritatively with his hands—"and things can go in a number of different directions. That's what we're looking at right now. . . ." Yeah, I thought—nodes. Around him people were nodding.

"We are history," he said. "The public life of our times is our life. We all have a dual citizenship—our private life and thoughts and our life as members of a community—not just a local community but our nation. Our nation's fate is a function of our decisions, our bravery, our cowardice. . . . The promise of democracy—and we still believe in democracy—is not a top-down thing. We don't act out a scenario that is dictated to us—not yet, not entirely. The scenario is a mosaic of all our individual actions. We, the people, managed to get Johnson out of the White House, and we can get the U.S. out of Vietnam. We can get civil rights for all our people. We can have a decent and a responsive government. We can help other countries achieve their own destiny instead of turning them into puppets. . . ."

I loved hearing this. It was great to feel as if you had a hand in History, a collective project, that what you did and felt made a difference in the large picture. The image of a destiny, the greatest cure for anomie. . . .

Someone remarked that America was trying to be the policeman of the world. Ken said, "I'll tell you why I think that is. I think the United States carries a sense of collective guilt for leaving the Old World—England, Poland, Italy, Ireland—and the Cold War is an act of collective expiation of that guilt. An attempt to show that we are not selfish in our upward mobility. The problem comes when the attempt to demonize Communism becomes a refusal to look at the moral contradictions of capitalism." Ken had an answer for everything. Actually, I wasn't sure I understood this one yet.

As I thought about it, Corey Tarnopol appeared at the edge of things, motioning for me to come with him. Reluctantly, I left the circle of illumination and followed him into the cricket-breathing night. The sense of bodies around, other adolescents, girls in blue jeans and peasant blouses. A pipe was produced.

Corey talked to me as he prepared the pipe. "Ken wants to be Al, that's his problem," Corey said. "Did you hear what he was saying about guilt and the Cold War? That's a lot of bullshit. We've got no guilt about anything. Americans are ruthless, which is why we came here to begin with. Anything we can't control, we kill. Here," he said, holding the pipe out to me.

In my hand the bronze pipe was heavy, as if it had been made out of a Chinese gong. Ceremonial. I held a match over the bowl, circled it around as I inhaled, the taste in the back of my throat. We passed the pipe back and forth. After the third hit, I began to feel a distinction between my head's presence in the air and that of my legs and feet on the ground. In the spirit of science, I lifted up one foot, which seemed as if it were at the bottom of a giant scaffolding on top of which I sat, directing things.

"Contact," I said. Corey was coughing.

"Have you been inside yet?" he asked.

"Inside what?"

"Inside the house."

I thought about inside the house; it seemed like a large concept. Very definitive. Either you were inside the house or you weren't. The house was bulging with light—it seemed to want to expand—yet it was only a small part of the world. Too small, actually, to be half of such a large equation. There was inside the house, which was this, and then outside, which was everything else.

"How do they do that?" I said to Corey.

"Huh?"

"Make the house . . . that . . ." I didn't finish the sentence, mainly because I didn't know what the rest of it was. "Mainly" . . . that was what they always said in *Mad* magazine.

"Come on, John," Corey said, putting his hand on my shoulder, "you freak. Let's go see the Lampkins' nice house."

Together with Corey Tarnopol I walked up onto the wooden deck at the rear of the house. Someone said hello to Corey and he said, "We're on a mission." We went into the house. It was like being inside a glowing beehive. Odd glare of lights. Corey in his green crewneck sweater and his heavy eyebrows. My fellow soldier, my fellow human!

"This is fucking incredible," I said.

The house was a study in beiges and greens, some kind of

Middle Eastern motif going through it, big windows, space managed for flow. I was aware of the occasional person registering our presence as we walked across the deep, spongy carpet. The crowd inside the house was a little older, amber glints of whiskey and ice cubes in crystal tumblers. . . .

Corey and I went up a set of stairs covered with the same carpeting and found ourselves in a long hallway under muted lights. On the walls hung framed photographs of Lampkins in various stages along life's journey, of Lampkin kids who had grown up and left home. We walked past rooms with and without lights on, doors partly closed, and came, at the end of the hall, to an unlit room, which we entered; it turned out to be a sunroom affording a view of the backyard where all the partying was taking place. Milky backyard light came in through the large windows, casting banded shadows across what appeared to be the floor's Navajo throw rug.

We sat down on two wicker chairs that snapped and crackled as we sat in them. Corey pulled out the pipe.

"What if somebody comes?" I said.

"What if somebody comes?" he repeated, with different emphasis.

In truth I was feeling a little weird, a little isolated, being away from the group like this. I liked hearing Ken talk. I wanted to be part of a Larger Project. I felt alienated enough as it was. The sense that one's destiny might actually be connected to the life of one's time felt like a form of salvation to me.

Corey used a cigarette lighter that was sitting on a small table to light the pipe; the flame shot out of it in a stream, hissing. We both registered surprise; it was as if the lighter were some local god of the sunroom. You pressed a button, and fire sprang forth. He handed them both to me. "Feed your head," he said, almost gagging on his lungful of smoke. The lighter was heavy and beautiful, in the shape of a seashell, and appeared to be made of gold. Wow. I lit up, the golden seashell spitting fire that bent back upright, bending down into the bowl only as I sucked air in through the pipestem.

Minutes went by; we sat, listening to the music wafting up. I felt as if we were in the control room of the party. There was a television, with framed photos on top, including one formal portrait of the Lampkin family; along another wall, over some built-in cabinets, hung about twenty more framed photos of the Lampkins. I'd never seen anything like it. These people had a need to be surrounded with pictures of themselves. It was like being in some ongoing tribute to the Lampkin Family.

"Look at these people," Corey said, as if he were reading my mind. "Would you care if one of these people got hit by a car?"

"What do you mean?" I said. It was a jarring question.

"If someone in one of those pictures disappeared from the world," Corey said, holding the seashell lighter and looking at it, examining it in the eerie glow from the window, peering into its golden finish. "Would it mean anything to you at all? If we left here and one of them got hit by a car, what difference would it make to you? Seriously."

This was a serious philosophical question, and I didn't want to answer it automatically.

"Look at that picture," he said, pointing to the formal portrait on the TV. "Look at it."

I got up from the chair and looked at the picture. A middle-aged man with a thin face, wearing a dark suit, looking into the camera, smiling—guiltily, it seemed. His wife was next to him, sitting down, with a bouffant hairdo and a pink dress with a wide white belt. A girl, standing, wearing a dress and belt matching her mother's, and a guy a few years younger than us, with oily hair combed down and across his forehead. The knot in his tie was clumsily done. What was I supposed to be looking at?

"How could you say you would care if they disappeared off the face of the earth? You would never even know they were gone," Corey said. He was preparing another pipe. "There's an endless supply of people who look like that. They could be anybody."

"Well," I said, "that's the point, isn't it?" I took a deep hit and had a small coughing fit. Corey was coughing, too.

"What?" he said.

"I said that's the point. If they could be anybody, then they could be you or me, too. So . . ." So what? "So you have to care about them."

Corey took back the pipe and lighter. "You're a sentimentalist," he said.

Corey's eyes were half shut; he was fingering the beautiful shell lighter. From below, Bob Dylan's voice floated up, singing, *"You used to be so amused about Napoleon in rags, and the language that he used . . . ,"* and I wanted to go back down and listen to Ken Randall and be part of the romantic reclaiming of America that he represented, instead of the dark, private, trippy inner journey up the Amazon of the self. . . .

Eventually we got up and started to leave the room. I noticed that Corey was still holding the lighter. He noticed me notice it. "Let's nationalize this," he said, putting it in his pocket, where it made a giant bulge.

"You're just going to take it?" I said. I couldn't believe it.
"Fuck private property," he said.

———

HOURS LATER COREY gave me a ride home. We got high
again on the way, and the house, as we approached, sat ticking
silently, like a clock. It was midnight; I hoped my parents
wouldn't be up. I didn't want to go inside and be seen, particularly. I wanted to stay out in the dark night. Good-bye, Corey. I
put the key in the front door and then felt the mass of the door-
knob in my hand, the feeling of permanence itself; somewhere
people designed and built things that used this kind of hardware. I stepped inside, into the carpeted living room, the
French chair, the Chinese fan on the wall, one lamp on the end
table. The living room was static, muted, a sword hanging by a
hair, like the set of a play in the middle of the night, but I heard
the sound of the television coming up from downstairs. Chris's
room was dark around the doorframe; he was asleep.

I had to go downstairs, just to say good night to Mom and
Dad. Be normal, I thought. Act normal. I breathed a couple of
times and went to the little stairs that went down into the den.
Six short, carpeted, creaking steps. They both looked up at me
smiling as I walked into the room. Hey, how was the party?
Great, I said. Fortunately they were pretty involved in watching
The Tonight Show, and I sat down for a moment and turned my
attention to it as well, the bristling, hyper-real present tense that
overrides all else, the glowing tube. . . .

Johnny Carson's guests are Don Rickles and Buddy Rich.

Rickles is talking about something incomprehensible, the face on his bald, turtlelike head set in a constant grimace of outrage and ridicule, strands of hair combed across the top of his head and slicked down, a figure from the commedia dell'arte, an evil puppet, a manic Jewish snapping turtle with no inhibitions. . . .

Johnny, with a seriocomic look, his kind of arch ingenuousness, an exaggerated formality, says to Buddy Rich, "I understand you have a musical specialty for us this evening."

"It's not evening, John. It's afternoon," Buddy Rich says, his tone implying "You are a lunatic, but I can cure you if you will listen closely." "You should be honest with your viewers," he adds.

"Yes," Johnny says, wanting to laugh but having to play it straight until he can't take it anymore. "But our show is aired at night." He says this in his "I'm being reasonable with you even though I have to explain things to you as if you were a child" voice.

"*You think anybody cares?*" Rickles screams, jumping in, grabbing the ball. "Your viewers are laying in bed wondering how a dummy from Nebraska pulls down half a million a year for boring his guests to death. . . ." At this Buddy Rich falls on his side in his guest's chair, laughing, and Johnny turns his hurt-innocence face to the camera or the audience, and there's a chorus of laughter and jeers for Rickles's cruelty, sympathy for Johnny. "What?" Rickles says, looking at the audience, his eyebrows arched in disbelief. "You paid eight dollars for tickets, and you're feeling sorry for *him?* He gets to go home and watch his wife walk around in a leopard-skin bikini while he sits in bed clapping his hands and hollering, 'Sing "Malagueña"! Sing

"Malagueña"!'" Rickles clapping his hands in imitation of Johnny sitting there in preorgasmic frenzy, and now Carson loses it, along with the audience and Buddy Rich.

Carson recovers after a moment, turns again to Rich, and says, "As we were saying . . ."

"I wasn't saying anything," Buddy Rich says.

"What is the name of the song you are going to play for us?"

"John, the piece I'm going to play is called 'Rhythm Is My Business.' It was a big hit for the Jimmie Lunceford band."

"Good," Johnny says. "I'm glad you have a business to fall back on, because after this show, NBC will make sure that you never appear on network TV again." And at that, Rickles and Rich crack up in laughter, the requisite ceding to the host the prerogative of pulling the plug and flexing his muscles, and the audience applauds, and everybody feels good, and Rich gets up and walks over to the stage area, where two straight-back wooden chairs are set up, facing each other.

He sits down in the one on the right, facing back toward the dais, profile to the audience. On the other chair lie a pair of drumsticks, which he picks up and twirls quickly in his hands, like a gunslinger twirling a pair of pistols. He holds them briefly up in the air, freezes, then brings them down and starts clicking out a tap-dance rhythm on the seat of the chair in front of him. He is hunched over, his gaze focused on the tips of his sticks as they hit the chair; at one point he kind of rears up a bit, still playing— readjusting his spine, maybe—then he bears down again.

"*Rhythm is my business,*" he starts half singing, half speaking, to the rat-a-tat accompaniment. "*Rhythm is what I sell . . . ,*" all the while beating out that rattling tattoo on the seat of the chair, like the tapping feet of a midget tap dancer.

"*Rhythm is my business*"—really speaking the words rhythmically, with just a little melody on top, like a dusting of sugar on dry oats—"*Rhythm, it sure is swell. . . .*" You watch him fascinated, the way anything self-contained is fascinating. "*When I do tricks with the sticks, The boys in the band all play hot licks. Rhythm is my business, Rhythm, it sure is swell. . . .*"

As soon as he finishes the lyrics, he sets up a little chittering rhythm just with his left hand, the stick making a blur like a fan, and with his right he starts going up and down the rungs on the ladder-back chair, beating one, beating two, back down again in steps. He lets the right-hand stick bounce up and down between the second rung and the third, a cross-rhythm against the left hand on the seat, a moiré pattern, pulsing, and as soon as he is sure we've seen it, heard it, like someone doing a yo-yo trick, he steps the stick back down to the seat and plays a series of intricate beats, pulling them all out of the excelsior of his little stick salad. Rich bends low over them, and then he takes his right hand and jabs the stick—*Pow!*—through the ladder-back and freezes—as if to say, "Look, here, behind the curtain, quick"—and then he goes back into the little tattoo, and the tap dance gets hypnotic, becomes the wallpaper of the solo. . . .

I sat watching it with a mounting exhilaration in my chest. What poise and wit and equilibrium, I thought. Totally in the moment. I was enjoying this show beyond anything I could imagine. It was the greatest thing I had ever seen in my life. It was so pure. It washed away everything. That moment of consciousness, though, put me back in the world of time, and I rejoined my body there in the room and became a separate person watching. . . .

Now Rich was playing the chair at angles, playing on one

leg, then playing on the leg on the other side, one leg, then the leg on the other side. Then he played with one stick on each leg, playing both legs at once, then he played the top of the chair with one hand and one of the rungs with the other, then he switched those off, adjusting his body attitude perfectly each time, never missing a beat, and finally he started playing a rumba beat on the seat of the chair and tapping out another rhythm with his feet; his entire body was a series of contrasting rhythms, gestures, and sounds echoing each other and then at just the right spot in the beat he stopped—*blam*—and in the same motion stood up like a little boy after his first recital, ankles together, bowing deeply, and the audience went crazy.

"Wow," I said. "Wow. That was great." My parents both looked at me, smiling.

The camera cut to Johnny, who was standing up, clapping his hands and shaking his head, wearing a faint smile of amazement.

"I never liked his band," my father said. "I went to hear them once at the Riverboat. They were so GD loud we had to leave."

Now Rich was back on the dais, on the couch; they had moved him over for the next guest, an animal trainer. Johnny was introducing the guest, trying to keep a straight face. "This poor guy," my father said. "They're leading him to the slaughter." Rich and Rickles avoided looking at each other, sitting there like the worst boys in the class waiting for the substitute teacher to come in. I was watching the television with an intensity that was due partly to the charisma of the image and partly to my sense that as long as all attention in the room was focused on the TV my own state would be invisible.

Now the guest walked out onstage, wearing a safari jacket and leading a giant turkey behind him. A giant turkey. "Oh, God," I said. "Oh, God," I heard myself saying. "It's not . . . ," I began to say. "The turkey is so big. . . ." Shut up, I thought. Rich and Rickles stood up and gravely shook hands with the guy, Carson watching them a hint nervously. Everybody sat down, and the animal trainer gave one sharp tug on the turkey's leash. The turkey hopped, fluttered its wings.

"Well, sir, welcome to *The Tonight Show*," Johnny said.

"Thank you," the man said, yanking on the turkey again. "He's a little flustered," the man said, almost to himself, embarrassed, frowning as he tried to corral the turkey into stasis. Already Rich was in hysterics, with Rickles sitting next to him, his eyes wide and focused straight ahead and his mouth muscles set in a rigid refusal to laugh.

"Can you tell us what you've got there?" Carson said, the camera tightening in on him and the trainer.

"This is a jumbo turkey," the man said. *"Meleagris majoris."* Carson, with a very serious expression, repeated the Latin name back to the man. "That is correct," the man said.

"And the *Meleagris majoris* does tricks, I understand." At this you could hear Rickles's demonic laugh, off camera. The audience was being swept by little gusts of giggles; God only knew what was happening with Rickles and Rich. I wanted to see.

"Oh, yes," the trainer said. "He does about twenty-eight different tricks." He yanked on the turkey again.

"Twenty-eight," Johnny said. "And you taught him these tricks yourself."

"Yes, sir."

"Can he do one . . . do one now?"

"Certainly . . . if I can get him to calm down. Amos," he said, addressing the turkey.

"Amos?" Johnny said.

"That's his name," the man said, trying to get the turkey's attention. The camera was now pulled back to show the entire couch; Ed McMahon was sitting with his hands on his knees, laughing helplessly, and Rickles and Rich were leaning on each other, laughing.

"Come on, Amos," Rickles said, laughing lewdly.

The trainer emitted a series of high-pitched, gargling noises, bending down and looking at the turkey, which was facing the audience, pulling its head back and forth. The man gurgled and squawked in short, sharp bursts, and with no warning the turkey ejected several finger-length turds from its anus, regarding the audience all the while.

Rickles leaped to his feet, said something that the network must have bleeped out, and then pandemonium erupted. The audience was screaming and hooting; Rich had fallen sideways on the couch, and the camera cut to a close-up of Carson's face, stymied, beyond shock, beyond surprise, a mixture of resignation, pity, and wonder, looking at the home audience now.

I was laughing so hard suddenly that I couldn't see. I couldn't stop. I was completely out of control, laughing and laughing. I didn't even know what I was laughing about. Laughter was a god, and I was swept up in the whirlwind. My parents were laughing, too, at first, and then I was aware that they had stopped, but I couldn't stop.

On TV Rickles pointed at Carson, hollering, *"You poor sap! When this is over you're going to be back on Saturday mornings* doing *Farmhouse Frolic*. 'Okay, kids. This is Mr. Ducky, this is Mr. Donkey. . . .' "

I was laughing so hard I thought I was going to choke to death, and through it I heard my mother's voice saying, "John . . . *John* . . . are you all right?"

"I'm fine," I said, tears covering my face. "I'm . . . fine."

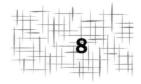

AT HOLLISTER YOU BEGIN TO take the seasons for granted, as if they were the acts of a play you've sat through many times. You talk about them with the other faculty. You almost begin to feel as if you own them. You adapt to the imagery, the pace, the reading periods. You grow used to the deceptive density of Connecticut. There's countryside all around, but it's warm countryside, inviting, a sense of hooked rugs inside, in front of fireplaces. Copper pots hanging up somewhere.

During these past few weeks I leave my office each evening feeling like a pogrom survivor who has spent the day hiding under the bodies of the dead. I am astonished, even affronted, on some level, to find the world still going out there, apparently unchanged. After spending the day meditating on the JFK assassination or the 1968 Chicago convention, fallout shelters, Kent State, Vietnam, I emerge, blinking, onto a landscape of tranquil trees and the pursuits of youth, like an amnesiac, amazed and disquieted by all this solidity and continuity. Was this ability of the world to heal beautiful or hideous?

I learned a while ago not to talk to Val about this question. Val has a kind of stability. Her socialism is the equivalent of religious faith. It is completely secular, but it gives her a deep spiritual keel in the water. She still believes in the coming Revolution the way Christians believe in the coming Rapture and Jews believe in the coming Messiah. For her, History is an organism wiser than, and independent of, the people who act out its dictates. It is something to serve. One serves History. I, on the other hand, lack faith in God, and I lack faith in History. But being close to so much certainty is comforting.

We share a hundred-year-old frame house, with a porch on two sides, at the end of a long gravel driveway under beautiful oak trees, just outside of town. This was Val's doing. She picked out the house, arranged the furnishings. If it were left to me, we would probably live in a cave lined with books and videos. I am unaware of my immediate surroundings most of the time. In fact, there is an old converted garage on the property that I use as an office, which is nothing if not a cave lined with books and videos. Val has a beautiful office on the second floor of the main house, filled with plants and light.

We met in Chicago nine years ago, at a conference entitled "The Labor Movement and the Cold War," sponsored by Northwestern. She was the belle of the ball among all these old Labor grayhairs and cheap suits, full of steely vigor and good late-thirties sexual energy. She stood out. And I guess I did, too, among the history professors and the researchers and the old foreign-policy-adviser guest stars. It embarrasses me now, actually, to think about how much that attention mattered to me.

We were introduced in the bar at the Hilton across from Grant Park, where so much of the 1968 rioting had taken place twenty-some years earlier. She had been to my keynote lecture that morning, which I called "Strike Three: Counting Labor

Out," in which I used baseball imagery to discuss the ambiguity of unions' role in the United States after World War II, how they were both progressive and reactionary at the same time—the connections between the unions and the Mob, and the Mob and the CIA, the split in the Democratic Party that came out in the open at the 1968 convention, between the New Left and the old working-class traditional constituency of the party, represented by the Daley machine. I compared the corruption in unions with the corruption in baseball, charted the erosion of their respective myths of virtue.

In all honesty, you couldn't really call it a lecture. It was more of a slide show with remarks. At the time I called the technique "Guerrilla Imaging." I used to do a lot of these things. In this slide presentation, I'd show simultaneous images of JFK and Mickey Mantle or (this was a good one) the famous image of Mayor Daley drawing his finger across his throat at the 1968 convention, juxtaposed with one of Mussolini grimacing, and all the while I'd be talking about the way these images worked on the National Subconscious or expressed the culture's Dream Life . . . you get the idea. I was asked to do a lot of these talks back then. I was a fad.

Val was at a table at the Hilton bar, drinking with two middle-aged guys, and one of the conference organizers, George Federman, brought me over. They were laughing at something she had said. When we were introduced, she said, "Ah-ha," smiling coldly, with an appraising look in her eye. "The light-show man. Hey—I didn't know Mussolini ran the '68 convention. That's some valuable archival footage." She gave me a Mona Lisa smile, and I thought, Uh-oh. Someone with a talent for finding the weakness. Accustomed to taking the offensive fast and finding out what the Other Side is made of. That was okay—I was used to some people thinking the presentations were BS. "He might as well have," I said.

They invited me to sit down, which I did, and I saw quickly that she wasn't so much bored as overfamiliar with the guys she was talking to and the whole setting. She and I started talking, or fencing, with each other, and the guys at the table were kind of left to themselves. I got the feeling that she knew how to handle that world, knew what it was and how it worked, and that I represented something different—maybe fraudulent, but fraudulent at least in some new way.

She had been holding forth for them, talking about how the Vietnam War had represented the United States' showing its true fascistic colors, which seemed to mildly scandalize the old union rank-and-file guys. She had this nostalgic thing going about the Weathermen and Angela Davis. She obviously enjoyed saying outrageous things, and she was really laying it on thick. At one point she remarked that the Black Panthers were the most important and progressive political movement in the United States since the Wobblies, and I decided to break in with a Sweeping Remark of my own.

"Huey Newton," I said, "was a worse thug than Jimmy Hoffa."

The other guys laughed at this remark, and she looked at me as if I had to be joking. She squinted slightly, and I imagined the roulette wheel of possibilities spinning behind her eyes: If I was joking, what kind of a joke was that supposed to be? Was I some kind of government agent or a provocateur? Was it just a random remark?

"In fact," I went on, "he had more in common with General

Westmoreland than he did with Gandhi. He just served authoritarianism from the bottom up instead of the top down."

"That is the most ridiculous thing I've ever heard in my life," she said, leaning forward. "It's a complete contradiction in terms." She seemed half amused and half irritated.

"Is it?" I said.

"How can you have authoritarianism from the bottom up?" The others sat watching us guardedly. "Westmoreland napalmed babies," she went on. "The Panthers fed them." This pronouncement drew her features together slightly tighter; a bit of glint went out of her expression.

"The only reason you can say that," I said, "is that one had state power and the other didn't. Give the Panthers a chance at state entitlement. See what you'd get."

"You'd get full employment and universal health coverage for starters," she said with a smile of satisfaction, looking at her buddies for support. They chuckled nervously.

"You'd get the Red Guards," I said. "And you would be the first person they'd come after."

"How do you figure that?"

"Because you hate authority, and they just represent a different authority. Hey, they love unions. Look what the Soviets did to Lech Walesa. . . ."

We took to each other like pit bulls. It was so much more fun than your average conversation at one of these academic conferences, where everyone is polite and trying not to make enemies and sniffing around for jobs. I could tell she was used to being around people who more or less agreed with her.

We had a good time that weekend. At one point I yanked her away almost physically and we did our own tour of the sites of 1968. Val had a strong intelligence and a no-nonsense quality to her that I liked. But in those green eyes, which were so ready to poke a hole in the nearest balloon, I could also see a side of her that went back to the cheerleader she had been, a mischievous side that she'd been adept at keeping in check her whole adult life.

I couldn't stop myself from needling her about her politics—about which she had never cultivated the least sprout of irony—and even though she would bristle, I could see that she liked it on some level. We started a long-distance relationship, which lasted for two years before she moved to Connecticut, we bought the house, and, after five years in it, got married. We are a well-known couple. Too busy and, finally, too old to think seriously about having kids.

If you put Val up against a wall and forced her to answer, she would tell you that she admires Fidel Castro more than any postwar leader, that she is nostalgic for Khrushchev, that the Soviets did only what they had to do to counter U.S. aggression, etc., etc. We used to argue about this kind of thing for hours, even to the point where I would question whether we were doing the right thing being together. Our differences have been both a strength and a weakness. At best we have offered each other, in various ways, an escape from our respective patterns. I have always wanted to be sure of things, the way she is. And I think I offer her some contact with a less deterministic side of herself that doesn't get much exercise in the gray asphalt yard of her historical imagination.

I always told myself that I wanted a family, several kids. But at the same time, of all the things in the world that I might conceivably want to do, reliving my life by watching children grow is at the bottom of the list, and maybe below the bottom. Having a kid, letting him crawl around, or two kids, taking them to soccer games, like Ralph Powell, and then getting the divorce, the adultery on both sides—forget it. I gave up. I made a separate peace. And yet as the years have circled around I wonder about it.

Val's answer for everything is activity and more activity. There's always something more important in the world than one's own petty feelings. She's always cooking up projects— legal-defense fund-raisers, labor-redress boards in public housing in Hartford. The phone rings at odd hours with calls from poor, semiliterate people in all kinds of trouble. Her latest thing is "The Reading Project." She coordinates maybe twenty volunteers, of whom four are part-time administrative staff and the rest are "mentors" who go in one of three rickety old RVs to sites in the poorest areas within a hundred-mile radius (yes, there are very poor areas in Connecticut) and sit for hours tutoring learning-disabled children to read. It is a great project—awards from the governor, etc.—but it makes me nervous, as many of her projects do. Where does it stop? Where do you draw the line? What if these people want something more from us? What if they come to the house unexpectedly? Too much contact with life has always filled me with dread. Maybe any contact with life. Anyway, Val has given up asking me to participate. Val and I both more or less do our own thing these days. We give each other a minimal emotional base that, as it turns out, doesn't demand much of either of us.

And yet sometimes I look at Val and she seems so preoccupied. I wonder where, or if, I've failed her, or if we've failed each other, by absolving each other of most of the vicissitudes of married life. The speed, the running, that kept me landing so lightly through my twenties and thirties that I thought I could walk on water, has slowed, and I feel myself getting wet around the ankles. In my weakest moments, I wish I had a family. I dread my later years, heading downriver toward the Great Waterfall, the roar growing louder in the distance; I dread leaving nothing behind on the shore. . . . But, of course, I did have a family, and I ran screaming in the other direction.

ONE EVENING I came home after a long and fruitless day spent trying to write about the Kent State shootings and getting nowhere. I pulled into our gate, drove along the gravel drive under the oak trees and up alongside the nice colonial house with the shutters on two acres of land. . . . I always marvel at it, as if someone else really lives here. I brought the mail inside and set it on the little Shaker table Val bought for the entry hall—all the usual junk, magazines, bills. Any interesting mail for me tends to go to my office.

Normally I go to the kitchen and put on some coffee so it will be ready for Val when she walks in. But on this evening I was feeling both heavyhearted and restless. I couldn't settle down. The furniture itself seemed sullen, as if it had clammed up when I walked into the room and refused to go on talking.

It was time to admit that I could not write the book. It was that simple. My grand overview of the surfaces of the Cold War had come to a grinding halt. Billows of smoke were coming out from under the hood. Everything I tried to write about—all my escape from the undertow of what I considered to be irrelevant personal life—had become hopelessly contaminated with nothing other than the sludge of my personal life. What irony, if whatever it was I needed to complete this book were hidden somewhere back under all the radioactive rubble of my life. *"Don't forget the CAN OPENER"* indeed.

I had concentrated on those surfaces as assiduously as a twelve-tone composer eschewed tonality. I could riff at will on this stuff. Bring up a topic, and I could say something that sounded original about it. The JFK assassination? Dealey Plaza bred such morbid fascination because heroes are usually killed on hills, brought down by someone below. This is the classic hero death, as expounded by Lord Raglan, et al. In Dealey Plaza, the hero was picked off by someone above—either in the Book Depository or on the grassy knoll—like shooting fish in a barrel, and then drained toward the drain of the railroad bridge like dirty water; it was obscene, a perversion of the usual hero death. Something wrong and profane and unresolved about it. You want more examples? Dylan going electric at Newport? The Folk Festival ethos was cotton—growing from the earth, pacifism—but Dylan showed up in leather, wearing the mantle of a slain animal, a carnivorous as opposed to an herbivorous aesthetic. The leather was polished and finished into a blazer, too, so that there was an urban edge to it—urban carnivorous, you could say, versus rural herbivorous. . . . What about the lack of Truman coins? For one thing, you don't put common sense on a coin. Money has nothing to do with common sense, which is democratic. Money is authority. Truman wore his authority backward, with the sign on his desk reading THE BUCK STOPS HERE. Completely wrong: The buck *starts* there. . . .

Fragments, all of it. And despite my best efforts to present an integrated, readable surface, there was an unanticipated seepage through a cracked foundation, this smell coming up from the basement, my own life forcing itself on me when all I wanted was to get away. . . .

No, I couldn't write this book. Once I admitted this, opened the door to this notion, put up my hands and surrendered, the reality of it began to enter, like marshals entering my house to confiscate everything, walking past me as if I were invisible. Anxiety, dread beginning to finger all my private assumptions . . . I would have to call Gordon, pay back the advance—thank God I hadn't spent that much of it—explain it to the History Department, explain it to everybody, endure the questioning of Silsbee and Rappaport or, worse, their sympathetic silence. I might even need to find some new line of work. Maybe I could sweep up around campus. Join the grounds crew. Do some honest work instead of peddling all these intellectual baubles and paste jewelry. It was amazing that I had been able to make it this far, running away from whatever I have been running away from. This, I supposed, was the point in the movie where the fugitive's horse finally keels over from exhaustion and dehydration and the fugitive takes off through the woods on foot in a vain attempt to outrun his pursuers, with the dogs baying in the distance. But who or what, exactly, was pursuing me? What debt did I owe? What business had I left unfinished?

I had been walking through the house, blindly, and had ended up at the den, an enclave of books, videos, and music where I spend most of my time. My little fallout shelter. Full shelves line every inch of wall space, and more is piling up in stacks on the floor. I accumulate this stuff at an amazing rate; there are four shelves of books just on JFK and Dallas, one shelf just of *Mad* books going back to *The Mad Reader, Utterly Mad, Mad Strikes Back* . . . runs of *Life* and *Look* magazines, *Believe It or Not!* books going back to the 1940s, three shelves of board games from the 1950s and '60s—*Go to the Head of the Class, Lie Detector, Careers.* . . . When guests comment on the amount of stuff, I say, "It's cheaper than insulation." Which, of course, it isn't. It is, on some level, a very expensive form of insulation.

As I entered the room I inadvertently kicked, and nearly tripped over, my father's violin in its case. It had been sitting on the floor at the end of the couch since I'd set it down the evening I returned from his funeral. I couldn't figure out what to do with it, and I wasn't yet ready to consign it to closet or garage oblivion, so it sat there, like someone's ashes in an urn, awaiting further instructions.

I sat down on the couch and picked up the case, set it on my lap. And what was I supposed to do with the violin? Estelle had given it to me, but I had no talent for it at all. I may have heard my father play it once. It was Chris who had picked it up and been able to play it with no apparent effort. Melodies sang forth from under his fingers with warbling, ecstatic expression, and my father would sit listening to him, shaking his head in wonder and appreciation.

I decided to open the case. Maybe, I thought, there was a clue for me inside. Maybe there was some vein of beauty somewhere inside me that I had never tapped in to, that could help me fly over this wasteland into which I had strayed.

The latch on the case was tricky. It was one of those where

you had to slide a little button to one side and a spring-cocked tongue would flip open, except the spring was gone, and I had to slide the button and pry open the tongue with a fingernail. It took a couple of tries. When I opened the lid a distinct, invisible whiff of mildew ascended to my nose. The violin lay there, snug in maroon velvet, like a relic of the Cross. Or a piece of driftwood from a shipwreck.

I picked it up out of the case, light and fragile-seeming as the dessicated carcass of a bird. The f-holes for sound resonance, the ebony tongue of the fingerboard cantilevering over the top of the body, the classic shape that speaks itself and says "violin." Its pedigree humbles you.

Secured to the lid, which was folded up at a right angle to the case itself and held in place by a maroon velvet ribbon at the foot, was the bow—long, sleek, and subtly curved, its filaments slackened like an old woman's hair let down for the night. I unhitched the bow and held it, turned the little gizmo on the end—I remembered how to do this much at least—and the hairs of the bow grew taut.

With my left hand, I brought the violin around, holding it by the neck, and set it on my shoulder in what I figured was the appropriate position, the black chin rest ready to receive my chin. I tried to reach my fingers around to press the strings down, and my arm twisted like a cruller. How did anybody play this thing? When I had it secure I brought the bow around with my right hand, inadvertently hitting the lamp on the end table. The bow is long, and a small rotation of your fingers as you hold it at one end can make the opposite end describe a wide, reckless arc.

I brought the bow around too quickly as well, and it bounced on the strings, like a plane undercalculating its descent rate and bouncing up off the tarmac. With difficulty I got it so that the bow hairs were resting on the violin strings. Then, slowly and deliberately, I dragged the bow downward and to the right, trying to keep it perpendicular to the violin, and a hoarse, feeble, tentative complaint issued from the strings as if I were indeed trying to raise the dead. You couldn't call it a note; it was a sound that contained several possible notes, all badly damaged. With the middle finger of my left hand I pressed down on one of the strings and pushed the bow upward, hitting two strings at once and producing what almost sounded like a note. The taut metal wire bit into the soft flesh at the tip of my finger. As I came to the end of the upward push, the note, provisional at best, disintegrated into a sickly croak.

Decisiveness, I thought, was probably the key to making an actual note. I immediately pulled the bow back downward across the strings and for a tantalizing moment produced a note that pulled into focus, recognizable—nameable, even, if I had known its name—before the bow skidded sideways and bumped into the finger that pressed the string down.

What a waste, I thought. My brother could play this.

My brother. The words burned in my mind as soon as I thought them. I had a brother. Another part of the life I had ordered away because it was painful and inconvenient. Life had been knocking, and I had been pushing it away. I had escaped into the Cold War. Or onto the Cold War. What was I going to do now that the door had slammed shut on my escape? Obviously there was no musical career waiting for me. I should, I thought, get in touch with Chris and give him this violin. That would at least be something constructive.

The last I had heard, from Estelle, he was in San Francisco, barely scraping by. I think he might even have been in some kind of group home or halfway house. Poor Chris, I thought. I had been a real shit. It had been eight years since we had spoken. I wondered if he had spent those years feeling the way I was feeling right then. Maybe, I thought, it was time to get in touch with him. Even as it suggested itself, the notion made me faintly nauseous with anxiety. Chris was the last link I had left to what passed for my personal life, which I had spent years running from. Yet, for the first time, I had a pang of sympathy for what he might have been feeling all those years.

As these thoughts blew around in my mind, something else came into view, tentatively, a scrap of paper floating on the breeze with a message scrawled on it. Maybe, it occurred to me, I had been writing the wrong book all along. Maybe I had really been needing to write some kind of memoir. My personal life had, after all, been constantly forcing itself into my carefully arranged frame while I had been trying to hide behind the surfaces of History. I had become a sort of cultural imperialist, annexing and exploiting historical turf I didn't really understand while ignoring problems at home. Maybe my penance for this long retreat behind History was to, in some way, redeem my personal life. There would be an ironic justice to that.

I sat with the idea for a few moments. It wasn't bad in the abstract, but what could the specifics be? What was I going to say—that I had spent my life as an intellectual origami artist? Nobody wanted to read my confessions. What would it prove anyway? What would I find out that I didn't on some level already know all too well?

Then I thought, What if I wrote a book about going to find Chris?

Instead of the Cold War book. Find my brother and write about the trip.

If I could reclaim part of my life, and help Chris, and get a book out of it at the same time, that would be an amazing thing.

I eyed this idea suspiciously, from a distance.

I could, conceivably, get in touch with him, make the trip, write the book in a couple of months, and present it to Gordon as a fait accompli, in place of the Cold War book. Everybody loved a brother book. I was something of a public figure. There might be some interest.

I tested the idea, the way you might test the ice on a pond with your foot, tentatively, to see how much weight it could take. Something about it felt vaguely wrong, but I wasn't sure what. It had an undeniable resonance, as if it were somehow what I had been looking for all along. Besides, there weren't a lot of other ideas offering themselves.

Outside, the car door shut; I could hear Val crunching across the gravel. I didn't want to tell her about my idea yet. Who knew where it would lead?

"Hello . . . ," I heard, coming from the front of the house.

"Hi," I hollered out.

After a few moments, Val walked into the room, wearing a denim jacket and peasant skirt—her trademark outfit—carrying an accordion folder and the canvas bag that she uses for a brief-case. "Hey!" she said, looking at me and the violin with a sur-prised expression. "Great. Are you going to try to learn it?" Back in Val's cheerleading days she had also been a camp counselor, and she is characteristically thrilled by any show of industry or initiative, any new activity added to the sign-up sheet.

I told her I had just pulled it out out of curiosity. She sat on the edge of the couch and set the file down, ran the back of her hand across her forehead.

"Are you all right?" I said.

"Yeah," she said, setting down the bag. "No coffee?"

"Sorry," I said. "I haven't been able to get it together today for some reason. You look beat."

"Well . . . one of the kids in the Project"—this was the Reading Project—"showed up with bruises on his face. It's obviously an abuse situation, but we're in a ticklish position there with the state agencies. Jack Fortier is stonewalling the whole funding connection with the Title One people, and when Mary Ellen brings in the documentation she gets rubber-stamped six ways from sundown."

Val has a way of speaking familiarly about people and situations I don't know anything about, and it always leaves me feeling as if I might as well not be in the room.

"But I think I know what I'm going to do," she said, looking into the distance. "I'm going to call up Franco and bypass the whole Title One swamp. . . ."

"Val," I said. "I don't know what you're talking about. I don't know who these people are."

"I know," she said, looking at me with those beautiful, cold, green eyes. "They're just . . . people," she said. Then she said, "Your eyes are red—are you okay?" The scent of sadness or misfortune in someone will dependably bring Val back down to earth. I have been guilty, on more than one occasion, of letting myself be weaker, more troubled, than I really am just to get her attention.

"They are?" I said. "I guess I've just been thinking about my father. And Chris."

Val expressed some sympathetic concern, but I could see that she was preoccupied, and before long she said, "Honey, I've got to get these boots off and make some calls," and she went upstairs to her office.

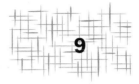

As of that evening, Chris and I hadn't spoken in eight years. But even for years before that, it had been almost impossible for us to have a reasonable conversation. Something in the dynamic called up the equivalent of microphone static. Speak a few wrong words and they would be run through the amplifier of the other's insecurities and blown back out, distorted and shrill.

Chris was a constant reminder for me of home—of confusion, indecision, badly managed pain. I had all I could do to control my own chaos. For Chris, I guess I was the embodiment of a world that hadn't prepared a stable place for him. This was already true when we were kids, for me at least, but it started really standing out in relief on visits I made home from college. Chris had turned into a skinny, high-strung adolescent; he cracked jokes compulsively while his eyes searched my face and he asked me questions about school. He and Mom had left my father and moved into the apartment in Rockville Centre. I wonder now whether Mom wasn't sick already. She always seemed to be apologizing in some way either for divorcing Dad or for marrying him in the first place. She seemed so preoccupied. Chris was stuck there with her, looking for his own way out, stealing her cigarettes, trying to make believe he wasn't scared. At some point he took a semester of classes at Nassau Community College, but he had no real direction.

It was an uncertain period for me, too, and I made myself feel steadier by acting like a caricature of a big brother. It makes me cringe to think about the self-righteous pep-talk letters I used to write Chris. "You have to focus," I would say. "Get out." "No one's going to help you." "Pull yourself out of that mess, like I did. . . ." I was talking to myself, of course. Eventually he did get out; he left and headed out to Berkeley, well after the big party was over. He attended classes there for a semester and a half, I think, before dropping out.

Somewhere during that period I had the revelation that would change my life. It was right around the time of the Dallas trip with Lee, a couple of years after I graduated college with my American Civilization degree. I was sitting in a coffee shop in Sheridan Square in New York, and I was reading Anthony Scaduto's biography of Bob Dylan, where he tells the story of how Dylan found out that the folksinger Ramblin' Jack Elliott was another middle-class Jewish kid like him—Elliott Adnopoz of Brooklyn, the doctor's son. I thought how funny it was that they both had these secret identities, and then suddenly I thought, *Of course.* . . . Muhammad Ali, Muddy Waters, Lenny Bruce—in order to function, all these guys had adopted new identities, Alter Egos. They kept their birth names hidden, like Batman, in order to go out into the world and operate. I thought, *I have to do the same thing.*

This is the weird thing: As soon as I decided to change my name, everything pulled into focus. I applied to graduate school and got a big-time fellowship from Duke, where I was viewed with suspicion by certain members of their very hidebound department, and yet, perhaps because of that, made a name for my unorthodoxy; I got the doctorate, published the first book, the whole bit. I really began then to consciously work out the notion that only the surfaces of history are real. The understructure is what is provisional and gets blown away with the wind. The surface is what endures and is where we must look for "meaning."

Chris was floundering during this time. He was all over the place—California, then with relatives in Eau Claire, then back in California. For a while he lived in an ashram. He was always casting around for some fad thing to believe in. After Mom died, it got worse. He would call me and tell me about the need for alternative energy sources, or about Krishna consciousness, or whatever his latest version of The Real Answer was, and I would just be unable to listen. "You're running away from yourself," I would say. "Why can't you stay in one place and build a life? Focus on what's in front of you. Stop chasing around. . . ." His groping made me extremely nervous. In some ways I think I was measuring my own success by its distance from his failure.

Finally he came out and asked if he could come to live with me. I remember that phone call. I was teaching at Bennington—this is a year or two before Hollister—and renting a renovated farmhouse that was much bigger than I needed, but it was what had presented itself to me. I was rolling on the career track; my first book was selling well. I was getting interviewed, flying all over to do lectures; I had girlfriends, I threw great parties. . . . The last thing I wanted was a giant chunk of my exploded past hurtling toward me.

I can't remember now if Chris was in California or Eau

Claire. It might have been New Orleans—he went there for a little while, too. The latest thing hadn't worked out, whatever it was. He called—collect—on an evening when I was running around getting my place ready for a party. He kind of sidled up to his question, asking me what I was doing, as if he was just calling up for a leisurely chat, which I knew he wasn't. "How's your head?" That kind of thing. I was impatient with this and basically told him to get to the point. He said he needed a place to stay for two months, maybe three.

"I don't want to be here anymore," he said. "Everybody acts like they're your friend, but they're a bunch of phonies."

I remember that I was standing in my cathedral-ceilinged living room, tapping my foot on the wood floor, and it made an echo that I liked to hear. It was twilight outside—the days were getting shorter. I had a vision of Chris camped out on the couch. "Well," I said, "isn't that what people told you when you went out there the first time? You thought it was going to be the answer to all your problems. When are you going to sit still and figure out what you want to do with yourself?"

"I *know* what I want to do," he said, frustration pulsing in his voice. "I want to study massage therapy. There's a school in Vermont—"

"Massage therapy?" I said. "What happened to yoga? What happened to leather work? What happened to that coffee-roasting thing?"

"I told you," he said. "They wanted, like, three thousand dollars just for the start-up stuff. . . ."

"Well didn't I tell you to ask them about that?"

"I made a mistake," he said, shouting through the thin phone lines. "Don't you ever make mistakes?"

"Look, Chris," I said, "I've got a houseful of people coming over here in an hour, and I have to get it together. I don't have time for this. It's always the same thing. . . ."

"All you ever do is criticize," he said. "Everything I do is stupid—"

"And when I give you advice it's never the right thing to say. What am I supposed to do, Chris? Just tell you everything you do is great and loan you money and let you stay in my house indefinitely?"

"It isn't indefinitely; it's just until I find a place."

I flew off the handle. I told him he was flailing all over, looking for all these cheap answers, and I wasn't going to be his next cheap answer. I told him he had to find his own place in life just as I had. I tried to rationalize by telling him it was for his own good and he'd never find himself if he lived with me. Words became worse words, a chain reaction, and before we hung up he was crying and screaming in rage and frustration. I haven't heard from him, nor he from me, for eight years.

Estelle kept in sporadic touch with him. I remember hearing something about Oregon, something about Denver. It got to the point where I didn't ask, and she knew better than to tell me. If she did, I would start ranting about Chris and when was he going to wake up and come down to earth, and I think Estelle just got tired of hearing it. I'm pretty sure she sent him money. Anyway, the last I heard, he was back in San Francisco, living in some kind of group home for a while. I had no idea what a group home was, or who paid for it, or if it was a drug-rehab thing, or what. I didn't really want to know. I didn't have room on board. I had been such an asshole.

Now I grabbed at the possibility that I might be able to undo

141

some of the damage. I could go to San Francisco and find him, tell him I knew how badly I'd acted and that my own answers hadn't turned out to be so great. I could give him money and help him get back on his feet a little. I envisioned walking with him in Golden Gate Park, eating in restaurants, having long talks and finding surprising places of agreement with him about things, maybe going to hear some music. I thought about walking along the steep streets of the city, the harbor lights at night. Maybe it wasn't too late to be a decent older brother to him.

But at the same time that these images flashed in my mind, another element was present as well. San Francisco would, I thought, be a great setting for the book. It really could work thematically—the old Beat and hippie hangouts as a background for a reckoning with the aftermath of the 1960s, as it plays itself out between two brothers who had taken different paths. . . . The ways in which the cultural and political assumptions of that time affected the choices we made . . . Gordon couldn't fail to see what a good idea this was.

Even as I thought all this, though, I had a moment of pause. I was aware of an anxiety that had formed within me, just under the surface, like tiny drops of condensation inside a wristwatch crystal, doubt that had entered through an invisible aperture. There was, I recognized, a deep contradiction in my motives. Part of me acutely felt a need to reclaim my life and make peace with Chris. Another part was arranging this as an opportunity to get me out of a jam with the book. Which was the real motive? I thought about this question, and I realized that I didn't know the answer.

Calling Estelle wasn't something I looked forward to, but I needed to do it to get a phone number for Chris. Estelle always wanted to have heart-to-heart talks with me—"find out what was ticking inside that big brain" of her stepson's—and it made me uncomfortable. God knows she deserved some kind of medal for living with my father. But get to know me? Why? I felt like the Phantom of the Opera. Touch this mask and die.

We got through the call okay. I avoided answering her questions about why I was contacting Chris. I simply said that it seemed to be time. Estelle didn't push me on it. There was one surprising piece of information, though: Chris wasn't in San Francisco. He was in Iowa.

"*Iowa?*" I said. "What the hell is he doing in Iowa?"

"Well," Estelle said, audibly rattled by the intensity in my voice, "I think he met someone he liked, and . . . I'm not sure just what his situation is. . . ."

I tried to camouflage the degree of my surprise, but after we got off the phone, I was furious. Why couldn't Chris stay in one place? Iowa was nowhere near as good a setting as San Francisco for what I had in mind. I chuckled uneasily as I realized how quickly my irritation with Chris could expand to fill the moment, even after all that time, like a self-inflating mattress. I would need to watch that.

I HAD DECIDED NOT TO tell Chris about the book idea. It would just confuse matters, I thought. The dissembling didn't sit entirely easily with me. But since when, I had begun asking myself, were motives ever entirely pure? Sometimes the best things happened out of a mixture of exalted and base motives.

143

But beyond that was the fact that, in all honesty, I didn't have a clue who my brother was. He had been someone, something, to use as a marker to measure how far I was from the center of the whirlpool that wanted to suck me under. I wasn't sure, in fact, that I really wanted to know who he was. That knowledge, I realized even then, would probably occasion me some type of grief with which I was unprepared to deal. But I would cross that bridge when I came to it. For that moment any action was better than no action.

I was nervous about calling; before I called, I picked up a few pencils that were scattered on the coffee table in the den and arranged them in a row. I fixed the bolsters on the couch, which were a bit in disarray. Finally I just pulled the rip cord and punched in the number that Estelle had given me.

The phone rang three times before someone picked up and a voice on the other end—monotone, guarded—said hello.

"Chris?" I said.

A moment went by.

"Yes?"

"This is John."

"John?" he said.

Another second or two went by. I began to wonder whether he knew it was me. "Your brother."

"I know," he said. After yet another moment he said, "I'm kind of . . . amazed to hear from you."

"Well," I said, "on some level . . . I guess I'm amazed that I'm calling you." That sounded wrong. It sounded as if I thought he didn't deserve the call. "It's been a long time," I added, helpfully.

"Where are you?" he said.

"I'm in Connecticut. Same old place. What are you doing in Iowa?"

"I'm . . . living here."

This brought us to a stop, as if we stood on opposite sides of a canyon, listening to the wind.

"Well, how's it going out there?" I said. "Estelle didn't seem to know much. . . ."

"It's going all right," he said, tentatively.

"Good," I said.

I figured I might as well just charge in with the edited version of why I was calling. "Look, Chris," I said, "let me tell you what I was thinking about."

"Okay."

"How would it be if I came out and visited you?"

"You want to visit?" he said. He sounded confused by the question.

I told him what I had in mind, that we could drive around, hang out, spend time together.

Chris was quiet.

After a few moments I said, "Are you there?"

"Yeah," he said.

After another minute or two of silence, I said, "Hey, if it isn't a good idea, you know, that's okay. . . ."

"No," he said. "It's not that."

Now I was flustered by his reaction, or lack of one. "Is something wrong?" I said.

I heard a short laugh, then silence. Then he said, "Well . . . I mean, why are you calling? Why now?"

"Chris," I said, groping for something honest, "Dad is gone, Mom is gone, and . . . you are my brother. I feel bad that we've had this—what?—this rupture. And I want to see if we can salvage some kind of relationship with each other. Eight years is long enough." As I said all that, I realized that I meant it. That in itself was reason for some kind of hope.

Chris was quiet again for a moment. Then he said, "When were you thinking about?"

"Well, actually," I began, "I had a weekend in mind. I thought about it and looked at the calendar, and I could do it the second weekend in November."

"You want to come out the weekend of the eleventh? November eleventh?"

"Whatever it is right there, yeah."

"I have to talk to Brenda first."

Brenda. "Brenda?" I said.

"We live together."

"Oh," I said. "Of course . . . I assume there are hotels around there, right?"

"It's not that," he said. "There's a Holiday Inn in Riverton. But you could stay here. . . . It's not that. Give me a day or two, okay?"

"Sure, Chris," I said. "Whatever you need."

When we got off the phone, I felt an odd sense of letdown, as if more should have happened. But that was okay, I thought; the first contact was bound to be a little strained.

When we spoke again, two days later, our conversation was more relaxed, if brief. The weekend would be fine, he said; he'd look forward to seeing me. After that talk I began to pay out the leash on a kind of exhilaration. I would walk through campus and think, I have a brother. He's in Iowa. I even let myself imagine holiday dinners—Chris coming to stay in Connecticut, with his girlfriend. Or me and Val out in Iowa, or meeting in Chicago. The idea that there was someone else who had seen what I'd grown up with, the life I'd kept buried under the floorboards like the Tell-Tale Heart, inspired both hope and anxiety. It was scary, like unilateral disarmament. I was considering dismantling defenses that had been built up carefully over decades.

Part of me knew I needed some commando raid on my own locked heart, some unpredictable encounter with my own brother. At the same time, though, I was panicked at the prospect, and already I was making every effort to control the experience in advance by planning a structure for the book. I outlined possible chapters, made lists of questions I wanted to ask, things I wanted him to show me. He said he worked part-time at the university and part-time at an antiques store, and I figured I ought to see those places. I went to Office Giant and bought a special hardback notebook and scribbled down a few scattered sentences as potential openings. I was going to make bringing him Dad's violin the central "errand" of the book. It made me feel prepared. I wouldn't merely be putting all my emotional chips on a visit that might or might not end well. I would be writing a book.

I HAD DECIDED not to tell Val about the book part of the idea either. Val is nothing if not humorless about the spectrum of possibilities that lie between right and wrong. In truth, it doesn't exist for her. Once the gavel comes down in the arbitration chambers of her heart and a decision is reached as to who is exploiting whom, expect no leniency. No, I would not tell her about my conflicting motives for tracking Chris down.

But, of course, she picked up something in my tone. One thing about Val: she doesn't like to look into herself that much, but she is very acute about hidden motivations in others. Watching me with a slight squint, a slight frown mingled with the faintest smile, she said, "How was it talking to him?"

"Good," I said. "Good." She kept watching me with that little squint. It made me feel as if I was in a dark basement hiding behind a piece of furniture while someone searched for me with a flashlight. "I mean, he was surprised."

"I'll bet," she said.

"I'm sure it's going to take some getting used to for him."

Allowing herself a little more of a smile now, she said, "Why *are* you getting in touch with him now?"

"Look," I said, "am I supposed to go through the rest of my life without ever talking to him again? At some point, if we're going to get back in touch, someone has to take the first step. What's so hard to understand about that?"

"Nothing," she said. "I think it's great. It just seems a little sudden, and I was wondering what made you decide to call him."

"Sometimes," I said, "there doesn't have to be some big reason. Sometimes things just happen."

She nodded; already she was leafing through the newspaper, standing at the kitchen counter. "When are you going out?"

"November eleventh," I said. "That weekend. I hope." She was reading something in the newspaper. "You think this is a bad idea?"

"I didn't say that," she said, turning the page, glancing over the Events of the Day. . . . "Do you think it's a bad idea?"

"I wouldn't have called him if I thought it was a bad idea," I said.

Now she looked at me and said, "Are you mad about something? You're snapping at me."

"I'm sorry," I said, and I was. Val is one of the most straightforward people I've ever known, and I felt bad about being so defensive. "Maybe I'm just nervous about seeing him again."

She was peering into my eyes, frowning slightly and nodding. "Well, that's understandable," she said. She stepped over and put her arms around me. "I'm proud of you for taking that step." I hugged her back, thinking, I don't deserve you, Val. But, of course, nobody knows what anybody deserves.

I received one more call from Gordon Kohl before I left. He had been sitting offstage, drumming his fingers audibly on his desk, waiting for my manuscript. For even a small part of my manuscript. I had been dreading the call, which I knew was coming. But I had a plan. I said that *John Delano's Cold War* was doing fine, but that I also had a great idea for my "next" book. I told him about my brother and where he was—in the heart of the heart of America—and how we had become estranged. His time in California, his search for something to believe in . . . I told him it would make a great brother memoir, using the backdrop of Cold War suburbia in which we had grown up; I mentioned bringing Chris the violin.

Gordon was guardedly positive about it, but his main remark was, "Let's get this one"—*John Delano's Cold War*—"in the pipeline first."

"Of course," I said quickly. "But what do you think about the idea?" I hoped I didn't sound as desperate as I felt.

"Anything you want to write, I want to read."

That was all I needed to hear.

———

I HAD DECIDED to drive. It had been so long since I had actually gotten out into America. I fly in here or there, do a lecture, whatever, but it's not the same thing as getting into the car and steering for the horizon. Preparing, I felt good, happy, for the first time in months. You can get so taken up in your career, your little corner of reality, that you forget to put yourself into context. So, I thought, that's what I'm doing, along with the trip to see Chris. The directions couldn't have been much simpler, at least until Iowa, when I would end up on small highways and county roads. I had never spent much time in the Midwest. I imagined Iowa as flat and barren. I packed enough clothes for a two-week trip even though I was going for only a long weekend, and I set the violin case in among the bags in the trunk, carefully, as if it contained one of my vital organs.

I headed off on a bright fall morning, pulling out of the driveway onto the street, which still had orange leaves all over, and onto the Wilbur Cross Parkway, going west. It was still the tail end of fall in Connecticut; the leaves hung on like decorations that had been carelessly left up after a party. As soon as I was on the road, I knew that I needed this in many ways. The turns and twists of the Wilbur Cross and all that countryside to get out into. Pennsylvania, Ohio, Indiana, Illinois. A feeling of release. Just not having to go into Driller Hall every day and confront that brick wall. To be away, for a little while, from the contending choices involved in the Cold War book, to just be in the present. That's all I ever wanted anyway. Of course, the way west in America was always an escape from History. The East is History; the West is . . . what? Possibility.

I wound through Connecticut, then hopped across the Hudson River, clipping off a corner of New York State, in full autumn colors at midmorning, crossing the Thruway heading toward Pennsylvania. Oh, driving in old America. It had always been important to me to drive, in earlier years. You felt as if you were claiming the country, claiming possibility itself. The sense that you could pull off at any exit and, if you really wanted to, change your life completely. That seemed to have become passé. The image of America as the province of the true liberated consciousness, that sense of becoming, of drama generated by the contrast and tension of the country's parts—of Jack Kerouac hitting the road, Walt Whitman, Bob Dylan's Rolling Thunder Revue, Norman Mailer's political-convention pieces, Martin Luther King's speeches . . . that was something in history books. Now everybody was making a separate peace. A game of musical chairs. Find your roots, stake out your position. This colleague just wrote his memoirs about growing up Irish. This one just got his papers from the Cherokee Nation. Finally it's going to end up with everyone in the country writing his own memoir, to be read only by himself. *E pluribus plurum.* The old paradoxical ideal of the one and the many, the many in the one, gone for good. But what about someone's identifying not with his own thin slice of the multicultural pie but with the multiplicity itself? Or is that some

Faustian oxymoron, doomed by its own terms to meaningless-ness?

Why had that become so hard? It was as if people couldn't identify with an image of America that was anything less than all good. The joke was that the generation of the 1960s had taken their parents' idealized vision of America to heights that even those Italian and Irish and Polish and German and Russian parents would have been too modest to advance. The parents presented America and its possibilities to their kids like a precious ancestral treasure—the Statue of Liberty, the sepia-toned photos of Ellis Island, the thrill at the enumeratable victories of assimilation—and it turned out to have flaws that the givers of the gift couldn't bring themselves to acknowledge, and there was shame in this, for the kids, as they watched the sixties unfold. My own parents! Duped! Look at what's in front of you! Genocide in Vietnam, devastation in the cities, hunger in Appalachia, segregation, duplicity . . . When they realized that America did things that were not just ill advised but hideous, they couldn't allow that into the tent. Instead of being encouraged to conceive of the country's fate as a constant process of becoming, of struggle between creative and destructive forces, like any organism, they had been told that the Kingdom of Heaven was in fact possible on earth. The negative elements, when revealed to the light, seemed too horrible to consider assimilating. The parents screamed that the kids were ingrates, that they should love the country, but the kids did—that was the problem. Nobody had warned them that humans were going to be human in America, too, just like in Europe. They had been presented with a transcendent vision of the nation's promise and destiny, but without the leavening sense of the undertow of the world's inevitable barbarism. Nothing could have lived up to such apocalyptic expectation. When it didn't materialize, the disillusionment was violent and all but complete. It would take another generation to complete it. I see it in the students; they inherited the sense of *If it isn't perfect, it's shit,* the sense of *Don't argue with my ideas; they're as good as yours*—a complacent corruption of an idealized egalitarianism. . . .

Vietnam at least was an occasion for an argument over the soul of the country. After that came Watergate; then, worst of all, the Reagan years—the mixture of a sentimentalized moral authoritarianism with wholesale rape of the economy and the environment for the profit of the oil companies and the military industry. . . . Some of the worst people in the country were the ones who most aggressively made the case for swallowing the notion of the country's virtue whole. But why cede to them the right to do that? Why do they get to define how to be American? Why not come along with the notion that being American means not taking one's own virtue for granted but questioning it? As long as the word still existed, you had a right to ask what it meant. "American"—didn't one at least still have the right to say, "What do you mean by that?"

I DROVE FOR five hours across heavy iron Pennsylvania under a bright early-winter sky, the hills and mountains painted a brownish gray, bare trees like stubble along their long, humped arcs, blanketing the iron ore, the heavy, dense minerals. As the day softened toward evening, I passed Cleveland and the winking

153

lights of Lake Erie, and dusk fell on western Ohio as the country started to flatten out a little. Driving amid the evening lights and trucks was like swimming in the warm water of a bay at sunset. The trucks passed me, heavy-shouldered, gears muscling them forward ahead of the mouth of night. The air hadn't been terribly cold in the afternoon, and I'd been driving with my window half open and the heater on; but as evening fell I put up the window and turned down the heat. I drove past the green interstate exit signs, the other cars, and was passed in turn, with a feeling of extreme warmth and comfort.

Iowa is too far to drive to comfortably in one day from Connecticut, and somewhere east of Toledo I pulled into a motel just off the interstate and settled in for the evening. Is there anything more pleasant than the feeling of being in a clean, warm motel room, in a king-size bed, while outside on the highway the cars rush past like a river? I'm not one of those who condemn the big highway interchanges, the clusters of fast-food places and chain motels and stores. It's fashionable to be superior to all that, to see it as a blight, but my feeling is of being incredibly well insulated by it. How fine to know that if you got hungry you could walk out of your room and not be on some windy forlorn urban street with shadows lurking in doorways, but in the middle of brightly colored winking signs, plenty of company, travelers like yourself, a desk clerk, coffee in the lobby, a market, twenty-four-hour gas station with bottled water and snacks. . . . You are buoyed up on a salt lake of goods and activity, the howling prairies and mountains and sad animals and owls pushed back into the darkness, while around you electricity sings and color and energy pulses, telling you that all is well. . . .

I hadn't remembered my dreams in a long time. That night

I had a lot of dreams, very close to the surface, none of which I remember except for one mexplicable image: a big monolith, or stone, like in the movie *2001*. Just that.

MY WAKE-UP call came while it was still dark. I got up slowly and walked to the window, pulled back a corner of curtain; outside, the air was whizzing and milky. I put on the television and learned that a blizzard was in progress. I got myself together, ate some quick Continental breakfast in the lobby, and headed out. There was a lot of snow already, and it was sticking.

Across into Indiana much of I-80 had been narrowed to one lane—the flatness, the sparseness of settlement—wind and snow in all directions, under a dim fluorescent medium that was not distant enough to be the sky; the sky had come to earth, and the gray vibration of the air was an unbroken continuity from the wet roadway up to whatever might be left of heaven. It was like some backward version of the desert, not a bareheadedness under God but a teeming vagueness that joined you to the Divine.

But as I drove west it lightened just a little, and then a little more, the air less like a swirling fluid and more like real air with a few slicing, sweeping flakes, what was left of the storm. Somewhere around Gary I stopped for a quick burger, and by the time I headed out again, past Chicago, the whole thing had passed. As I drove into Illinois I could see the huge, massed, ominous grayness receding toward the east in my rearview mirror.

As I neared the Mississippi River I passed the signs for the old steamboat and railroad towns—Rock Island, Moline—and then I was heading slightly downhill until there before my windshield was the bridge, and I slowed down as I crossed the River, opened the window all the way and stuck my head out in the freezing air. And then I was in Iowa, in the late-afternoon sunshine and shadows, looking for my brother's house.

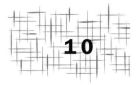

10

THE EXIT PULLED ME OFF the interstate and onto a two-lane road that ran smoothly up and down hills, past houses with wide porches—the outskirts of Riverton. I was a little surprised by the hills; I had been under the impression that Iowa was flat, but instead the landscape rolled and dipped. In the distance, as I skirted downtown, I could see the dome of what was probably an impressive public building. I approached some railroad tracks just as the gates were lowering for a long freight train; car after rumbling boxcar trundled by, the road beyond the tracks in its dappled light visible in semaphore bursts between the hitchings.

I made a lot of mental notes so that I could describe this in *A Brother's Errand,* as I was now calling the book. The closer I'd gotten to Iowa, in fact, the more anxiously I found myself trying to form what I was seeing into a narrative shape as I experienced it. In truth, I was scared out of my wits. It was coming home to me, in a new way that I experienced in my stomach, that I was about to see Chris again, within half an hour or so. There are a lot of situations in which I know what to expect. I'm fine in front of a class, or on a television show, or lecturing, or being interviewed.

I know how to read the dialogue, in a sense, as it's happening and edit it, shape it. But sit me down with someone who stands a chance of seeing beyond my surface and I'm not sure what I'm supposed to do. His reactions are unpredictable.

So as I drove along I was doing my best to control this experience, too, by framing it in a way that would allow me, literally, to have the last word. I even had a lead paragraph that I was working over in my mind. *"Some debts need to be paid,"* it began. *"It was getting on toward late afternoon as I approached my brother's house, and I had the sense of a long journey coming to an end, a new phase ready to start. I was about to do something I should have done a long time before: I was about to make peace with my brother."* Melodramatic, yes. A measure of the panic I was feeling underneath.

After the train passed I crossed the tracks and headed southward, with the last of the low sun coming in the passenger window and smacking me in the corner of my right eye. Highway 8, a two-lane road, led me out of town and, in short order, into the countryside, curving west over rolling rises and dips, through hills covered with endless fields of brown cornstalks mostly covered with snow, farmhouses nested in stands of trees. Out in the middle of nowhere, a house alongside the road with a sign in front advertising guns and ammo; in a chair next to the sign, a dummy dressed in camouflage gear, holding a Confederate flag. I passed through a small town where I saw Amish people dressed in black, riding bicycles.

Eventually I turned off onto a country road that curved gradually to the left up a long hill and through a patch of forested country, and I knew I was getting close. In spots the trees nearly made a canopy over the road, and mailboxes at roadside signaled the openings of driveways that led into the woods and disappeared. And now the road wound downward again and out into flat, open country, and at exactly .7 miles outside the edge of the woods, as Chris had told me, alone in the bare country, I saw a two-story white frame house set back, in a field, from the right side of the road, next to a lone tree, both casting long shadows toward me in the late sun, and, breathing deeply, I turned into the snow-crusted dirt-and-gravel drive.

No sign of life from within as I parked and closed the car door. I wore a sweater and a jacket, but I was freezing, and I stepped quickly across the shallow snow in the shadow of the house to the two wooden steps that put me up onto the small porch, then across the hollow-sounding planks to the front door, and pressed the button for the doorbell. The sun had dropped behind the house, and I was pounding my hands against my sides. I couldn't see any lights on inside. After what seemed too long a time, I rapped hard on the wooden door (there was no storm door and no knocker). Then I noticed the faded Post-it note to the left of the door, with nearly unreadably faded red Magic Marker letters saying PLEASE KNOCK. As I was noticing this the door opened and there, looking up at me blankly, stood a woman about a head shorter than me, with brown hair pulled back and clipped in a barrette, wearing a sleeveless blouse, which surprised me, given how cold it was.

"Brenda?" I said.

"Yeah," she said, warily, looking up at me.

"I'm John."

"Chris is at the store," she said, without changing expression. "He should be back soon."

She just stood there and looked up at me. For a moment I thought she was going to ask me to go away and come back later. There was no *How was the drive?* or *Why don't you come in and wait?* Behind her in the darkened living room I saw a sofa on a bare floor; in the distance, bright light from another room. Apparently this was going to be it in the way of greeting. After another moment she stepped aside, holding the door open, and I entered the house.

Without another word she walked toward the back, toward the room from which the light was emanating. I considered the possibility that it wasn't really Brenda, but who else could it have been? In the absence of any other direction or invitation, I followed her through the dark room, across the wooden floor, to the kitchen. The walls were also bare; it felt as if they had just moved in. It wasn't the arrival I would have chosen.

By the time I joined her in the kitchen, Brenda was busy stirring something in a pot on the stove. "There's coffee over there," she said, looking down into the pot. I saw the coffeemaker on the drainboard. "The cups are on top."

Something warm was a good idea; I walked over and opened the cupboard and pulled out one of four mugs that sat in the otherwise empty shelf. The coffee was strong and hot, and I was grateful for that. I glanced around the kitchen. This is where Chris lives, I thought. Standard-issue fixtures, fluorescent-ring lamp overhead. The cupboards were painted white, but in places they were chipped through, and I could see a layer of yellow paint and one of red.

"Have you lived here for a while?" I asked.

"A few months," she said, still stirring. She nodded to her-self. "It's a rental," she added.

I stepped over to examine a photo magnet on the re-frigerator, a young man in army camouflage, holding a rifle. The kitchen table occupied about a third of the room; it was big and heavy and round, with unmatched chairs, Salvation Army castoffs. Chris had been struggling. He was still strug-gling.

IT WASN'T MORE than five minutes before I heard the front door open. I stepped back out into the living room in time to see Chris closing the door behind him. He wore a corduroy coat and an open-necked plaid flannel shirt, and he was carrying a large paper bag from the store. A full head of thick brown hair, no hat. He never wore a hat. There he was.

He put the bag down on a chair and looked across the room at me.

"How was your trip?" he said.

I looked at him from across the room. "It was fine," I said. "I hit a storm in Ohio."

"Yeah, we saw that on TV," he said. "But you got here all right."

"Yeah," I said.

We stood wordlessly for a few seconds, and, as we did, an entirely different encounter was happening, simultaneously, in my mind—a kind of shadow encounter in which even as we stared at each other and exchanged hollow pleasantries, we crossed the room and embraced each other, hugged, and wept. The scenario played itself out half consciously inside me, footage destined for the cutting-room floor, silent tears draining away. . . .

Then Chris picked up the bag again and we walked together into the kitchen and he put the bag down on the kitchen table. In almost the same motion, he picked up the cup I'd been using and brought it to the sink, and Brenda, with whom he had still not exchanged any words, said, "It's his."

"Sorry," he said, setting it on the table again. He started unpacking the groceries from the bag. Neither he nor Brenda said anything else, and I couldn't think of anything to say either. I offered to help him put things away, and he said, "Nah, we're all set." I didn't particularly want to sit down while he was doing this, so I stood there, feeling uncomfortable. He had gotten stockier, bigger in the shoulders. His flannel shirt and jeans looked well worn but clean. He still moved with nervous energy. His eyes didn't meet mine once while he was unpacking. There was something incongruous about the situation, like looking at something close with one eye and far away with the other; the brain can't bring them both into focus. Somewhere in myself I was grasping almost hysterically for a handhold. Feelings that I recognized from afar, but without actually feeling them, rushed past inside me like closed boxcars on a speeding train.

Chris got the things put away and folded up the paper bag and stashed it alongside the refrigerator, exactly as Mom used to do it (Val put them under the sink). Then he said, "When is the chicken going to be ready?"

"I just put it in," she said.

"John and I are going inside."

She didn't respond, and he approached her and said something in a low voice that I couldn't hear, and she nodded a little, still staring down into a skillet that she was greasing. Then he walked past me out of the room, and I followed.

"Brenda's real shy," he said.

We went out to my car and he helped me carry my bags—I decided to leave the violin in the trunk for the moment—to the room where I'd stay, just off the living room. Half the floor was crowded with shopping bags and boxes, as if they had moved in the week before. In the corner nearest the front of the house was a daybed, made up with sheets and pillow; in the other corner, Chris pointed out a door that led to a tiny bathroom.

After I got situated, Chris asked if I wanted a beer, and I followed him into the kitchen again; he pulled two out of the fridge and opened them, and we took long slugs, then stood regarding each other.

"You've put on some weight," he said, smiling for the first time since I got there. Chris's body had thickened as well; he had the beginnings of a double chin. He had always been skinny as a whip.

"You have, too," I said. "I guess Brenda's cooking agrees with you."

Brenda didn't react to this and, in fact, made a point of walking a bit too closely around me to put something on the table.

"Why don't we go inside," Chris said.

When we got into the living room, I asked Chris if something was wrong with Brenda, if everything was okay. He shook his head. Things were fine. As we stood in the middle of the floor, Chris looked around distractedly, as if he was trying to decide what to do next. There was nothing small to start on, no thread of a previous conversation to pick up: *How is so-and-so? Did he ever finish the blah-blah?* I asked him about his neighbors—if he had any, who lived nearby. He said he'd taken the day off from his job working in maintenance at the university the next day so that we could drive around some. Sometimes on weekends he also worked at an antiques store, but he'd taken the day off from that, too. He asked me how teaching was going, and I told him a little about the Cold War book. Naturally I didn't mention *A Brother's Errand.*

Dinner was ready before long. We ate at the kitchen table, just the way we had growing up. The dinner was simple—baked chicken, canned green beans sautéed in butter, white bread sliced diagonally across the middle. It was a long, awkward meal. Something odd came off of Brenda. I tried to draw her out a little. I asked questions, but she answered them more or less curtly. Almost as if some previous conversation they'd had was a subtext for everything else that was going on. Or maybe it was just that everything that was really important was so far beneath the surface that any possible conversation seemed like small talk.

At one point I asked how they'd met, and he said he'd come through with a friend from San Francisco on the way to Chicago. The friend had a friend in Riverton who did something at the university. They went to a bar, and Brenda was there with some of the friend's friend's friends.

"Chris just kind of floated in," she said, looking at me now. "People notice him when he walks in a room. I did."

It was surprising to hear this about my little brother; I tried to imagine him the focus of admiring attention. Chris smiled over at me and made a muscle with his arm, like a bodybuilder, and I laughed, grateful for the glimpse of normalcy.

I asked some question—I forget what—about the university. Smiling and glancing down, Brenda pushed the food around a bit on her plate. "It's kind of disgusting, you know, looking at some of the goings-on."

"What do you mean?" I said.

"Up and down in the pedestrian mall," she said, smiling and looking at me now, "there's colored people with that stupid hairdo with it all in knots. Their heads look like big black tarantula spiders. And they're all there on scholarships, and they all got pretty little white girlfriends. And it kind of makes you sick." And she smiled at me simply, almost defiantly.

"You don't need to go into that," Chris said.

"He asked me a question," she said, going back to the food on her plate.

It came out of nowhere and seemed to be directed at me for some reason. I didn't know how to respond. I wasn't out there to have a fight with Chris's girlfriend. But what kind of person was this anyway? At odd moments I would catch Chris staring at me with a questioning look.

AFTER DINNER CHRIS suggested making a fire and went to get some logs from the back porch. Brenda washed the dishes and went to bed without saying good night. I sat on the couch in the living room as Chris arranged the logs, putting bunched-up newspaper underneath. A single end-table lamp threw a somber light that petered out before it reached the upper corners of the winter-darkened room. Through the front window, a stretch of road gleamed under a cold silver light strung up on a telephone pole.

Here I am with Chris, I thought. I tried to remember whether I'd ever been in a situation with him where he had been arranging things like this, playing host. I couldn't remember any. For that matter I couldn't remember the last time I had actually seen him. I was used to thinking of him as a lone satellite somewhere Out There, and it was touching to see him in a space that was his. I tried to fix the images and details in my mind so that I could describe it all in the book. He pulled a box of matches off the mantel and lit a corner of newspaper under the logs, and the newspaper writhed as the orange flame consumed it, beat its trail up into the tangle of twigs and more papers. Chris squatted, watching it, his face dimly illuminated by the flickering fire. When it was going strong, he came and sat in the lone easy chair. "This reminds me," he said, "of when I used to look at your monster magazines."

This was a surprising thing to say. It was a bit disorienting, in fact. "What monster magazines?" I said.

"*Famous Monsters*," he said, looking at me. "Or *Monster World*. I remember one had the Wolfman on the cover. You had a bunch of *Playboys*, too. After you left I used to go through all your stuff."

"Why does this remind you of that?" This was the first I'd heard about him going through my things. It was weird to think about him still at home after I left, looking at my stuff.

He laughed, thought a moment, and said he didn't know. "When you were gone I'd look at the stuff you left and I'd imagine we were looking at it together. I liked the monster magazines, and the cards with the pictures of the Martians with the big brains."

"You're kidding," I said. I remembered those Martian cards, suddenly and completely. I hadn't thought about them in years. There were something like fifty of them, and they formed an entire narrative of a Martian invasion of Earth, and Earth's counterattack. They were hilariously gory—giant ants sticking their pincers into people's throats with blood spurting—a boy's delight. They would be a perfect topic for a unit in a class—the Cold War obsession with invasion, with aliens. . . .

"No," he said.

"Where is that stuff? Where are the cards?"

"I don't know what happened to them."

It was a strange feeling to have that memory called up after so long, sitting out there in the middle of Iowa. Suddenly I wanted to see those cards in the worst way.

"One of the Martians was shooting a kid's dog with a ray gun, right in front of the kid," Chris said. "That one scared the shit out of me."

"Yeah," I said. I could see it as if I were looking at it. "The title was 'Destroying a Dog.' The cards were numbered, and the numbers were in little yellow and red asteroids in the lower-left corner." How did I remember this? "Do you remember 'Beauty and the Beast'?"

"That was the one where the Martian was coming in the girl's window?"

"No, that was—I can't remember what that one was.

'Beauty and the Beast' was where the Martian had his arms around the girl and she was screaming." Maybe Chris had it the right way around, actually.

"She had on a bright red sweater." Chris said.

We sat quietly for a few moments. I imagined Chris looking through my things, all those years ago, and felt a pang of sadness, mixed with a faint irritation at the presumption. Still, he kept himself warm by looking through my stuff. Chris sat, staring into the fire, thinking God only knew what.

"Do you remember," he said, "when you were in the play where you played the hypnotist? You hypnotized a girl. I don't think Dad was there that night, just me and Mom. You wore an old coat, and you had a big guy who was your assistant. Everybody was watching you, and I remember thinking, John can do anything."

"I remember that kid's name," I said. "Eddie Muller." I couldn't believe that came back to me unbidden, so quickly. That name hadn't crossed my mind in thirty-five years. "I don't think I remember anything else about being in the play. How do you remember this stuff?"

"You had models, too," he said, getting almost agitated. "Do you remember Frankenstein standing on his grave? Dad made the airplanes and put them in the drawer in their bedroom dresser and you got them out and we played with them and broke the one that had two wings. Dad got so mad he hit you and broke his hand. You painted Frankenstein's face green and had blood coming out of his mouth. . . ."

I remembered none of this. Well, I remembered the plane with double wings—a World War I fighter molded in translucent burgundy-red plastic, with Maltese crosses on the wings and fuselage. That was all.

Chris got up and went to the kitchen to get us a couple more beers. An odd, sinking feeling, a kind of vertigo, washed over me as I sat there in the firelight. I had been so used to being invisible—to thinking of those parts of my life as being unwitnessed. Even Val didn't know about most of this stuff— she never asked. For which I was, mostly, grateful. . . . But I felt ambushed by these images. I was surprised at the emotions they called up. I ascribed this mainly to fatigue from two days' driving.

Chris came back and handed me a bottle, then he sat down again.

"I know you're pissed off at me for not coming to the funeral," he said.

Another abrupt change of direction.

"Well," I said. "Yeah. I guess I was." Albuquerque. The desert and the mountains at the same time. Exposed and trapped, simultaneously. And then that diner where we went to eat after the interment, with the yellowing travel posters. I never wanted to go back to Albuquerque.

He seemed to be waiting for me to go on. "I was mad," I said. "Estelle could have used some more support."

"I didn't really have the money to come," he said.

"Oh, come on, Chris," I said. This pissed me off. "Estelle would have paid for your ticket. I would have paid for your ticket, for God's sake. . . ."

He looked over at me now, his expression blank, then he looked down at his hands. "I didn't want to ask Estelle," he said. "I don't think she has that much to spare."

I sat there thinking about this. There was, of course, every good human reason in the world for him not to call me after eight years and beg for plane fare to our father's funeral. But I

169

didn't believe that was the reason he hadn't come. I felt my eyes closing with exhaustion and fire crackle; I shook my head awake.

"I was remembering," he went on, "Dad at Mom's funeral."

"What about it?" I said.

I knew what he was talking about. I remembered it just fine. They had put a straw-colored wig on her in place of her beautiful hair and tried to puff out her sunken, wasted cheeks. They did it badly, though, and she looked like the Golem in the silent movie. After the visitation, for our last look before they closed the casket, the three of us walked up to the front together, Chris and I on either side of Dad. It was a year or two before he met Estelle. Chris had his hair long at the time, and he was wearing a bright, flowered polyester shirt ("Mom liked bright things," he said). Everybody else, of course, was there in somber Italian funeral clothes, what was left of the big extended family.

They were people I saw almost never—my Aunt Mae, Uncle Johnny and his family. Uncle Rudy was there—he would be dead a couple of months later, as I remember—a shriveled old man with big glasses now, still with the wart next to his nose, his red hair turned white and almost gone, looking up at people from his seat, an oxygen canister next to him on a little cart. His sons were there, too, as was my cousin Johnny—in their twenties, all of them looking like funeral ushers, old men in training, standing in a circle in their dark suits, smoking cigarettes outside, laughing at jokes, always at somebody's expense, never their own, the air bright and hot outside the shade of the funeral-home carport, sunlight glinting off their expensive wristwatches, the blue cigarette smoke rising and disappearing.

They had totally accepted the world they had been handed, the balance between the opportunity, the material goods available in the New World, and the insularity and suspiciousness of the Old—deal only with family, with people you know. . . . At first the greetings, the obligatory hugs, and then later the covert looks back and forth between them, laughing at Chris in his flowered shirt. . . .

I had thought Dad would holler at Chris for coming dressed like that. I had seen Chris first, though, and because I was nervous about Dad yelling, I yelled at him myself. When Dad finally did see him, he didn't say anything; he just looked Chris up and down and shook his head and turned away. And I thought, *You old shit.* What difference does it make how Chris is dressed? Isn't he bleeding like the rest of us? Isn't his grief enough? This, after I had given it to Chris myself. . . .

But that wasn't what Chris was talking about. We walked up the aisle, conscious of the relatives and friends around—I noticed a few of those slit-eyed Sicilians looking at Chris and knew what they were thinking ("What is he, a fag?")—until we arrived at the casket, with the flowers on both sides like some kind of flower organ, the breath of Mother Earth trumpeting flowers under the fluorescent lights in that airless chapel, the rouge on my mother's distended cheeks. My father's hands were crossed in front of him at waist level. Chris was smiling—maybe this was some Hare Krishna period for him, death is not the end, etc. Inside myself I was saying, I am not going to be the cryer here. I am not going to be the weak one. None of these wise guys is going to look at me and think, "He is the weak link, just like his father." Instead, as we approached, I stole a glance and saw my father's red eyes, gazing down at his dead wife, my mother, the saddest look I've ever seen on anyone's face. He was a little boy again looking at his own mother, dead, and I saw him at the exact moment that he started to cry, a high-pitched wail of pure grief, almost unrecognizable as a human sound; it was an animal sound, that of a coyote, or a dog caught in a trap, hooting and keening in mortal pain.

Automatically I brought my left hand up and began stroking his back to comfort him. As I did that, Chris did the same thing, and we both stood there, both tearless for our own reasons, trying to comfort our father. His body was shaking, his head bobbing up and down on top of his convulsive sobs. The harder he cried, the more we rubbed his back, until all at once he shrieked, *"Get your goddamn hands off of me!"*

I jerked my hand away. The hair stood up on my arms and neck. The gaze of everyone behind us in the chapel fell like a sunlamp on my back as I stared down, frozen in shame, at my mother for the last time. . . .

"You're being quiet. Are you okay?" Chris was addressing me from his chair nearer the fire.

I was tired, I realized, and that is what I said. I was fucking exhausted. I had driven two long days to get there, and feelings were coming up that I didn't think I could handle without some real sleep. As we called it a night, Chris did something surprising. He stepped toward me and hugged me. Mechanically I put my arms around him, too, but my muscles were stiff and tense. I realized that I had no idea whether I was happy to see him or not.

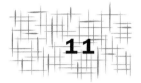

11

IN THE BEDROOM I FIRST turned on the overhead lamp, then I closed the door behind me.

The daybed occupied one corner of the high-ceilinged room; next to the head of the bed on the bare wood floor, a fruit crate partly covered by a green cloth supported a table lamp. The room had looked warm and clean, if cluttered, in the last of the afternoon light, but now it looked desolate and provisional. With all the shopping bags on the floor, it felt like a storage room.

As tired as I had been, as soon as I'd said good night and closed the door to the bedroom behind me, I was no longer sleepy. My mind started buzzing. I realized, for one thing, that I had forgotten to give Chris the violin. I was shaken, on some level, by the conversation, by the whole experience. I felt sort of emotionally roughed up, a mixture of exhaustion and overstimulation.

There was a tiny half bath off the corner of the room, with a toilet and small sink. I went in to brush my teeth and get ready for bed. We had gotten through the evening all right, I supposed. I think I had been expecting something coherent and immediate and kind of apocalyptic, emotionally speaking. Actually, "apocalyptic" was not the word—I meant cathartic. There you go, I thought; I'm a true child of my generation—confusing apocalypse with catharsis. Revelation with purgation. If you admit to something, it wipes the slate clean. Apocalypse is easier to deal with than a slow unfolding. Psychologically. For some people. You know—let's get it over with. . . .

I hadn't anticipated the emotional effect those shared memories would have on me. I had a palpable sense of how much time had gone by, and yet the images we had called up were so immediate. . . . Maybe this would all make a good beginning for *A Brother's Errand*. The initial discomfort, the slow unfolding of trust . . . I thought of a dedication: *"To my brother, Chris. With whom I shared the Cold War years."* I almost started to get choked up thinking about it.

The front window had an old-fashioned roll-up shade lowered to the midpoint, which I pulled down the rest of the way. The side window was covered by a sheet affixed with thumbtacks. I brought my bags over near to the bed, then, restlessly, I poked around some more. A box at the foot of the bed contained books, and I looked in it; a weird assortment, books on UFOs, astrology, nutty-looking stuff. In a smaller box, I noticed a familiar book jacket—my book of JFK photos; I had given it to Chris just after it came out. For the cover they had made a composite portrait of Kennedy's face from about two hundred tiny photos of him, arranged mosaic style; the result was somewhat blurry, but totally recognizable. *The Road to Dallas: JFK in Focus.* By John Delano. I opened its hard cover (later they brought it out in paperback, too; that was when everything got a paperback sale almost automatically), and there was the inscription I had written: *"For Chris—from your brother, John. October 3, 1988."* Jesus, I thought. Was that the best I could do? I set it back, then plucked one of the spacy-looking paperbacks more

or less at random from the other box and brought it over to the
bed table to look into before I went to sleep.

The bedroom was coldish, but they had put plenty of covers
on the bed. I turned off the overhead lamp and got in, picked up
the little book, and just looked around the room for a moment or
two. My mind ran to the winter farmland outside, the miles I had
crossed in the past two days, the cold white lights strung up on
poles here and there in the farmscape. . . . It was like being on the
moon and gazing back at Earth across all that distance. I wondered what Val was doing. I had called earlier and left a message;
she was attending some labor-mediation seminar.

The book. I picked it up and looked at it; *The Twelfth Entity*
by Hezekiah Werner. A cheap paperback, the cover a montage
of hieroglyphics and unrecognizable planets; across the top the
words *"Provocative . . ."* —*USA Today.* Inside the cover the
name "Yeager" written in black ballpoint pen. I opened the book
at random and started to read.

*THE ASSYRIANS KNEW a secret, though. Our
friend ANUK—you remember him as the parallel to
BAR-AT in the Five Books of Ham—had brought the
entity close by once before—too close, in fact, for comfort. The planet, following its 6,000 year ellipse, had
taken its planal tangent and actually grazed the earth,
altering its polar alignment and creating its younger
brother, the moon (JOR).*

*When the Book of Revelation mentions the Four Horse-
men, Judas Abraham is in fact referring to the twelfth
entity and its three trailing asteroids! The Island of Pat-
mos, where "John" (Judas Abraham) wrote the Book of*

*Revelation, is actually located under the Third Ecliptic
of Solea*—the exact path taken by the twelfth entity on
its fateful journey. . . .

What was this crap? I turned the book over, glanced at the
back cover. Is this what Chris was reading? What kind of psychic state would induce someone to take gibberish like this seriously? People were walking around in some vacuum of
belief, the old post-JFK paranoia, looking for the Missing Key
that had been Kept Secret by the ones who Controlled Everything. . . . I sat forward, tossed the book back into the box,
swung my legs over the side of the bed, and looked around. I
was restless, completely awake. All the bags . . . Usually it oc-
curs to me to bring a book when I travel. I don't know what I'd
been thinking.

You don't, I knew, just go marching into someone's life after
eight years and act like you've been there all along. I knew that.
Chris didn't seem to be in a state of great need, exactly, or dis-
turbance. He kind of phased in and out. Brenda was a puzzle.
The room I was in was telling me nothing, except that they
seemed to be occupying the house only provisionally. Brenda
had said they'd been there for months, yet there were no decorations on the walls, no pictures. No real sense that they lived
there. I understood that it was a rental, but still, you would think
that they'd do something to make it their own in that amount of
time. It was eerily quiet.

The wood floor was cold when I stood up. I stepped quietly,
barefoot—I didn't want to make shoe noise—and approached
one of the bags, squatted down, looked in it. It contained more
books, paperbacks. The other bags around it did, too, apparently. I never remembered Chris reading that much. This was

an amazing quantity of books. Maybe they belonged to someone else. Maybe they belonged to "Yeager." Whoever "Yeager" was.

I dug around in the bag and saw that it didn't contain books all the way down; underneath four or five paperbacks were some cardboard boxes labeled DRIED PEACHES. Wherever he had been before this, he must have moved in a hurry, packing up the food with the books. Maybe some guru in California told him dried fruit was healthy. Chris was always a sitting duck for anyone with a scenario, anyone who had it Figured Out.

Listen to yourself, I thought. I hated that sound; it was so judgmental, so dismissive and sarcastic. I took a deep breath. If I could learn to stop trying so hard to control and manipulate and judge, the trip would serve some purpose at least. I would practice that now, as I went through my brother's stuff.

Another bag contained more paperbacks on top and more fruit underneath, this time dried apricots. The next bag was the same idea, but with bags of thermal socks instead of fruit. After I looked into each bag I carefully replaced the books as they had been. Two more bags had cans of tuna and deviled ham. Most of the books I found were the same mishmash of psychic weirdness, astrology, Sumerian religion, space travel. . . .

I knew, of course, that I shouldn't be doing what I was doing. It would be a nice scene for *A Brother's Errand:* Me furtively digging through my brother's belongings, looking for clues. It occurred to me that I might want to stop. I've wondered about it many times since that night. What, exactly, was I doing? Did I think I was trying to get closer to Chris, or was I trying to distance myself on some level? There is an ambiguous relation between information and understanding. Reading someone's mail, for example, erodes intimacy. You gain information, but you lose intimacy. And once you went that route, there was never enough information. Each fact, after all, suggested ambiguous interpretations. You became paranoid over every tiny and tinier hole in the netting of what you knew. But once you get started going through someone's secrets, there's no real reason to stop.

The closet presented a slight logistical challenge, since the bags had been placed so that you would have to move most of them in order to reach the sliding mirrored doors. Trying to remember the way the bags were arranged, I carefully picked them up and, one by one, started moving them to the side so that I could get to the closet. They made paper-bag sounds when I tried to lift them, so I had to half lift them and half slide them across the floor to clear a path.

Very quietly now, I rolled the closet door, on its plastic wheels, to the right.

A number of hanging clothes in plastic dry-cleaner bags. Up top, on the shelf that ran along over the clothes, what looked like boxes wrapped in dark green garbage bags. Under the clothes, partly hidden by the plastic cleaners' bags, on the closet floor, stacks of what turned out, on examination, to be identical books, arranged spine in. Next to these were piles of papers, also partly hidden by the clothing bags.

Squatting down, I plucked one of the books off the top of a stack. It had a crude, almost homemade look about it; a plain white cover with the title *Judgement Day* in large black script, with the extra *e* in the first word and a drawing of a noose and a lightning bolt on either side. No publisher on the spine. No author, for that matter. The rest of them were apparently the same. There must have been two hundred copies stacked on the floor. It looked self-published. Had Chris written a book?

I started paging through it; it had all the signs of self-publication—plain, cheap stock for the cover, same for the paper, slightly off-square typesetting, a spine that cracked almost immediately. It looked as if it had been photocopied from a typescript, reduced, and bound. At random I opened it and read a little:

> THE TRAITORS RAN *down the long street, pursued by the small group of patriots. Although their numbers were bigger, the traitors had the Fear in their hearts that all men do who have betrayed what they know to be Sacred. One of the cowardly group pulled to the side and fired back into the group of patriots. Reed Johnson was hit in the shoulder but continued running in pursuit along with his Brothers.*
>
> *"We'll hang him in the Square for that," said John Littleton, his emotions running high.*
>
> *"No," said William Jones. "Remember—we don't seek personal vengeance. We seek justice!"*
>
> *The traitors ran into a warehouse, elbowing each other out of the way to be the first to seek shelter.*
>
> *"Look at them," said Reed Johnson. "Out only for themselves!"*
>
> *"We'll have them soon enough," said William Jones. "Or we'll die trying."*

Jeez, I thought. You could see why someone had to pub-
lish this himself. I flipped ahead some, toward the end of the
book.

THE PEOPLE'S TRIBUNAL *was held in the lobby of*
the same hotel where the New World Order Congress
had met. The Star of David, which had been lawlessly
appropriated so long ago, still hung there, though now
its glory had been properly restored to the true Aryan
Israelites. The members of the Tribunal, led by William
Jones, had indeed managed to restrain most of the ex-
cesses of the mobs who had demanded street justice.
But not all. Outside the hotel the evidence was all
around; the bodies and blood that had been spilled
were a kind of pus that had to be purged before Heal-
ing could begin.

"Brothers and Patriots," William Jones began, rapping
his gavel three times on the podium. "The Long Night is
at an end. The God of Our Fathers who has watched in
grief over a lawless time of misagennation, will now see
His Law vindicated. What we punish here, no matter
how revolting, no matter the anger that rises within our
hearts, we punish because it has transgressed His Law."
A cheer went up from the crowd. . . .

I flipped it closed, looked at the cover again. *Judgement*
Day. The prose had a weirdly familiar sound or cadence—a
mixture of fanaticism, semiliteracy, and self-righteous, inflated
language. It resembled, in fact, the sound I remembered in

my father's old John Birch Society pamphlets—a desperate desire for purification hooked up to an ill-concealed blood-lust. . . .

I opened it up one more time, to a place nearer the beginning.

"I DON'T SEE why we can't," Willie Jackson shouted. "The honkies do it all the time."

"Shut yo mouth Willie," Malcolm Lummumba said. "There will be plenty of white women to go around. I got me one picked out. And Rubinstein said they got plenty money for bail between now and then."

"I'm gonna get me one of them little Jew college girls," another of the slovenly group yelled.

"Sheeeit," another laughed. "There ain't no challenge in that. Them Jews love to get it from one of us black bucks. I'm going to get me a real white woman. . . ."

At this there was an eruption of hillarity, with the dark forms slapping each others' hands, hi-fiving each other. . . .

I closed the book and looked at the cover again. I noticed that my hands were shaking slightly. What was Chris doing with a couple hundred copies of this?

I sat on the floor, turning it all over in my mind. I had made a wrong turn. Maybe, I thought, I didn't need to know the answer. Whatever complications this represented, I wanted to continue the visit without them.

Like someone trying to put stuffing back into a chair that was unraveling, I crawled the three feet back to the closet and replaced the book exactly where I had found it. As I did this, I noticed again the papers stacked up to the right, under the clothes. And once you get started, there's no real reason to stop, is there? But is there a reason to go on? Did I need to know what was under there? Did I even want to know? How would I know the answer to any of those questions until I knew what was under there?

So, breathing through my nose, I pushed aside the bottom of a wool overcoat and took one of the small pamphlets, four pages folded over and stapled in the middle, pulled it out, sat down on the floor, and looked at the front.

Krieg
White Power

Directly under that, a caricature drawing of a stereotyped black face wearing a quizzical expression, a noose around his neck and exclamation points and question marks radiating out from his head. Off to the side, meant to be in the distance, a drawing of a tree and a bonfire.

"*What could be more American than a good old-fashioned BARBECUE?*" the caption read.

"*Organize your own COON HUNT . . . advice from Daddy Dixie, page three.*"

No advertising; obviously run off in someone's house, on a home publishing system. A drawing of a dissolute face with a big nose and beard stubble, wearing a yarmulke with dollar signs on it, and over it the word *"YIDMAN,"* in Hebrew-type letters. The figure wore a baggy Superman costume; in place of the *S* on the chest, a big *Y* inside a Star of David.

IN NATURE A parasite is the lowest form of life. It procreates itself at the expense of the Host Body. It creates nothing. It drains the system of its Vital resources.

Since the beginnings of Time the Jews have been the parasite on the Host Body of Western Civilization. The Aryan Race discovered the laws of gravity. We discovered the uses of the wheel, of fire, of building materials, algebra, medicine. We are the race of Shakspeare and Aristotel, of Beethoven and Michaelangelo. What have the Jews contributed? A parasittic money-lending system that has sucked the vitality out of the great work of our Civilization.

In order to make themselves on an equal with the White Race the Jews who control the entertainment world and the mass media have tried to drag us down to the level of the nigger. We live in a time in which the achievements which are the Foundation of Western Civilization are systematically dennigrated in favor of false gods. Morals have disappeared.

Wake up!

Not this, I thought.
Not this.
Chris, I thought. Chris, you fucking moron.

I might as well have opened the refrigerator and found a severed head.

I was trying to regain my bearings. All the nerves along my arms and legs were screaming at me to get out, to bolt right then and not look back, as if all my worst suspicions about the kind of trouble and complication Chris represented in my life had been confirmed. There was a reason I hadn't talked to him in eight years. All right—a lifetime of blaming everybody else for your problems, and this is where it ends up. What was next? Cannibalism? I could find the Holiday Inn in Riverton. Go. *Go*, I thought.

Of course, maybe the stuff wasn't even his. Maybe it was Brenda's. Or . . . somebody else's.

But then what was he doing with someone like that? Even if it wasn't his, he was living in a nest of snakes. How could he not have known about it? And if he knew about it, how could he have stuck around?

But where was there for him to go?

This question was hard to get rid of. If Chris was involved in this kind of cesspool it meant that he was sick. Unhealed wounds had turned to gangrene. And, on some level, I was at least partly responsible. There was no escaping that.

I don't know how long I sat there, on the floor, in a fever of anxiety and indecision. What was I supposed to do here, I kept asking myself? I realized something else, too: This was probably the end of *A Brother's Errand*. I wasn't going to be able to write that book either. My sentimental idea of being his Great Savior after years of making him feel like an outcast. It made me want to throw up. The fact was that I had been counting—irony of ironies—on Chris to pull me out of *my* hole.

Whatever Chris's involvement was, if I went home without

even seeing what this was about, I was going to be in a hole that I'd never get out of.

Finally, after what seemed a long time, and sick to my stomach, I put the pamphlet back where it had been. I slid the mirrored door back into its closed position. I grabbed two of the bags and half lifted, half slid them back into their original positions. Then, before I did any more, I stepped over them, slid open the closet door again, and carefully took one copy of the book and one of the pamphlets. Then I closed the closet, walked over to my suitcase, and hid them away.

When I was finished putting everything back, I got into the bed, under the blankets. I couldn't bring myself to turn off the light, and I lay there, with my heart pounding—awake, awake, awake.

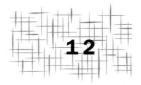

12

I MUST HAVE DOZED OFF eventually, because I was startled awake by a shift in the light, the room different, filled with light as a sail fills with breeze. The side window, with the sheet over it, illuminated the room; shadows of bare trees twitched on the thin white cloth in silhouette, as a draft around the frame ruffled it slightly. I smelled bacon cooking. I looked at my travel clock: only seven-thirty. I pulled the shade up a notch and looked out the front window at the long, early shadows on the snow, the brilliant light, the sun coming straight in. The previous night came back to me like a vision of storm clouds on the horizon. The air in the room was cold, but I was warm under the blanket. I had no idea how I was going to proceed with this day. Maybe, I thought, I would just stay in bed.

CHRIS WAS IN the kitchen, mixing pancake batter in a bowl. He had laid out the bacon in parallel strips on a paper towel, the way Mom used to do it.

"There's coffee," he said, still looking down at the batter he was mixing up. "Your mug's over there."

"Great," I said. I poured myself coffee, making a conscious effort to breathe naturally. I looked out the kitchen window at the field. I would find a way to address the question, but first I would drink coffee.

"You still take it black, don't you?" he said.

"Yeah," I said. "You have an amazing memory."

"I washed out your mug last night."

I stood against the doorjamb of the kitchen and watched him beating the batter, the empty eggshells on a paper towel on the table next to the bowl. Chris was intent on what he was doing. He picked up the bowl and turned to the stove, clicking on the electric burner and putting a chunk of butter into a skillet.

"I remember you used to like pancakes a lot," he said. "So I figured I'd do you up some."

"Thanks," I said.

"Are you okay?" he said. He looked at me with a puzzled smile. "You seem a little quiet. Usually you're the idea man."

"I think I'm just kind of wiped from the drive."

He nodded. With a fork he dragged the hunk of butter across the surface of the skillet; small bubbles formed in its wake, like a comet's tail. I was watching my brother make breakfast as if through a Plexiglas window. I was feeling my way. I was hoping that I'd somehow be excused from dealing with this. Like jury duty. But I knew that wouldn't happen. The key, I thought, would just be to get out into the day and let it develop naturally.

Chris finished making the pancakes, and we ate. At one

point he asked me what I wanted to do; I shrugged and said, "Anything." Then I added that I wouldn't mind seeing the antiques store where he worked. You'd be amazed at the Cold War artifacts I find in these places—campaign buttons, Red Scare literature of all types, fallout-shelter supplies, old magazines. . . .

Chris nodded and said, "Let's see. I thought we'd maybe drive around, get some lunch somewhere. . . . Over in West Branch is where President Hoover was from. I thought maybe you might want to see that."

"Sounds good," I said stiffly. "Where's Brenda?"

"She gets off to work around five-thirty," Chris said. "Oh—I have something for you."

"You do?" I said. What was this now?

"Wait here," he said, getting up and leaving the room. As he did, I remembered the violin, again, but this obviously was not the right time to present it. After a few moments Chris walked back into the room and handed me something small, a brightly colored card, a postcard.

I fiddled with it, righted it; the lettering on the front was surrounded with flowers and filigree; it was an antique postcard that said *"To My Dear BROTHER"*—the lettering was raised and slightly glazed and set among flowers and sprays of greens, and the word "brother" was spelled out in what looked like holly or mistletoe. I turned it over; the postmark said "June 14, 6 pm, 1909." The address, to Mr. J. D. Yoder in Parnell, Iowa, and the message were rendered in a faded, spidery penciled hand. . . .

"I got it at the shop," he said. "That's what made me remember it."

I looked at it.

"It's just like, a gift. It wasn't real expensive or anything." He stood there with his hands in his pockets.

"Thanks, Chris," I said.

WE HEADED EAST in Chris's old red Colt hatchback. The car seat was cold through my jeans, but the sunlight came in warm through the windshield. The morning sun, the ribboning two-lane road across the rolling open country, the barns out across snowy fields, farmhouses nested in stands of trees, silos facing into the low orange light like a de Chirico tableau—it all seemed so fresh and pristine. Yet at the same time I wondered, in all the cluelessness of my Northeastern heart, how many of those postcard farmhouses concealed fanatics, cranking out leaflets and newsletters on home publishing rigs. Did fear collect in all those wastes? Was the apocalyptic or prophetic mode a natural response to all those open spaces? Visions, absolutism of every sort . . . Something has to step in to fill the vacuum.

I used to wonder about that, with the Cold War—if the sudden absence of the Enemy in the wake of World War II generated some intolerable anxiety in the world. The Cold War gave everything a kind of balance again. It lent the world an overarching myth to which everybody had to relate. Even if you rejected the myth, you were still reacting against it. It's better, from the standpoint of balance, to have one God and one Enemy than it is to have hundreds of competing polarities. With the Cold War gone, the world was faced with the chaos of actual, unpolarized experience, the proliferation of unlicensed Gods and Devils. . . .

A tense quiet filled the car. Even in the most relaxed situations I have no stomach for silences. Silence is like shade; weird mosses and algae proliferate. Words hack back the jungle; they make a temporary clearing. So I asked some questions and got Chris to start talking, and as he talked, I sifted his words for clues, for something that would help me know what the truth was.

He talked about the places he had passed through in the last eight years, a wandering trail that led out to San Francisco, then to Denver, Oregon, Eau Claire (he stayed with my mother's cousin for two weeks—I hadn't even known Mom had a cousin out there), and back to San Francisco. It sounded as if he had progressively lost his grip on what he was doing. Every place seemed initially to promise an Answer, which would inevitably be followed by a letdown. To that extent it was more or less what I had anticipated. But at the same time, actually hearing him tell about it was different from imagining it in the abstract.

"That second time in San Francisco," he said, "I had just . . . I don't know. I had started to disintegrate." He drove, squinting out across the long fields with winter crop stubble in long rows. "I spent days in the library," he said, "looking at the art books. Whole days. I had no place to go. I'd get lost in the pictures. I liked the Impressionists. Like Monet and . . . I guess he was my favorite. Everything was in such a nice light. I panhandled, and I'd go down to the luncheonette on the corner and get a malted if I was hungry. I slept different places. I stayed for a few days at a time with Jeremy, this guy I met the first time I was out there.

I slept in a park once or twice. Just . . . crashed places. I washed dishes for a week once.

"I used to wish I could call you," he said. "I didn't really have anybody to talk to. You had told me I shouldn't be dependent on people. I wasn't going to call Dad. Actually, I did once, and he said some of the same things to me that you did. Word for word, almost. About how I was floundering and needed to find direction."

Hearing this was painful. The thought that I had acted or spoken like Dad was very hard to hear.

"I didn't know what I wanted to do," he went on. "For a while I wanted to look at the paintings in the library books. But then after a while I thought, What am I doing? I'm looking at a picture on a piece of paper. Suddenly it was like whatever had let me disappear into the pictures was gone, like it evaporated. Somewhere in there I went up to North Beach. I was just drifting. I couldn't find any reason to do anything. I was getting kind of disoriented.

"I met this guy, they called him Electric Jesus. He was playing guitar and singing in this place in North Beach. He had a thing where he played in a window, like a big storefront; he played facing into the place, but the bandstand was open from behind onto the sidewalk, and they put speakers out there to get people to come into the place. I had been walking around for, like, two or three days, and I hadn't slept, and I just went in and sat at a table and listened to Electric Jesus play. He wore these long robes like you see in the Bible, and he would make these patterns on the guitar . . . I don't know how to explain it. I sat there and listened, and it was like the patterns were the first coherent thing I'd seen for days. It was like he could modulate what you were thinking just by shifting these patterns. You'll think this is weird, but for a while I actually thought maybe he really was God. Like, you know, if Jesus came back, it would probably be in a place like that, and he'd be using music to get to people, and . . . I don't know. Like, you wouldn't see Jesus at some big political thing or on TV. He'd just show up someplace, and you'd have to find him. . . ."

Chris had no particular expression on his face as he talked about this, except for an occasional embarrassed smile. As he drove, his hands kneaded the steering wheel. I found that my own hands were in fact clenched into fists in my pockets; my shoulders were tensed up practically around my ears. What chaos, I thought.

"I ended up staying at his house for probably, like, two weeks. I stayed on a futon on the floor. It was almost like a shack—the floor was just plywood—and it got to the point where I wouldn't even get off the futon. I'd just roll onto my side and stare at the plywood. It was like looking out the window on an airplane. Sometimes the grain looked like sand dunes, or clouds in the sunset. Sometimes it was like I was looking at electric currents going through the wood. Faces would come out of the pattern. If you looked away and looked back it could be hard to find them again, and it got to the point where if I saw one that I liked I almost couldn't look away. I would just stare at it."

It was almost too much to listen to. Part of me wanted to reach over and embrace my brother, tell him I was sorry. At the same time, I found myself drawing back from him in horror, as if from the edge of a cliff. Chris had lived out the entropy I'd been trying frantically to avoid my entire life. But he was my brother; I had to do something. An embrace was necessary. But

how did you embrace without falling off the cliff? How did anyone manage it?

———

HERBERT HOOVER'S HOUSE wasn't much to look at. West
Branch had a small, well-kept downtown, maybe a hundred
years old, with clean streets, brick buildings, and a small, new,
brick-paved plaza with exhibits on Herbert Hoover's life.
Beyond that, a lawn and a little preserved section of a late-
nineteenth-century village, a collection of tiny houses, a
barbershop, a general store. Two or three couples walked
around, looking into the preserved buildings. I wasn't, in truth,
that interested in Herbert Hoover to begin with, and I found it
difficult to concentrate. Chris poked around, looking at the
exhibits, hands in his pockets. I had a whiff, the briefest image
that couldn't quite rise to mind, of us as kids at a museum. After
a while we drifted out and back to the car.

"Well," I said, as we got into the car, "what time is it?"

"It's eleven-thirty," Chris said. "We could go to Stone City
for lunch. Or Cedar Rapids."

"Wherever you say," I said. We left town the way we'd come
in. I opened the window a little; the air was warming. We
headed north on a two-lane road that soon led us into open farm
country again. Skimming the surface. I needed to talk to Chris
about what I'd found, but I was embarrassed that I'd gone
through his closet, and I didn't want some big confrontation. I
was treading water, looking for a landmark. . . .

"You know," Chris said, "when you called I was kind of . . .
astonished."

"Yeah?" I said.

"I thought you were mad at me," he said. "There were so many times when I wanted to talk to you. I used to think about if we were together in different places, walking down the street, you know, like I was going to meet you someplace for lunch."

I felt myself wincing, covering up inside.

"Like, I would try and imagine what you would tell me to do. But also I was mad at you at the same time. I blamed you for where I was. For a long time I thought I didn't need anybody. Almost like human contact was an illusion, and I tried to train myself out of wanting it. It would just get blown away, like the only thing that was real was me."

He was quiet for a moment, driving. "I never felt like I could talk to you before," he said. "After we talked on the phone, I kept wondering, Why now?"

I was aware of opening my mouth and closing it, like a boated fish gasping in the air. Go ahead, John, I thought. Do something decent and brave. Tell him what a dead end his big brother has come to and what a mess his life has become. Tell him straightforwardly about snooping in his closet, apologize, and tell him you are concerned about what he's involved in.

I felt as if I were looking down from a high-diving board into a small turquoise rectangle of pool. I felt the board flexing and quivering under my toes, my shaking knees; I was trying to screw up my nerve.

"It's confusing," he said. "But I'm glad you called."

We were coming to the outskirts of a town now—a four-way crossroads with a yellow blinking light, a burger joint, a gas station . . . then trees, small prefab houses, paved streets going off the main road at right angles, speed limit forty-five, then thirty-five, the slow coagulation of human presence . . . a sign: WEL-COME TO SOLON.

"Solon," I said. The streets were lined with cars now; something was going on.

"We're in Solon," Chris said. After a moment he said, "Shit—look at this."

We were getting close to downtown; people had roped off vacant lots, and there were signs saying PARKING $2. Over the road, attached to two telephone poles, a giant banner read SOLON BEEF DAYS—NOVEMBER 11–13.

We looked out at all the people milling around. After a moment, as if on cue, we both said, "Solon Beef Days." I was sitting there in the car with my brother, laughing. Another glimpse of some hypothetical normalcy. A reprieve, a deferment. . . . I'll take it, I thought. I needed a little time to regroup. We parked in one of the two-dollar places.

Downtown Solon was about the size of West Branch, maybe a bit smaller, and flooded with people. Huge tents had been set up right in the middle of the street and in the parking lots; under them, people sat eating at long metal folding tables covered with paper tablecloths. Hot-air blowers and braziers had been set up strategically for warmth. Billowing clouds of smoke careened skyward in the brilliant sun from a wagon where the beef of Solon was being grilled in giant converted oil drums, turned with oversize forks by men in denim shirts and white aprons. The sun was brilliant and warm, and some people even walked around in shirtsleeves—weird, after how cold it had been the day before.

At the far end of the main street they had set up a couple of rides for the kids, and on the back of a flatbed truck they had a big plaster replica of a bull. Chris and I made our way to the line at the giant beef-shrine truck, where you had a choice of T-bone, strip, or rib eye. We ordered rib eyes, and they came immediately—the biggest piece of meat I ever saw, lifted by giant fork from the grill, dripping fat, it must have weighed a pound and a half—slabbed onto a plate, which was then loaded up with a baked potato, beans, coleslaw, and a piece of white bread. At the end of the line we got sodas, and I paid for it all—eight dollars apiece.

We sat at one of the long tables, at the other end from some men in their fifties, with deeply lined faces, plaid flannel shirts and quilted hunting vests, smoking cigarettes. I unrolled my plastic knife and fork from the paper napkin they came in—somebody had done a lot of work rolling those packages up—and asked Chris if he'd ever been to Solon Beef Days before.

He shook his head. "I didn't even know they had Beef Days." After a moment he added, "It's weird they have it this time of year. You'd think it would be too cold." He took a slug off his grape soda. "It's almost never this warm this time of year."

"I was thinking the same thing," I said. "It's like a mirage or something." This warmth, this abundance, this oasis . . .

I cut into my steak and realized with a sudden impact that I was starving. I was so hungry. The steak was delicious; it carried the flavor of the charcoal; the thinnest crust of char briefly resisted every bite before dissolving. I began wolfing the food down, trying to fill the space, scratch the itch. It was a hunger I felt in my arms almost. Where had it come from? I ate like an animal. As I ate, I looked across at Chris, who was also eating as if he'd been starving, and I thought, Is this what it is to have a brother? Chris, my brother; I practiced the phrase in my mind.

Could we have been doing this all those years? I thought. All those years.

Chris was quiet, spooning up his beans. I glanced around at the crowd under the tent. Everyone was more or less poker-faced, despite all the consumption of delicious fats and blood. The mixture of bacchanalian carnal abundance and Protestant reserve. In spite of myself, I thought about photos I'd seen of public hangings—people in the crowd wearing straw hats some-times, regarding the camera with a burgher's unflappable sense of entitlement, as the body of some unfortunate man swung from the gallows. Then I remembered the pamphlets and suf-fered a pang of nausea, like when an airplane rides a thermal and the bottom drops. . . . What a mess, I kept thinking. What a mess. What was I going to do?

I looked again at Chris. He didn't seem like a fanatic, like someone who had been taken over entirely by one set of con-cerns. Yet he had been operating on his own for so long—who knew what kinds of influences he'd been exposed to? Around us the voices of people greeting one another, the big hot-air blow-ers at the corners of the tent, and beyond us the acres and miles of barren cornstalks, copper and bronze in the midday sun. He did seem more relaxed, or something. Less defensive, maybe. At one point, though, I got a glimpse of the old Chris. We had been talking about this and that—the antiques store where he worked, Brenda's brother Kenny, who he said had been a good friend—and I mentioned the university job. He shrugged and frowned.

"It reminds me of California," he said. "Everybody's in, like, a dream world. They're phonies."

This was the kind of thing Chris used to say all the time—

"everybody" this, "they" that. . . . That kind of easy generalizing reminded me so much of Dad, and it irritated the hell out of me. That I did it all the time myself—that I had, in some ways, made a career of it—was no help. As calmly and detachedly as I could, I said, "That's a pretty broad statement, isn't it?"

"Well," he said, "I mean, they're just running around playing games. They all think things are one way, and if you don't think like them you don't have the truth. They think what zog wants them to think, and then they walk around acting like they're so smart and cool, and meanwhile their parents and the citizens are paying for it."

"What's zog?" I said.

He looked at me, then down in his plate. He shrugged his shoulders. "It doesn't matter." He ate some more beans.

We were quiet for a while; I didn't particularly want to push it. I suddenly felt very tired. The intensity that swelled up so easily, like a genie waiting only for a small amount of friction to be applied. . . . In my heart I think I didn't really want to know what Chris was into, or not into. I was getting ready to settle for leaving Iowa without some huge blowup. But if I just left that way, I would leave with nothing. With less than nothing.

"You know," Chris said, "they have places out here, restaurants, where you grill your own steak. You pick out a steak from a refrigerator, bring it with you into a room with a pit grill, and stand there and grill it up."

"Yeah?" I said.

"There's one in West Branch. We walked right by it." West Branch, I thought. Suddenly I imagined myself looking back from Connecticut on this table in this tent, and on West Branch, and on the whole weekend. It was parenthetical to my life. I

wished I could take the forceps and lift it out with no damage to
the surrounding tissues. But I knew I couldn't. I needed to
reach out to Chris past any point where I was comfortable. But
where did you start? Where did it end? I would find a way, I
thought. I had to. Just give me a few more minutes, here. . . .

After we finished our steaks, we got up, threw away the
plates and napkins in a big garbage barrel, and started heading
out. I was going to figure it out. I was going to strike the right
balance between what seemed necessary and what I seemed capable of. As we walked one last time through the crowd on Main
Street, we stopped at a table where they were selling Solon Beef
Days T-shirts. On the front was a stylized drawing of a bull with
a ring in its nose and a crown on its head holding a torch aloft—
the Statue of Liberty. Big letters circling the bull read SOLON
BEEF DAYS.

"How much?" I asked the man behind the table. He pointed
to a sign on the building behind him. Ten dollars. I pulled out a
medium for Val. I turned to Chris and asked him if he wanted
one, and he shrugged, hands in his pockets, looking down at the
table. He had the saddest expression on his face. I knew what he
was thinking. I was going to leave, and this mirage would disappear. I was thinking the same thing.

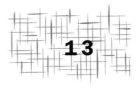

13

BY THE TIME WE LEFT Solon it had passed two o'clock, and the sun was already starting its slide toward late afternoon. We were heading down now toward South Liberty to visit the antiques shop where Chris worked. In the chill of the car, I turned over the possibilities in my mind. Knowledge was a splinter; partial knowledge was a splinter half in and half out. It snagged on everything it touched. I kept imagining and disqualifying ways of approaching the questions I needed to ask. I had no blueprint for what was needed here. But it was about to be taken out of my hands.

Downtown South Liberty consisted of an early-twentieth-century Main Street lined with one- and two-story brick buildings. The sky, by the time we got there, was a deepening, brilliant blue over the rooftops. The street had a deserted feel about it; half the stores appeared to be vacant. On the corner stood a brick bank building from the 1920s, with Roman columns and a big hand-painted sign over the entrance: L & N AUTO PARTS. We pulled up in the shade across the street from it, in front of a place that looked as if it could once have been an auto showroom or a big feed store, set between two abandoned storefronts; large letters painted in yellow on the bricks above the windows read YESTERDAY'S TREASURES.

On the way down, Chris had told me a bit about the guys he worked with. But as we got closer to the town he seemed a little withdrawn, a little uncomfortable. Now, as we walked to the store, I felt my own discomfort, wondering what Chris had and hadn't told them about me and about our history. I supposed I was the big brother who had abandoned him, coming to meet what was more or less his new family.

Inside, cement floor, a big chilly room tinted with cigarette haze, a graveyard of discarded items arranged in no particular order, as if they'd been dragged in and set down at random and then left there—old farm tools and candy machines, standing wire racks filled with water-damaged paperback books, ancient showcases with filmy glass tops and chipped wood sides; under the glass a confusion of old army medals, campaign buttons, cigarette lighters, pocketknives, wooden nickels, ballpoint pens with the names of lumber companies and electric businesses and plumbers, farm-supply companies—all forgotten by commerce and History. . . .

As we made our way through the maze of cases and junk, a voice from the rear of the store said, "Look what the cat dragged in." Three men were sitting in a miasma of cigarette smoke around a small electric space heater. Chris kept his hands in his pockets.

A big guy in a stained, quilted hunting vest and cap was smiling at us, seated on an upended wooden milk case. Sitting in a chair, leaning on a desk by a computer, a heavy man wearing a red plaid flannel shirt and a red mustache, with large, smudged, black-rimmed glasses, watched us steadily as we approached.

The third was a skinny guy with squinting bloodshot eyes, a mesh cap, blue T-shirt under a gray zip-up sweatshirt, some kind of tattoo on the back of his hand, mustache, smoking. He was introduced as Kenny Yeager, Brenda's brother. It took me a moment to remember Yeager as the name inside the spacey paperback I'd looked in the night before.

Tentative nods around the circle. Nobody put out a hand to shake. Chris said, "This is my brother, John."

Kenny took a drag on his cigarette and said, "Hey, brother John." He wore a faint, slightly mocking smile. The five of us stood around awkwardly. The ceiling was a raw arrangement of steel I-beams; in one of them the tufts of a bird's nest were visible.

After a few moments, Kenny pulled something from his pocket and held it out to Chris. "Here," he said. Chris took it, examined it; it was a pocketknife. "You said you were looking for one, and I found one."

Chris opened it up, looked closely at the blade, closed it. "It's a Buck?" he said.

Kenny gestured with his chin. "What does it say on it?"

Chris peered at the knife again. "Thanks, Kenny."

Just to say something, I asked whose store it was, and Kenny gestured with his head in Red's direction. But his eyes trained in on me.

"So you're a professor, huh?" Kenny said. His skin was reddish and leathery; his eyes were gray. "What do you teach?" He made it sound like a challenge.

"Cold War history," I said.

"Cold War history," Kenny said. "Cowboys and Indians, huh? The white hats and the black hats." He stared into my eyes as if I was supposed to know what he was talking about.

"That's one way of looking at it," I said, cautiously.

He gave a short, derisive snort, holding my gaze, and took another drag on his cigarette. My response was, apparently, some kind of new information for him, which he seemed to be trying to decode as he stared me down. He was making me very uncomfortable. The unwarranted familiarity . . . After a couple more inconclusive probes, he tried something a little more aggressive.

"Up at the university," he said, "they got a 'professor' "—he put quotes around it with his tone of voice—"who tells the kids that we should have gone Communist back in the 1950s. What do you think about that idea?"

I wanted to laugh. Was the Cold War going to follow me everywhere, now that I was trying to get rid of it?

This subterranean amusement must have shown in my expression, because Kenny's face was suddenly very serious. "Did I ask a stupid question, Professor?" he said, looking me in the eyes.

"No," I said. "The professor— There are a lot of people on either side of that question," I said.

"I asked you what you thought about it," he said. "I know there's people that think different things."

Now his aggressiveness was really starting to bother me. He was backing me against a wall. I had no idea what his problem was. Chris said nothing. "I would say that I don't even agree with those terms," I said. "For one thing, I don't know what he means by 'go Communist.' "

"You don't know what it means to go Communist?" he said, looking at me with his eyebrows raised. "You're a Cold War professor, and you don't know what it means to go Communist?"

Okay, I thought. What am I supposed to do here?

"Are you enjoying yourself in Iowa?" Red said abruptly.

It was out of left field, but I recognized it as an attempt to normalize things. "Yes," I said. "It's good to see this guy again," I said, indicating Chris with a tilt of my head. Maybe, I thought, the stuff with Kenny would just blow away if I ignored it.

Red asked whether I'd been to Iowa before, and we talked back and forth a little. Kenny busied himself stubbing out his cigarette in an ashtray, a preoccupied frown on his face. I couldn't tell if he was deep in thought or listening to the conversation. As Red and I talked, Chris stood quietly with his hands in his pockets, looking uncomfortable. At one point I asked Red how long he'd had the store.

"Since he couldn't make a living anymore doing what he was raised to do," Kenny said, jumping in again. "Since some people with funny names come in and decided he didn't have a right to work the same land his granddaddy did." He looked at me challengingly, as if to say, "Do you have a problem with any of this yet?"

I found, to my surprise, that I was suddenly short of breath, hyperalert. "I'm not sure what you're saying," I said, trying to keep my voice steady. "It sounds kind of abstract."

"*Abstract?*" Kenny said. "Why there's nothing abstract about having your land taken away from you and being told you have to give all your money to a bunch of porch monkeys to buy drugs while your wife is shopping at the Salvation Army. There's nothing abstract about that."

"Shut up, Kenny," Red said in an even voice, looking at me.

I should, I guess, have simply turned around and walked out. But I was almost shaking with anger. Why? Was it just the stupid prejudice I was reacting to? Or were there free-floating squads of anger roving around inside me, with their own agendas, looking for the right vehicle? Whatever the cause, the anger was rapidly compounding itself; I was angry, and I was angry about being angry. . . . So this was Chris's new family. If the source of the leaflets hadn't been clear enough before, it was then. The erasing of the humanity of others—the black face with the noose, the drawing of "Yidman"—the serving up of convenient enemies to carry the weight of your frustrations, and now, because of someone else's inability to deal with the world as it was, I was being placed in this defensive position, another convenient enemy. . . . The arrogance, the assumption that one has all the obvious answers and that a different conclusion could only represent either stupidity or a vicious duplicity . . .

"What's wrong with you?" I said, as evenly as I could. "Why are you trying to start a fight with me?"

"Hey," he said, with an "innocent me?" expression, "I'm not trying to start any fight." He was holding his hands up as if to say, "See?" "If you don't like what I'm saying and you want to fight me, I'm not going to disappoint you, but, hey, I'm just saying what I think. There's still a constitutional right to that, isn't there, brother John?"

"Is that how you think of people?" I said. "Porch monkeys?" I felt myself skidding toward a guardrail in my mind. Some deep, wide vein of anger in me was ready to ignite. It was an ignorant remark—but I had heard ignorant remarks before. You turn and walk away from them. But something in his smug ignorance was getting ready to send me over a line. . . .

Somebody needed to say something, and somebody did. Looking at Chris, Red said, "Maybe you need to clear out about now." He didn't say it angrily; it was intended to forestall something. But I wasn't sure, in fact, that I wanted to leave. The anger felt too good; it scalded and burned and scratched an itch. . . . All the unmanageable emotions that I'd been feeling in the last twenty-four hours were happily assuming a more comfortable form. Something easier to deal with, something that pointed outward. It was a relief to have a place for it to flow, instead of damming up inside me and boiling me alive. Was this what people experienced in a lynch mob? It felt good; it was a relief. . . . I was engaged in a staring contest with Kenny. Come on, I thought; give me a good excuse and I will fucking kill you. . . .

"I said clear out," Red said. "Kenny, go on in the back and get a beer and relax. *Now.*" To me he said, "I'm sorry, but you need to clear out. I don't want to say it again."

His face, behind the impassive front he'd learned to assume, was a bit agitated; I could see that. He was breathing just a bit heavily, I thought. Now it was either turn and leave or up the ante to some unacceptable point. I thought, Well, this is his store. Yes, and I could kick him in his throat in his store. And even as I thought that, I thought, Where is this coming from? And because I didn't know the answer, I turned and started for the door. I didn't know where Chris was, but I assumed he would be following me. As I walked out I heard Red's voice saying, "Go on and get him out of here."

Outside in the crisp, cloudless air, the shadows fell long and deep on the street. The facades of the buildings, the weird, impassive masks, the stage set. I wanted to hit something, to break something. As I walked past the deserted facades, I saw my reflection in a window; I glanced at it briefly and kept going, toward the car. Whatever the stuff in the closet was, it was out in the open now. I would find out whether I wanted to or not.

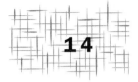

14

NOW WE DROVE.

"All right," I said. "What was that about?" Chris still hadn't said a word. "Who are these people?"

"I told you who they were," he said.

"That's not what I mean," I said, "and you know it." I watched the side of Chris's face as he drove, the clenching of his jaw through the skin, the muscle and joint working. He was mad, too. I could see it in the side of his head, see him wondering what I knew and what I didn't know. He turned his head to look at me as we rolled along and then he turned back to driving. I was suffocating under all my partial knowledge, my fears and guesses; it was becoming as intolerable as staying under blankets in the heat of a fever. You toss them off, you want to get free, breathe; otherwise you will cook in the heat of your own body. Of course, then come the chills, every whisper of contact with the air a step into the void, muscles gripping your bones, and you will wish you had all your blankets back, and more. . . .

"What kind of shit are you into, Chris?"

He straightened a bit behind the wheel. Hard to read his expression because I couldn't see his eyes.

"What does that mean?" he said.

"Is it some kind of militia group? Are you going to go shoot some porch monkeys?"

He was frowning, driving.

"What are you talking about?" he said. "That shit with Kenny?"

He thought he could hide behind the thin scrim of my not knowing what was in his closet. Was he relying on something as mechanical as my lacking a piece of information?

"I saw the stuff in your closet, Chris," I said. "I went to hang up my jacket"—this was my preemptive lie; it came to hand without my even having to think; it just materialized—"and I saw your leaflets, and the books. So don't act like you don't know what I'm talking about."

Chris continued driving, frowning—a delayed reaction was in the works. He was processing the information, trying on and discarding the logical possibilities.

"You went through my closet?"

"I was looking for a place to hang my jacket and a couple of shirts," I repeated, embellishing. "That's what closets are for. Don't act like I'm some kind of criminal for trying to hang up my jacket."

Chris stared out the windshield. To fill the silence, I went on, shoring up my position. "I didn't go in there looking for *Judgement Day*, Chris. I didn't think to myself, 'Maybe my brother has a closetful of hate literature. Let's have a look.' You understand? I didn't drive halfway across the country for that."

"That stuff isn't mine," Chris said.

"Yeah?" I said. This was a possibility. Maybe it was true, maybe it wasn't. "So whose is it? Kenny's? Your new brother-in-law? Mister Let's-Shoot-the-Porch-Monkeys? What are you even doing around people like that?" My embarrassment and frustration were generating steam clouds of self-righteousness as they hit the air. I remember the sensation of that conversation: It was like running down a steep hill. You have to go faster to keep up with your own momentum.

"What do you care about it?" he said. He looked over at me.

"What do I care about it?" I said. "Why do you think—"

The car swerved violently to the right, and I had to brace myself on the seat with my left hand as we pulled into a long gravel lot with a grain elevator at the end. Chris hit the brakes hard, and we stopped.

"Why are you so interested in what I'm reading all of a sudden?" he said. "You never gave a shit before." His face was red. For a moment I thought he was going to hit me. "What do you care who my friends are? I ate garbage, and you wouldn't even talk to me."

He was staring at me, with his jaw clenched tight. His face had turned a blotchy red. "I had to sleep on people's floors and . . . and beg. I had to beg. You didn't even care. Now you come out of nowhere and act like you can tell me what to do."

I watched him carefully; he looked as if he might snap. But I said nothing. There was nothing I could say. What he said was true. After a few more moments of dangling silence, Chris threw the car into gear again and lurched us out onto the road.

NEITHER OF US spoke again; everything was sliding through my hands faster than I could grab it.

For years I'd acted as if he wasn't even my brother, and now I was getting ready to walk away again. What had I risked here? Had I just been playing around? What had I been prepared to offer Chris? I had to take a step, even if I wasn't sure I could follow through. No; I had to be ready to follow through. At one point I became peripherally aware of some change of mode in Chris, and I glanced at him and saw him scuff tears away from his face with the sleeve of his coat.

It was already getting dark when we arrived back at the house. The sun was lowering into a smeared bank of clouds, orange and egg-yolk colors. I had a brief image of a beach at dusk, flags flying across the strand, the last of the crowd combing through the garbage, fighting off the seagulls for a scrap of pizza crust, a bluish glow still hovering in the air, reflected off the snow. . . .

We parked, and Chris opened his door, got out, and without a word started for the house.

I caught up with him at the porch.

"Chris," I said. I grabbed him by his arm. He wrenched it away from my hand and turned to face me from the step above as we stood in the last of the pale light. His brown corduroy coat was missing its middle button; the buttonholes were frayed and stretched with age. Some of the stitching had come loose where the right sleeve joined the shoulder. His shirt collar had little anonymous black crests stitched on a white background, a thrift-store special; underneath it his T-shirt had worn out around the neck, which was dirty under his now-middle-aged jowls. This was my brother.

"Listen to me for a minute," I said.

He looked at me expressionlessly.

"I've fucked everything up," I said. "I know it. I know if I'd been there, you wouldn't have gotten into this stuff. Please let me help now. Let's sit down and talk it through." A light breeze was blowing, and it had gotten very cold again. "You don't want to do this. These people . . ." I fished for the words. "This isn't what you want. Come to Connecticut, and you can stay with me and Val. We'll figure out a way to make it work. Or we'll find you your own place." I would worry about the practical consequences later. This was necessary. "I'll put you up, and we'll deal with it. I'm your brother."

"What's Brenda supposed to do?" he said. "Disappear?"

Brenda, I thought. Brenda. And Kenny. "Chris . . ." I struggled. "These people . . ." I was shaking my head, trying to find the right words, but nothing came out of my mouth.

"You don't know a fucking thing about it," he said. "You don't know how I feel about anything. You don't ask me, you just—"

"But they're racists," I said. "They're *Nazis*."

"So what?" he said. "What are you? You're nothing. You don't even help your own brother. At least they take care of me and act like I'm worth something. . . ."

"*I'm sorry!*" I almost screamed at him. "I'm here *now*. Give me a chance to help."

He looked at me evenly, breathing through his nose. Come on, I thought, reach across to me. . . .

He opened his mouth to speak, hesitated for a moment. "I don't care," he said. "I don't care. Go home and don't call me anymore."

Then he turned and walked inside, leaving the door open behind him. I stood watching him, dumbfounded, as he disappeared. I wanted to holler out, "What are you talking about? I'm your *brother*. You can't just turn your back on me. . . ." But even without hollering, I heard the echo coming back.

I GATHERED MY bags. Chris had vanished. When I brought my things out to the car in the last of the light and opened the trunk I saw the violin case. I had forgotten about the violin completely.

And what, I wondered, was I supposed to do with it? Put it away, out of sight, in a closet somewhere? Or keep it visible as a monument to my cowardice and wasted chances? A final acknowledgment that the lid had closed on all possibility. I wouldn't open it again. For what?

I picked it up out of the trunk and carried it across the cold, hard ground to the house, stepped across the porch, and, as I reached the door, stopped for a moment to listen. I heard no footsteps from inside. As quietly as I could, I opened the front door a crack and set the case down on the floor just inside. Then, without looking, I closed the door again and stepped quickly back to the car.

I sat in the car, staring at the house for what felt like a long time. Eventually I pulled out of the gravel driveway into the night.

III

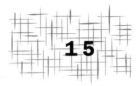

15

THESE VALU-CENTERS ARE THE big thing in Connecticut now. Stuff stacked to the ceiling like in a freight depot, still in the shipping cartons, bare girders holding up steel shelves. Val is an advance guard, way down the aisle, getting stuff for the party. She amazes me. She really knows what to do in a store. For someone who hates capitalism so much, she bakes a good pie with its fruits. Whereas, despite my romance with American culture, I find myself paralyzed in the face of so much production. I poke around for the discards. One more paradox of our relationship. I catch up with her as she's comparing two swollen rolls of crepe-paper streamers, like two psychedelic grapefruit, one electric green and one screaming red.

"I remember them," I say.

"What?" she says, looking at me abstractedly.

"The Psychedelic Grapefruit. They played at my high-school prom." Lame, lame, lame.

"Should I just get both of these?" Val says, as if I had said nothing. Actually, I didn't even go to my high-school prom.

"How much are they?" I ask. "A dollar thirty-nine? Why not?"

She reaches around me to toss them into the basket and proceeds down the aisle.

Val is shopping for the Reading Project Christmas party. She gets real busy around the holidays. Since I returned, I have been trying to participate a little more, trying to salvage something in our marriage at least. I have evolved a plan, in fact. I'm going to propose that after New Year's we go off someplace together for a couple of weeks and reconnect. I see no reason why we can't decide, together, to have a life, instead of just sharing living space while we both do our separate things.

I have been going through a pretty severe depression, I suppose. A month after the visit, I keep turning it around in my mind. Would everything have been all right if I had never looked in his closet? What about if I had talked to him about it first thing in the morning? I avoided getting to it, and that was why everything had gone to shit. I feel as if I had a chance to do something for Chris, and for myself, and I was unable to make the right choices. I have written two letters to Chris. I'm hoping that I'll hear from him.

In the meantime I have been doing some volunteering with the Reading Project. I don't know if it makes a difference or not. Maybe it does. You do these things, I guess, despite not really knowing what the effect will be.

Malcolm sits, reading slowly, his mouth painfully sounding out the words, one by one.

He looks up at me imploringly. "Look at the first letter, Malcolm," I say. "You remember what that is, right?" He's looking at it, kicking his heels on the floor of the RV in some discharge of electrokinetic energy that can't find the right channels. . . . He looks back up at me, his eyebrows raised. I can't tell if this look means he almost knows, or he doesn't know

and is expecting me to answer, or if he's thinking about some-
thing else completely. . . .

"Look again, Malcolm," I say. "That letter is M*."*

"Emm!" he says.

"Okay! Hold your mouth like that! Right like that . . ." I put
my fingers on his mouth and pinch his lips together. "Make that
sound right there. . . ."

"Mmmm," he says.

"Right," I say. "That's the sound M *makes. Remember the*
first word in the sentence?"

" 'My,' " he says.

"Right."

" 'My name is Malcolm!' " he says triumphantly, a note that
turns almost instantly to defiance, then into a troubled, absent
frown. . . . The moods pass over his face like cloud shadows in a
time-lapse film. He looks back at the page, then off into space.

Gordon will not take back the advance for the book, although I offered it. He still wants a book. I have no idea what I
can say that will be of any use to anybody. I think I'm going to go
on antianxiety medication, maybe.

I even tried calling Chris one night; the phone had been dis-
connected. Estelle doesn't know where he is. But I am deter-
mined to do what I can to salvage things with Val. That much at
least I can do something about.

IN THE CAR on the way home from Valu-Center, Val is going
over her checklist in the passenger seat, her salt-and-pepper

hair cut short, wearing half-moon glasses, a peasant skirt, and a big turtleneck under her denim jacket, which she's had since I've known her. She's so beautiful. She has such strength and focus. Sometimes it drives me nuts.

"Why don't we go out tonight?" I say. She is crossing something off her list, the pen cap in her teeth.

She looks at me with a faint smile, as if she can't believe I'm serious. "Honey," she says, "I've got to prepare the CIO talk."

The CIO talk. I must know about this, but it is apparently irretrievable in my memory.

"When is that again?" I say.

"Tuesday," she says.

"Well," I offer, "it's Saturday now. . . . Maybe we can just go out for a couple of hours?"

She replaces the cap on the pen with a beleaguered air, sighs, frowning, and looks out the windshield as I drive. I am opening a can of worms. Starting trouble again. This is what her look says.

"Fine," she says. "Where would you like to go?" She isn't smiling.

"Well, look," I say, "I mean, I don't want to if I'm just dragging you by the neck. I just thought it would be something good to do. You know, if we both wanted to. Don't make me feel like I'm forcing you."

"I don't know why you're doing this now," she says. "I've got a major talk to give, the Project party is coming up, Jason Liborio is in jail *yet again,* not to mention that you're trying to write a book—"

"But it's never the right time," I say. I hate this exasperated sound in my voice. "What I'm saying is that we have to make time for us, the same way we make time for all this other stuff, or we'll just . . . never have time." I shouldn't, I feel, have to plead this case so hard. Obviously we've had this conversation before.

We have gone on exactly one vacation. Her friends couldn't believe it. "You did what?" This was seven years ago. We went to San Miguel de Allende. I think that's where she got the skirt she's wearing. The idea of vacation doesn't fit into Val's cosmology.

WE ARRIVE HOME, unpack the bags, and I am trying to figure out how to open the subject again in a way that won't grate. I want to tell her that I know I've been blown way off course. We have, I will say, been making life too easy for each other. This can be the beginning of a new chapter.

We are in the kitchen, putting away the cans. The news is going on the small television by the cypress hutch; once in a while Val goes over to the butcher-block island and jots something down on one of the innumerable slips of paper that she cuts up from regular typing paper with her desktop paper cutter, to remind her of What Is to Be Done. There's a burned-out bulb in the lamp next to the pantry, which I keep forgetting to replace. I need my own list sheets; maybe it's a sentimental conceit that I keep acting as if I can remember it all without the notes. Maybe, as a concession to the New Regime I'd like to institute, I'll start making lists myself. As a tacit acknowledgment of Val's methods.

"I hope it's okay if I steal one of your slips here," I say, stepping over next to her and sliding one of the irregularly trimmed sheets off the pile and also rubbing up against her a little. "I am instituting the Val Method of List Management in recognition of its Superior Wisdom in the field of Organization." I hope this is coming out somewhat charming at least. I start writing down "lightbulb pantry" as she steps away, goes to the fridge, and looks inside.

"I didn't buy cranberry juice," she says, staring into the humming white chamber.

"That's just the kind of thing the Val Method is designed for," I chirp. "It is now being added to the John Delano list—"

"We need to talk," Val says.

"Yeah," I say.

She is standing looking at the floor, with one hand against the refrigerator door, propping herself up.

She's just standing there, looking at the floor.

"Are you okay, Val?"

"I'm moving out."

The cabinet above her head next to the refrigerator displays three-year-old tins of nutmeg and coarse-ground black pepper.

"I don't know how to tell you."

Still looking at the floor.

"I'm sorry," she says. "I just. I just."

"What?" I am groping for some kind of orientation. "Where are you going?"

She wipes away tears.

"Lisa is going to Cuba for two months, and I'm going to stay at her place." This name I recognize; it is her friend in Hanesport, twenty minutes away.

I am feeling along a wall in my mind for the switch that makes things visible and articulate. Parts of me are supposed to be hooked up but aren't. Sense breaks down. It is well known that you can't leave, say, a videotape on pause for too long; the tape is under tension and will eventually stretch. Most machines have some sort of cutoff mechanism to deal with it. That makes all kinds of sense. Ordovico or Viricordo . . . where the hell was that from? Spooooool . . . No, that was Beckett. . . .

"In Hanesport?" I manage to say.

Val is looking at me, frowning a little. And now I'm sitting on the floor, which should be comfortable and restful but is not. I see the oven door, the bottom of the refrigerator, the hem of Val's skirt, things I don't usually see. This view of things tells me something is not as it should be, and I don't want to hear it. I roll onto my hands and knees and stare at the pattern on the linoleum tile.

"I need some time alone," she says. "We both need some time alone."

"Are you going to come back?" I say. Who designs this stuff?

"I don't know," she says. "Get up, John."

SIX AT THE top. I copied it out dutifully, looked up the commentary.

A Goat butts against a hedge.
It cannot go backward, it cannot go forward.
Nothing serves to further.
If one notes the difficulty, this brings good fortune.

223

I have started throwing the coins in my study, among the ruins of Cold War American Civilization. Don't laugh. The *I Ching* has survived the ruins of more than one civilization. It's a guilty pleasure; Val hates the *Ching*, with its gnomic, ambiguous images and its unflappable refusal to take sides. I pulled it off the shelf a couple of months ago, just after she left, from its place between Jung's book on flying saucers and my signed copy of *Be Here Now*.

I am hardly the first person to note the resonance the lines seem to have to the situation at hand, whatever that situation may be. As I looked at this particular commentary, I was struck by a truly eerie appropriateness. *"It cannot go backward, it cannot go forward."* That was my situation in a few words. So simply stated. *"Nothing serves to further."* The *Ching* doesn't lie. Sometimes I try to check up on it. I'll open the book to some entry that I didn't throw, or I'll go back one entry from the one I turned up, to see if that would be just as applicable, and it never is. I tried it now. This was hexagram 34; I turned back to number 32 to see if it would have been just as good. Six at the top . . . let's see. . . . "Restlessness as an enduring condition brings misfortune." Actually, that one's not bad either. . . .

Almost spring, the smells of the ground and trees peeking out and then going back behind the curtain again. Hints. I don't know; I get some kind of comfort from the *Ching*, and I figured it was as good as anything to hold on to through what promised to be a long season of grief, drift, and waiting. It was something to engage in conversation. I remembered more than once, with a pang of sadness, my father sitting at the computer in that room in Albuquerque, the loneliness he must have felt.

Since Val left I've rattled around the house like a dried pea in an empty shoe box. After a couple of weeks we got together for lunch at Cilantro's, in Stamford. I don't know what's going to happen. I'm living with the uncertainty, I guess, but I hate it. But on some level I also need it; I know that.

What is extraordinary is that I heard from Chris. He had written on one of those blank postcards that you get at the post office, with the postage already on them. It was postmarked Des Moines.

> *Dear John—*
>
> *I left where I was. I'll call you when I get to Seattle. Thanks for bringing the violin.*
>
> Chris

That was it—no other information, no clue about what had happened. But just the fact that I had heard from him was more than I had a right to hope for. And that he had gotten out of that snake pit was a form of salvation in itself. I wished I knew more. There was hope after all. Then, once I had read it over a few times, I thought, What if he shows up and wants to move in with me? What if he becomes a permanent dependent? The old panic. I envisioned him moved into the guest room, felt myself cranking up, and I thought, Stop it. Take it as it comes. At least Chris had managed to get himself out of his trap, I told myself. How were you doing?

I went back to number 34. It did seem tailored perfectly. And there was that end line: "*If one* notes the difficulty, *this brings good fortune.*" Even when you are most stuck, acknowledgment is a kind of a charm. Not trying to change conditions directly, but accepting and acknowledging the facts of the case.

As a precondition, say. A humbling. Was it true? Was there grace to be had in sitting still and acknowledging that which you least wanted to acknowledge? The harder you tried to struggle and get free, the worse you were stuck. I never wanted to be the goat in the hedge. But in what hedge, exactly, had I been stuck all these years?

———

IT LIVED IN my mind as a place without history, a treeless plane, a shadowless tableau, where everyone was somehow provisional, interchangeable with one another. The houses all alike, the apparent absence of surprising things to be discovered in the shady corners of the past. Total possibility, total disorientation . . .

I hadn't been back to Atlanticville since Mom's funeral, fifteen years ago. She and Dad were both now covered by the ground, by the shadow of history. Those who act, I thought, cast a shadow; those who can no longer act are put in shadow. All right, I thought, I will go back there and cast my own shadow. While I still had a chance. For better or for worse, I had left there, with all its associations; I thought, it is time to go back and see it again, take its measure.

My father and Estelle had hung on to the house for two years afterward, even after Dad had moved out to New Mexico. They kept waiting for some input from me, but I didn't want to get involved, and eventually they sold the house themselves. I professed to be unconcerned. It was fine with me. One less bridge into the burning past. I hadn't wanted to get involved in the sale, the actual transferring, the ceding of the ground. I didn't want to know too much about the way the past could change on you. I wanted to leave everything exactly as it was and thereby make a definitive break. The plan had not worked as I had wanted it to. Something was wrong with the logic.

I picked a weekday; I wanted to avoid, to whatever extent I could, any chance encounters with anyone who might remember me. I didn't want to spend my time recounting what I was doing and where I'd been. I wanted a private communion. I wanted to see that shadowless tableau. Prove to myself that I was strong enough, separate enough, to face it now. Maybe the years would have cut it all down to size and I could be free of it all, once and for all.

So on a morning late in April, I made my way down to I-95 and across the Whitestone Bridge. The day had started out a mixture of sunny and cloudy; it felt like winter and spring alternately—warming on the surface, but when the sun went behind the clouds you could see that it was still a winter day at its core, like a piece of meat that was defrosted on its surface but remained frozen inside. By the time I got to the Whitestone the clouds had disappeared, and I looked at all the spangling water of Long Island Sound off to the east, the glory of the distant billows of clouds, the boats sailing in the good breeze, oblivious to my errand, life irrepressible as always. You had to love it for its blind irrepressibility even as you hated it for its obliviousness. Actually, I wasn't sure about that—blind irrepressibility isn't an easy thing to love. Maybe it doesn't even deserve to be loved. The life force itself was neutral. It was bellicose, oblivious of that which wasn't healthy. It stepped on toes. Still, wasn't it better than the death impulse? And there I went again, the constant cleaving into opposites. . . . Maybe it just was not a matter for choice—maybe you didn't get one without the other. And yet there were times when one had to make a choice. . . .

Once on Long Island, I took the Cross Island Parkway south, past all the yachts and pleasure boats in the bay and beyond that the old Gatsby Long Island to the east, Plandome and Roslyn and Great Neck, the rich neighborhoods to which my father grew up aspiring in borderline Garvey's Neck. That would be a pilgrimage, I thought, for another day. All the North Shore estates, the Tudor solidity, the giant trees, the lawns, the winding streets with no sidewalks. I remembered driving with my parents and Chris through those neighborhoods—University Gardens, Lake Success—and feeling my father's yearning. The family had made its toehold in the New World, and he was stuck, with his face against the sheer rock cliff of upward mobility, feeling around with his hand, looking for the place to grab for the next step upward. Maybe that was why he'd cracked. I'll never know. I suppose I had made it. I had unloaded Mom, unloaded Dad, unloaded Chris because the weight was too much on me. I had no kids; kids would have been too much weight on me. Everything was too much weight on me.

The Cross Island led straight to the South Shore, and I turned east on Southern State Parkway. Now it was still green along the parkway, but the grass shoulders were sandy at the edges—a harbinger of nearby Jones Beach. I opened my window and immediately smelled the salt tang of the ocean in the air. It was always one of the redeeming things about going there.

I drove east along the parkway, knowing that in a few miles I would come to the exit for Atlanticville. I braced myself for what was coming up. It was going to be a shock to see the house again, I knew that. I remembered the turns and twists of this road; they were burned into my muscle memory. I could negotiate them in my sleep. I had, in fact, done that any number of times in high school after a long night in the city. The litany of towns along the South Shore, the newer communities that belonged to the sons and daughters of the refugees from Brooklyn and the Lower East Side; you memorized the conductor's poker-faced recitation: "This is a Babylon train, stopping at Jamaica, Lynbrook, Rockville Centre, Baldwin, Freeport, Merrick, Bellmore, Wantagh, Seaford, Atlanticville, Massapequa, Massapequa Park, Amityville, Copiague, Lindenhurst, and Babylon; change at Jamaica for all other stations." That litany was one of the secret handshakes of the born Long Islander, at least the South Shore variety.

I was no more than a mile or two from my exit when I saw a sign that surprised me; it appeared on the right, with the brown background of the historical attraction rather than the green background of plain geography: ATLANTICVILLE HISTORICAL MUSEUM—EXIT 21. I almost laughed out loud. A museum? Of what? With a sign on the parkway? Of course, there had been the "Atlanticville Museum" in the old firehouse, where they'd cart us once a year in elementary school. The unvarnished wood floor, a few fuzzy blown-up etchings of Indians that had lived in the area, a few arrowheads in a glass case, the original bell from the firehouse behind a wood railing, a dusty diorama of an Indian shaking hands with the Town Founder . . . It was kind of a joke to us, as kids. Certainly nothing to merit a sign on the parkway. They must, I thought, have expanded it. I decided now, on impulse, to go to the museum first. Why not? I had the whole day in front of me. And I was a historian, wasn't I? I had a professional interest. I'd drive by the place, and, if the spirit moved me, I would drop in.

Doing so entailed passing up the exit I would ordinarily have taken and exiting instead a few miles east. I felt a slight pang when I passed the turnoff, as if I were somehow abridging an important ritual. Then I told myself not to be silly. I wasn't, after all, trying to relive my exact feeling of the past. I was coming to confront the past with new eyes. So this willingness to alter the pattern was in the spirit of the trip.

Exit 21 came up, and I peeled off and coasted up the ramp's slight incline to the top. Jerusalem Avenue to the north; Sunrise Highway to the south, and there was another sign for the museum, this one slightly smaller and with the words arranged in a logo, with an arrow underneath pointing to the right, south. I followed it, down Old Pinecrest Road, through the beautiful midmorning, a slightly older area, past the brick bungalows and the occasional larger wood-frame house with a porch and big yard. I passed the old junior high, crossed Sunrise Highway, and passed the rear parking lot of St. Bernard the Inquisitor, where we used to attend church in the gym and where, one night in a car with Roy Burton and Jimmy Scoleri, Janis Cahill drank so much cough medicine she went blind for two days. That was the night when Diane Pellegrino brought along the biker-looking guy from Mepham whom nobody liked but who had such great pot and who carried a book of Hart Crane poems.

I was getting close to Merrick Road, the dividing line into the residential areas along the swampy harbor and shore area, when the residential pattern suddenly broke on the left side of Pinecrest and opened out into a big lawn, and a moment later I saw the sign, carved into a giant slab of wood set on two legs—

ATLANTICVILLE HISTORICAL MUSEUM—and beyond that, behind the professionally landscaped grounds, was a state-maintained-looking building of stone and glass facade. Stunned, I turned into the drive, with its miniature, matching ENTER sign. Where had this come from? I thought. The drive led me inward to a fork with another sign that said VISITOR PARKING, with an arrow pointing left, and BUSES, with a sign pointing right. I followed the left fork and parked in the nearly empty parking lot.

I went up some wide flagstone steps, pushed open the glass doors, and stepped into a beige-toned entry area with a sternum-high counter, behind which sat a woman about my age, perhaps a few years younger. There was an atrium effect with a skylight, and an artificial waterfall at one end of the entry area. She was smiling, and she greeted me by asking me to sign the guest register and informing me that the suggested adult donation was six dollars. "Have you been here before?" she asked. I tried covertly to search her face for clues—was she, I wondered, someone I'd gone to school with?

"No, I haven't," I said.

"Well," she said, unfolding a brochure and spreading it out for me on the countertop, "let me get you oriented. We are here," she said, pointing with her pen to a beige patch on the brochure's floor plan. She moved the pen to a pastel green square. "This is the 'Native American Roots' area here. You'll find all kinds of artifacts and a history of this entire part of Long Island before the Europeans came and just afterward. This blue area here next to it tells the story of Atlanticville's incorporation and its growth in the early years of the twentieth century, up to World War Two."

She pointed the pen to an oblong red zone. "This is my

favorite part of the museum. It's called 'Postwar Boom,' and it tells the whole story of the development of Atlanticville after the war and into contemporary times."

"Wow," I said. "This is just . . . unbelievable. When was this place built?"

"They had the ribbon-cutting ceremony eleven years ago."

"Eleven years ago?" I was shocked. I felt like Rip van Winkle. "Is the old Atlanticville Museum still there?"

"You mean the firehouse?" she said. "Their collection was folded into ours when this building was planned out. They moved the firehouse building itself to Bethpage Park. You remember the firehouse museum?" she asked with unfeigned awe.

"Yeah," I said. "We used to go there every year in grade school. Did you . . . grow up here?"

"No," she said, blushing slightly. "My husband and I moved here twelve years ago when our boys were getting ready for junior high."

I nodded.

"Where did you live?" she asked.

"We were south of Merrick Road, in the west part of town. The development between the harbor and Merrick Road."

"Really?" she said, with emphasis. "Saxon Estates."

"Saxon Estates?" I said

"That's what the developers called it," she said, nodding.

I had never known this. Saxon Estates—it was comically out of proportion to what it was. I imagined my parents going to look there, deciding to buy a house in Saxon Estates. . . .

"We're trying to get National Register status for the original model house," she said. "Saxon Estates was only the second development on a Levittown-type pattern on Long Island. It was really a pioneering effort." She looked at me and smiled. "I'll bet you didn't know that."

"I didn't."

"The model is down on Merrick Road by the Department of Parks building. It's occupied by an insurance agency. Did you grow up in one of those split-levels?"

I nodded again.

"Wow," she said. "One of the originals. You have to see our diorama. Come on," she said, opening a gate in the counter and coming out. "It's slow today."

Together we walked through the first display area, with the Indian artifacts, including a big canoe in the middle of the floor with a couple of full-size wax Indians paddling it, and kept on to an entryway with the words "Postwar Boom" expertly stenciled on the wall, above some text. Recessed lighting, the whole deal. This was something.

We entered the room, which was large and lined with blown-up photos and glass display cases, one of which contained a full-size cutaway of a fallout shelter. She led me to the center of the room, where, laid out in the middle, was a giant tableau, under glass, that resembled a sprawling architect's model. It must have been twelve feet square; along its side were the words "Atlanticville in 1960." Low platforms had been set up on each of the four sides for kids to stand on, and explanatory over-lays had been strategically stenciled on the glass. We ap-proached it, and I tried to get my bearings.

It all seemed kind of random at first, but then the pattern began to emerge—the grammar of the streets, the syntax of place and time—and I recognized Merrick Road as the large artery through the middle. Every house, every building was, apparently, in place, in amazing detail. I made out the library; little cars lined the streets, little people populated the sidewalks, little trees festooned the older areas. Dividing the tableau, perpendicular to Merrick Road, was Powers Avenue, the main original north-south street, which ran past the front door of St. Bernard's, and the old Powers Avenue School, where I went to kindergarten, and the library. At the intersection of Powers and Merrick stood a tiny, accurate model of the original Brown's Hotel, which they demolished the year I left for college. I used to love that place—it had a wide porch, and I would sneak in and use the bathroom sometimes, if I was walking downtown; inside, it felt like a Wild West saloon.

I walked around the table to the far end and easily located what I was looking for. Stenciled on the glass were the words "Saxon Estates," and in smaller letters "Constructed 1951–1952." Under the glass were all the streets between Merrick Road and the harbor, lined with identical houses, the grid I carried in my mind—Laurel Avenue and the streets running off it like ribs: Quahog, Manhasset, Wonalancet, and Alder Drive leading in its S shape across to Upper Willoughby, all lined with toothpick-thin trees. And there, between Wonalancet and Pequod Streets, was the house where I used to live.

"It's meant to be just how it looked when President Kennedy was elected," she said. "See how skinny the trees are?"

"Yeah," I said. It appeared to be an exact replica, but something wasn't quite right, on a subliminal level, and after a few moments I realized what it was: They had made the houses different colors, but they hadn't gotten the colors right. Mrs. Leary's house, for example, across the street from us and down one, was maroon with white shutters, and they had it dark green. I looked around the corner on Pequod and down five houses from Laurel, and there was Bobby Mayer's house, which was incorrectly colored yellow instead of the "natural shingle" effect I heard his mother bragging to my mother about one day in Bohack's supermarket. How did I remember this stuff? Our house, on the other hand, was correctly painted white, but with green instead of black shutters. "This is too weird," I said to my companion. "I used to ride my bike down that street. That was my house."

"That's what everyone says," she said, smiling cheerfully. "It's all different now," she went on. "You wouldn't recognize it. That's a very desirable area. The houses sell for upward of three hundred thousand dollars."

"Oh, come on," I said, turning to her. I didn't believe it. She raised her eyebrows and nodded at me. "My parents paid twelve thousand for that house," I said.

"That's right," she said. "That was price-level two. You were facing on Laurel. Price-level one was the corner lots; they sold for twelve five ninety-nine. Price-level three was all the side streets. Most of those sold for eleven five ninety-nine." She smiled, proud of herself. "I'm finishing my dissertation," she said.

A muted beep sounded from up front, and she said, "Oops—customers. Excuse me for a moment." She headed back to the front desk and left me alone with the tableau. I stood and surveyed the neighborhood where I grew up. I kept expecting feelings, scenes, to come forth in memory, one by one— "Hey John, remember me?"—a miniature *This Is Your Life*. But all that came was a series of names: Vitale, Bullock, Leary,

Riordan, Kleinman, Randle, Marchese, Krevens. As if I were looking back at a planet from which I had blasted off. Were they all still there? I wondered. They couldn't be.

This tableau was reminding me of something else, though, bringing something else up. It came to mind without too much effort. Kandor, I thought. The name made me smile. It was a piece of *Superman* history. Superman's father, Jor-El, was a great scientist on the planet Krypton, and he knew that his planet was about to explode. He sent his son, Kal-El, off into space in a rocket ship, to land somewhere else, where he would have a chance of making it; shortly afterward Krypton exploded. Of course the baby landed on Earth, where he was discovered by kindly Ma and Pa Kent. It turned out that he had superpowers and superstrength because Earth was smaller than Krypton, and so gravity was not as heavy on him. He led a double life, adopted the secret identity of Clark Kent—everybody knows this.

But Superman also maintained a secret retreat in the frozen arctic north, called the Fortress of Solitude, where he would go to hang out by himself. He had exhibits on the lives of all his friends, memorabilia of his life—his own private museum, which nobody else visited. One of the items he kept there was a giant bottle containing a miniature city. The evil genius Brainiac had shrunk it and imprisoned it in the bottle, and it was all that was left of the planet Krypton. This was Kandor. Superman had vowed to return it to full size and let it live again, but so far he'd had no luck. I sometimes wondered if he didn't have some kind of subconscious stake in keeping it enclosed like that, keeping it manageable, immune from change; it was all he had left of his past, after all. . . . Actually, that wasn't true, not exactly. When

Krypton exploded, chunks of the planet were hurled out across the universe, and some of them landed on Earth. When Superman came into contact with these chunks, called Kryptonite, he began to weaken and get sick, and, if the exposure was sufficient, it could kill him. . . .

After a while I got ready to go. On the way out I stopped by the fallout-shelter cutaway—life-size wax figures of a man and a woman, a folding cot, big cans of food with black-and-white labels, a gas mask hanging on the wall. A small card next to the cutaway read MATERIALS DONATED BY MRS. S. PELLEGRINO. The Pellegrinos had had a fallout shelter? Amazing. Diane had never mentioned it, not that I remembered at least. Next to it was a display with an old photo of Brown's Hotel, with some mustached men in derbies and vests standing on the porch, and next to that, photos of the demolition. I could have spent more time there, but it was making me restless somehow. I walked out of the Postwar Boom room, past the new visitors, who were busy in the Native American Roots section. My friend, back behind the front counter, looked up as I approached, saying, "I thought you might want some time alone for your trip down Memory Lane."

"Are there any postcards of that tableau?" I asked.

Her features made a "what a shame" expression, and she shook her head. "Everyone asks that, too, and I've told them they ought to make 'em up, but they haven't yet. You're free to take a photo if you want, though. . . ."

"I didn't bring a camera."

"Why don't you go over to Renek's and get a little diposable camera?" At my puzzled look, she said, "The drugstore. Right around the corner on Merrick Road."

I PICKED UP a camera at Renek's. Downtown was all different. I say "downtown," but it wasn't really a downtown; it was a strip of stores along Merrick Road, like a cluster of crystals on a long string that stretched from Queens all the way out to the tip of Montauk Point. Mid-Island Department Store was now a triplex movie theater. Henry's Hardware was a Toys "R" Us. George's candy store was still a candy store, but not George's. The German deli next door to George's was still going at least.

I figured I'd head over to the house first, before I went back to the museum. I would grit my teeth and get it over with. I drove west on Merrick Road, past the bank that stood where Brown's Hotel had been, and the expressway interchange that had filled in the canal and obliterated the tiny seafood place with the cement floor where my father had taken me to eat clams, and eventually I came to the intersection of Merrick and Willoughby, where the Ivy Barn gift shop used to be, where now a Korean vegetable market stood, and I turned into the old neighborhood.

I drove slowly, stunned by what I saw. Instead of the treeless architect's diorama I remembered from childhood, I drove through a settled, leafy enclave. Laurel Avenue was nearly covered by a canopy of trees that had been growing on the curb strips, some of them for fifty years. Off to the left ran the side streets, and they, too, were shady and pleasant. I slowed even more and inched along. Many of the houses had been altered—dormers here, a camelback addition there—so that the uniform feeling was much less pronounced. Rare, in fact, was an original split-level that hadn't been altered in some way. People had managed to make these places their own. On the right I passed curving Alder Drive, where I'd gotten lost as a child; it still wound around off to the left, into the noontime suburban dream.

I slowed for the stop sign at Wonalancet Street, then I eased off the brake and rolled forward, slowly, until I pulled up at the curb across the street from the house where I'd spent my childhood. I put the car in park and let it idle for some moments before I turned the key and shut the motor and sat there, in the silence. From the driver's window I looked across at the house. It was still painted white, with dark green shutters. The garage was open and empty, and no car sat in front of the house. The flagstone walk my father had put in leading from the driveway to the front door was hidden behind a row of neatly trimmed shrubs. The lawn was well groomed, which I was happy to see. My father had put a lot of work into that lawn. He used to make me mow the whole thing twice—once in horizontal rows and once in vertical rows—because he thought that would give it a more even appearance. We had shouting matches about it. In the middle of the lawn the sycamore tree still stood, but much larger now. I couldn't believe how big it was. I opened the car door and stepped out.

I stood there with the nubbly surface of Laurel Avenue under my loafers. I looked up and down the avenue, to the left and right. A light spring breeze ran through my hair. I reached back into the car and grabbed the camera, then I started across the street. On the grass curb strip, another tree grew. I couldn't get over how the trees changed the feeling of the neighborhood.

From the sidewalk I regarded the house. I remembered when the sycamore tree was only a little taller than I was, and thin enough that I could get my ten-year-old hands around the trunk. As it grew in and the roots humped the lawn slightly in places, my father insisted that I bring the mower up to it directly, face-on, and push down on the handle slightly so as to raise the mower blades. Otherwise they could cut too closely and dig up the soil under the grass, like a razor burn.

I stood there, unsure exactly how to proceed. Did I want to look inside the house? Meet the new owners? Look around at the backyard? It was a moot question; no one appeared to be home. And anyway, I wasn't sure I wanted to see someone else's furniture and curios scattered around inside the house. The day was quiet and still, except for the distant hum and moan of an airplane somewhere up in the ethereal blue, invisible through the leafy spring branches. I stared at the house and tried to remember how badly I had wanted to leave A-ville, what a victory I thought it would represent. I thought I might come back and see the ruins of a vanquished, or at least diminished, foe, as if from a helicopter, and be grateful to have made it out with my skin. It would have stayed the same, and I would have moved on and grown. Was that what I'd been looking for? A sense that I had prevailed? That it might kneel to me and acknowledge that I had at least escaped? It seemed instead to have gone on and grown and become a good home for someone else, whom I didn't know, and to be unconcerned with my presence. Had I left it behind, or had it left me behind? And there I was, again, still stuck, like the goat from the *I Ching*, in the old Either/Or. Why not both true? I thought. And neither? Both and neither.

This seemed right to me. And suddenly I had a strong feeling that I wanted to stand there, on the property where I'd played, on the lawn I'd mowed. I wanted to touch the tree, to stand under it and spend a few moments mulling this koan I'd been presented. Maybe I'd find whatever it was I needed, whatever I'd lost. I had the feeling that all I needed was to see whatever it was for a moment, just to see it, or feel it, and I would be healed, like a pilgrim at Lourdes. Touch the tree, I thought. I started across the lawn.

As I approached the tree the front door of the house opened. A man stood behind the storm door, holding a child in his arms, watching me. I had assumed that no one was home. Maybe that was wishful; it was unsettling to see the door of the house open with a stranger behind it, although I don't know what else I might have expected. More or less automatically, I redirected my steps, diagonally across to the opening between the hedge and the flower bed, where I could get through to the front door and introduce myself.

I smiled and waved as I approached the front stoop. The man, who was not smiling, appeared to be in his late twenties or early thirties. He had Asian features and wore a polo shirt and chino slacks. As I approached he set the child down and said something to her, and she disappeared.

"Excuse me," I said, climbing the first two steps of the brick stoop and holding on to the iron railing. "I didn't mean to disturb you. I didn't realize anyone was home."

"Can I help you?" he said.

"Of course," I said. "I'm sorry. I used to live here. Back when the house was first built." I introduced myself.

He had, it turned out, bought the house two years before,

from the people who had bought it from Dad and Estelle. After a few exchanges he stepped out onto the stoop with me; he never did invite me inside, and I averted my eyes from any glimpse at the interior. He was formal, polite, and volunteered no information—never, in fact, even told me his name. An insurance salesman, I figured, with inspirational posters on his otherwise bare office walls, climbing up through some middle-management scenario. As we talked, I looked toward the street from the stoop and remembered my father and my grandfather having a fight once because my grandfather had come to the house and pointed out a couple patches of crabgrass in the yard. "That's the only thing he notices," my father told my mother afterward. . . .

"The lawn looks great," I said to this man now.

"Landscape Solutions," he said. "They're over in Merrick. They do a good job."

He seemed to be waiting for me to leave so that he could get on with whatever he was doing. But it all felt so inconclusive to me. I didn't want this visit to be over yet. This guy would have plenty of time to get back to his life. Who knew when I'd ever be back here? I wanted *something* to take with me, some image, something to hang on to, something tangible. . . . Life seemed to have turned into a nonstick surface, and I was sliding off everything I touched.

Stalling, I said, "Would you mind . . . could I take a look around back? Would that be all right?"

Nervously, he agreed, told me to meet him around the side of the house. He went inside, and I walked around to the side steps, where Dad and I used to sit after our "workouts"— throwing a baseball or a football back and forth in the backyard.

The new owner emerged from the door and walked me around back.

"Do the Harkavys still live next door?" I asked.

"No," he said. "They moved two years ago. They went to Florida."

The forsythia hedge was in bloom along the side of the backyard. They had built a shed in the far corner, an ugly thing painted red, with a big Pennsylvania Dutch hex sign on the side. Two beach chairs sat in the middle of the yard. What was I looking for? I didn't know. The chestnut tree was gone. I glanced at the kitchen window, through which Mom would watch me while I played.

I felt a wave of sadness and depression wash over me. What was I doing here? What good was this doing? What good was all this past? All it did was make you grieve for everything that wasn't there anymore. Or that never had been there in the first place. Oppressive. Like witnessing a crash scene. It was too late to do anything about it now.

As I thought these gloomy thoughts, I noticed something— a large circle in the grass, maybe fourteen feet across, inside of which the grass was slightly less green than the surrounding lawn. It was on the right side of the yard, near the forsythia, and I remembered, suddenly, what it was. It was where the pool had been. Dad had dug out the lawn himself and made a bed of sand to absorb the water; he bordered it with bricks and put the pool in the middle of it, a big blue-vinyl-lined aboveground pool. When we got older, he got rid of the pool and replanted grass, but it never grew in in exactly the same color as the rest of the grass. It still wasn't the same; the shadow of the pool's image was still there. I don't know why, but this made me feel a little better.

And then an image came to me. It was so intense it was almost as if I could see it in front of me. I must have been ten or eleven years old, and Chris was five or six, and we were both in the pool with Dad. Dad had invented an activity for us, which we loved. The three of us would start walking deliberately through the water, in a circle, counterclockwise around the circumference of the pool. It would be slow going at first, but we would keep going as steadily as we could, in a circle, and slowly a current would form in our wake, in the direction in which we walked. As the current gathered momentum, we could walk faster, and that would make the current stronger, and we would walk faster and faster, until something close to a whirlpool formed. As I stood there now, I could see the three of us in the pool, under the summer sun, all wading in a circle, and Dad singing "The Caissons Go Rolling Along." The current would get stronger and stronger and at a certain point Dad would give us the signal and all three of us would holler as loud as we could and lift our feet and we would be borne, whirling, around the pool, floating on the current we had created. . . . I was almost transfixed; I could see us there; I could feel the sun on my face as I floated with Chris and my father.

I closed my eyes in the sun and remembered that moment in and out of time. My poor father, I thought. He bought the house, planted the lawn, showed me how to throw a ball. . . . I didn't know whether to be glad or sorry. Neither and both. Dad, I thought. Here I am. Here's Chris. Is this all right? Thank you, I thought. Thank you is an important thing to say. Is this all right? Please let this be all right.

The owner of the home cleared his throat—he actually cleared his throat—and said, "Uh . . . I'm going to need to get back inside, with my daughter, now."

"I know," I said. Good-bye, Dad. "I know." Then I remembered one more important thing. "But—please," I said, holding out the camera to him, "would you take a picture of me over here? This is where the pool was." He looked at the camera in my hand, frowning. I would stand right in the middle of the circle.

"Please," I said. "Just one. It's for my brother." I would write him again and tell him the whole story.